After Dinner Conversation
"Best of 2023"

Philosophy | Ethics Short Story Fiction

After Dinner Conversation – "Best Of" 2023

After Dinner Conversation publishes fictional stories that explore ethical and philosophical questions in an informal manner. The purpose of these stories is to generate thoughtful discussion in an open and easily accessible manner.

ISBN 979-8-9896194-0-5
Library of Congress Control Number: 2024930313

Copyright © 2024 After Dinner Conversation
Editor in Chief: *Kolby Granville*
Story Editor: *R.K.H. Ndong*
Acquisitions Editor: *Stephen Repsys*
Design, layout, and discussion questions by After Dinner Conversation.

https://www.afterdinnerconversation.com

After Dinner Conversation believes humanity is improved by ethics and morals grounded in philosophical truth and that philosophical truth is discovered through intentional reflection and respectful debate. In order to facilitate that process, we have created a growing series of short stories across genres, a monthly magazine, and two podcasts. These accessible examples of abstract ethical and philosophical ideas are intended to draw out deeper discussions with friends, family, and students.

Table Of Contents

The Worst Thing You Can Do is Nothing

C.S. Griffel

* * *

Stanislav did not want to join the army. It was his mother who said he must. Stanislav's father didn't argue. Father had once been brave enough to fly a fighter plane in World War II, but that had been a long time ago. One glorious act of bravery in a man's youth tells you nothing of his future. Reality can steal the wind out of any man's sails, given enough time. An unhappy marriage, a brother in the gulag, and the loss of a child far too young left the family at the mercy of a tired and embittered mother who no longer wanted the burden of feeding a teenage boy. His father should have told her no. But he didn't. When Stanislav had peered into his father's eyes, pleading silently for a lifeline, some kind of support, his father's dead eyes turned away with a shrug of the shoulders and sigh that said, "What can I do?" So, at seventeen, Stanislav shipped off to the army. His parents never left the three-room apartment in the far eastern Russian port city of Vladivostok. It had been twenty-six years since he boarded a train for Moscow. That was the last time he had taken the seven-day journey or ever would again. Stanislav called his father once a month, just to make sure neither he nor his mother had died.

Life for a Soviet soldier was about the same as it has always been for soldiers. Hard. The training is hard, the sergeants are hard, the food is barely passable and never quite enough. But what could Stanislav do? That was life. If he were a soldier, life would be hard. If he were not a soldier, life would be hard. So, Stanislav worked hard for himself and for his country. And now he was not just Stanislav. He was Comrade Lt. Colonel Petrov, an engineer who had the knowledge and skill to oversee the USSR's most cutting-edge satellite monitoring system, a defense against the nuclear might of the Americans.

Stanislav's trip to work was no simple matter. After his train ride, he had to pass through the first of many security protocols that kept the Soviet defense systems secret. The first was a gate where it was a simple matter of showing his military identification card. Next, it was a shuttle ride from the gate to the massively impressive and intimidating Soviet structure that housed the defense monitoring system. There was a lot of speculative chatter on the bus ride. A few weeks earlier a young pilot flying for the Soviet Air Defense had taken down Korean Air flight 007 which had veered into restricted Soviet airspace. The Americans claimed it was a commercial flight that had veered off course. The *Politburo* informed the citizens of the USSR and the world that it was, in fact, an American spy plane and a direct provocation to war. Everyone knew this was a lie.

The USSR admitted nothing to the Americans.

A fat-faced major speculated, "Do you think the Americans will retaliate?"

"Perhaps," replied a steely-eyed captain with the look of one who knows the exact path he needs to take to climb over fat-faced idiots for a promotion, "Reagan is a warmonger, hungering for a reason to drop the bomb on the Soviet Union."

Stanislav looked away from the cackling group of men that sounded more like hens than roosters, but whispers of "Hiroshima" and "Nagasaki" snuck into his ears. Japan was not far enough and World War II not long enough past for the Russians to forget what had happened and to take the lesson to heart. *They had done it before.* What could Stanislav do but protect his homeland?

While on duty, Stanislav was the officer in charge of the *Oko* early warning system. His duty day consisted of watching men watch computer screens to make sure no one sent a missile at Moscow. With the tension over the Korean airliner and a reportedly trigger-happy American president, now seemed as good a time as any for Armageddon. The world, he knew, especially America, also leveled a suspicious eye at the Soviet Union. Evil empire. That's what they said.

He thought of Raisa and their children, Dmitri and Yelena. Were they evil? Raisa was the kind of warm, endearing, laughing mother his had never been. He thought of his frail father, once a mighty pilot that had helped the Americans and the Brits defeat Hitler. Now he was the ghost of a person who had once existed. He even thought of his mother. She was bitter and sharp, her beauty wasted in hard toil and a loveless marriage, but *evil*? He could not fathom this. What Stanislav wanted was to not get blown up. He didn't especially want to blow anyone up either. He wanted to put on his uniform in the morning, wear it with pride all day, and then go home. He wanted to eat a bowl of hot soup and laugh at his children's stories. He wanted to smoke a good cigarette and drink a glass of vodka. He wanted to slip into bed with Raisa and whisper and make love and go to sleep.

The ideological war was above Stanislav's pay grade. Let the idiot politicians fight about that. But why must it always be at the expense of the men who wore the uniform? When it came to it, it would be he, not the shitheads in the Kremlin, who had to make the call. It would be he, or his comrades at the *Oko* who had to bear the weight of knowing they had sent a nuclear missile at some poor sucker's family in America, a man that went to some boring job and just wanted to make it home to his wife and kids, but who had been blown into radioactive dust somewhere over Nebraska. *Ne-braz-ka,* it almost sounded Russian. Stanislav bore no ill will against the man somewhere in Nebraska. But what could he do?

Stanislav exited the shuttle bus and entered through the next layer of security before making his way into the recesses of the building to his work site, one of the most secure in the Soviet Union.

"Good evening, Comrade Colonel," said the guard checking identification.

"Ya, good evening, Comrade," Stanislav replied.

He exchanged all the same good evenings he always exchanged, the only difference being, this was supposed to be his day off. Comrade Oblonsky could not come in today. He was called before the Comrade General at headquarters. Stanislav didn't know why. He found it better not to ask too many questions. Also, he wasn't especially interested in Comrade Oblonsky, who he found to be rather abrasive and loud.

"Status?" Stanislav asked the outgoing officer in charge.

"All systems normal." Of course, they were.

It was just after midnight, halfway through his shift that the alarm sounded. Stanislav tensed up, but one alarm was not a reason to panic. Yet.

"What is the report, comrade?" Stanislav asked his subordinate.

"The satellite shows five intercontinental ballistic missiles from the North American continent have been launched."

Deep in his gut, Stanislav Petrov knew something was not right. But there it was. Alarms were sounding ominously throughout the bunker. The computer screens were flashing red imminent danger warnings. He knew the protocol. He knew what he was supposed to do, and he also knew that he shouldn't do it. But here, in this building he was no longer Stanislav, husband to Raisa, father to Dmitri and Yelena. He was Lieutenant Colonel Fucking Petrov. He had orders, dammit. And he was surrounded by others who would be watching him. Hesitating to follow protocol was no light matter. He knew it could mean prison. Or worse. It could be treason. Worse yet, it could mean millions of his own people would die. Worse yet, it could mean World War III. But this time, America was not the only country to own a nuclear weapon.

Ha. *A nuclear weapon.* Those words were a joke in 1983. In 1983 one American minuteman nuclear warhead contained more destructive power than all the bomb blasts set off during the entire course of World War II put together.

"Comrade Colonel?"

"I need confirmation."

"Comrade Colonel, headquarters already knows about the attack. They are waiting for your confirmation to respond. They are ready to begin the launch sequence."

Respond in kind. Those were the orders. Every moment he did not obey them was one more step down a path from which he could not return. What would happen to Raisa and the children if he lost his job? Would he have to watch them slowly starve? That was the slow kind of torture he would gladly die in a mushroom cloud to avoid. If he were imprisoned? If he were killed? He pictured the tiny apartment they shared, two small windows letting in only the shadowed light from behind another apartment block. Were he to be sent to prison or killed for this action—or rather *in*action—the children would be taken. Raisa, alone, would have no one to see she took her medicine or to bring her a bowl of soup on a frigid Moscow winter day when no sunlight came through the windows to warm the interior of their home.

The blaring alarms and insistent lieutenant snapped Stanislav's mind back into focus. "Comrade Colonel, what are your orders?" *One wrong decision and everything turns to dust.*

The phone at his right blared insistently. This would be the call with the answer about the satellite monitoring system. The mathematicians and computer analysts confirmed that their satellite alert system was running properly. There was nothing wrong with it. No reason to believe it was malfunctioning. The ground monitoring analysts could not confirm whether an American Nuclear Minuteman missile was indeed coming for the USSR or not. They could not confirm the second one either. Altogether, the satellite warning system detected five Minutemen. None of them could be confirmed by the ground monitoring system. The ground monitoring system could not say they weren't there either.

"Are they coming?" Stanislav screamed into the phone. On the other end was the major in charge of the ground analysts.

"Conditions are bad, Comrade Colonel. Our view is obscured. We cannot confirm."

"Keep working. Keep looking."

The insistent lieutenant spoke up again, "Comrade Colonel, what do you want to tell headquarters? They insist on a report." He looked into the blinking and frantic eyes of the lieutenant. Stared into them really hard, knowing what he was supposed to do and what he should not do. He stuck his hand out for the phone.

"This is Lieutenant Colonel Petrov. False alarm." The lieutenant blinked at him in shock.

The satellite monitoring system was new. Brand new. The algorithms said what they said. That American missiles were right now hurtling through the sky toward a Soviet target and that they would unleash untold destruction. But he didn't trust the system. Something was wrong. Why five? If this were truly a first strike that would launch the world into war, why not enough to flatten the Soviet Union? That's what he would do. If he wanted to start a nuclear war. He would make sure the enemy was decimated beyond the ability to retaliate. Five missiles would inflict devastating damage, but not enough to wipe them out. Not without getting in a devastating swipe back at America. It didn't make any sense. They would wait.

But the alarms were blaring, and the entire control was

looking to him to do what he was supposed to do, yet they were too well trained to disobey his direct orders in case they were the ones later scrutinized.

"Call the ground to air monitoring system again."

"Yes, sir," the lieutenant dialed, "here they are, sir."

"This is Petrov. Status?"

"Cannot confirm, sir." *Dammit, dammit, dammit.*

Mushroom clouds exploded in Stanislav's mind. He saw a dead world with burned husks for trees, nothing living but the cockroaches shambling over piles of ash and bodies.

"We wait," he announced. He had no love for the Americans. None. But he could not get past his feeling that this was all some great cosmic mistake. The air in the control room felt too thick to breathe. The smell of sweat permeated every inch of the room as terrified but controlled intelligence officers monitored their screens, sure Stanislav had just condemned them to swift and immediate death.

The phone rang again.

"Headquarters," said the insistent lieutenant, offering the phone to Stanislav.

"Petrov," he paused to listen, "No. It's a false alarm." He handed the phone back to the lieutenant whose eyes told a story of disbelief.

They waited. Stanislav had made the decision, and they all had to live with it. He bet Moscow, all eight million residents, on his gut. If he was right, eight million would be a drop in the bucket compared to the lives saved. Not just human lives, but Life itself.

They waited, and nothing happened. The moment of projected detonation passed, and Moscow was still there. The collective sigh of relief was visible and auditory.

The mathematicians and computer engineers would study the algorithms and try to determine what went wrong with one of the most advanced technological systems on planet earth. There would be hell to pay. But right now, Stanislav was still breathing. He wasn't dust particles in the atmosphere. Neither was Raisa. She was hopefully sleeping peacefully in their bed at home.

Stanislav rode the train home, as he always did. He got on the train at one of the furthest stops so there were often seats available. As the train stopped at each platform the railcar filled up with factory workers, bakers, waiters, nurses, doctors, teachers, and all manner of folks heading home to efficient, if not beautiful, Soviet apartments. The Soviet machine did not stop for the nighttime. An old woman entered the car wearing, as many older women still did, a scarf wrapped around her head in the old way. Stanislav stood to let her sit. He stood among the people in his uniform, reveling in the fact that they were alive, though they themselves did not.

The walk from his stop to his home took fifteen minutes. Warmth attempted to linger in the late September dawn. Stanislav was not a man given to poetry, but if he were, he would have written a poem about the way the soft pink dawn of late September in Moscow lights the normally cold, gray buildings in warmth, rendering them almost beautiful enough to remind one of Heaven, if such a place existed. Which, of course, it did not.

Stanislav opened the door to his apartment cautiously, not knowing if it had been a good night or a bad night. Perhaps Raisa would be sleeping. The children would be.

"Stas? Is that you, my love?" It had been a good night.

"Ya, my little bird. It's me. Who did you expect?"

"KGB," she quipped back. He laughed. *Maybe tomorrow, my love. But not today.*

Their kitchen was the first room on the right upon entering the apartment, so Stanislav stopped there first, pulling a pot of soup out of their small refrigerator. Raisa had actually worked up enough energy to make a large pot on Sunday, with enough left over to make meals for most of the week. He placed the pot on the stove, turned the heat on medium low and left it to warm.

Raisa lay inclined on the sofa, a tattered brown affair that had already been used when they first married. Raisa crocheted bright white, lacy doilies to lay across the arms to hide the dingy fabric, and a multicolored afghan of greens, blues, yellows, and pinks lay over the back. Raisa made everything more beautiful than it would have been left to its own devices. On that old sofa, she had sat reading traditional Russian fairy tales to their children. On that sofa, they had watched the news of the world pass by on their television. Lunar landings, American failures in Viet Nam, the Munich massacre. There they had hosted friends, drunk too much vodka, smoked too many cigarettes, and postulated about the meaning of it all.

"How was your night, my little bird?" Stanislav asked as he leaned down and kissed his wife on the forehead. She looked tired now, but she was still beautiful.

"It was good. Mrs. Kuznetsova stopped by with cake and tea last night. She complains that her son never calls her. She complains about the price of bread. She complains about the brightness of the sun and the darkness of the night."

Stanislav laughed, "She complains to have something to say. She needs an excuse to talk to someone."

Raisa nodded her head in agreement. "Yes, yes, you are probably right. And anyway, for all her complaining, she makes the loveliest cake, and her tea is strong and sweet. So, I can't complain." They both laughed at her little joke. "How was your day, Stas?"

"Fine." *My day is classified, my little bird.*

"Just fine?"

"Yes. It was the same as always. The computers watched the sky while the men watched the computers while I, I did nothing."

He glanced out the tiny window at the brightening day. He knew they knew. Tomorrow he would face the consequences.

* * *

Discussion Questions

1. Do you think Stanislav's response would be typical? Do you think most people in his role would refuse to launch a nuclear attack, even when protocol and duty demanded it?
2. If you were in Stanislav's position, what would you have done?
3. In the story, the nuclear attack was a false alarm. However, would your opinion of Stanislav's response be different if he had turned out to be wrong and the attack had been real? Is your opinion of his response contingent upon the outcome?
4. Do you think Stanislav should be reprimanded for failing to follow protocol, even though he turned out to be correct?
5. This is based on a true story that took place on September 26, 1983. Does knowing it is a true story change your opinion of the incident or of Stanislav in any way? If so, why?

The Chair of Opportunity

Cory Swanson

* * *

Taylor put his clothes back on and waited in a well-outfitted room. It was far posher than any doctor's office he'd ever been in and he wasn't sure why he'd been given a physical, much less one more thorough than any he'd ever had before.

When they'd called Taylor in, he'd assumed they were concerned with drug use. Guys like him who looked like he did were often treated with suspicion. Maybe it was his tattoos or his shaved head. It was fine. Taylor had nothing to hide. Sure, he liked a good time, but that was usually limited to a glass of nice scotch and a good book. Often, he listened to music, too, and perhaps it was his tastes in this regard that had raised his employer's suspicions. He liked flashy guitars and loud drums, artists who perhaps were guilty of the sins he felt he was being accused of.

Whatever. Taylor could take it. He sat in a chair that

appeared to be several centuries old. *Late Baroque*, he thought, admiring the ornate carvings on the legs and arms. They were nearly as complex as the skull and flame tattoos on his forearms, artwork of which he was particularly proud. The ink had taken time and money to accrue, but he didn't have much else to spend money on. No wife or kids. Taylor liked this freedom. It fit his ethos.

The heavy, oak doors on the other side of the room opened and the frail form of a man in a wheelchair rolled in. The man thanked his helper, who dutifully exited, closing the doors behind him.

"Taylor Albright," the man intoned, his voice aged yet firm.

"Mr. Oakstand," Taylor replied, rising from his seat at the presence of his boss.

"You don't have to get up," Oakstand said, motioning for Taylor to sit, the medical report in his lap. "Especially since I can't do the same."

Taylor had never met his boss before. The company had many layers of management, and he worked in the lower levels, checking software for bugs alongside an army of technicians identical to him in skill and position. It didn't bother Taylor. The job paid for his books and fine whiskey and tattoos. He'd never been asked to take a physical before, not when he'd been hired or at any time in between. It seemed like the kind of thing you did for manual labor, or if you ran heavy machinery.

"I suppose you're wondering why you're here," Oakstand began.

Taylor nodded at the understatement.

"Let me begin with my admiration for you. You're fit and

in good health. Your mind is certainly a strong muscle, your ability to cognate among the best I've encountered. You're young but not too young to have a fully mature frontal cortex."

Taylor nodded, unsure what to make of this talk. "Thanks," he said, hopeful it was the right response.

"The tattoos are not quite to my taste, but not a deal-breaker."

Taylor didn't know how to react to this, so he chose not to react at all.

"Your organs are all functioning optimally. No family history of cancer or addiction?"

"Not that I know of," Taylor said, his discomfort growing by the second. "There's a chance some distant relatives have had problems, but nobody ever told me about it."

Oakstand rubbed his hands as though they were cold, the report in his lap. Taylor had seen pictures of the old man before, mostly from when he was younger. He had that Jack Nicholson air of power balanced with good humor, something Taylor imagined had lent to his success. CompCorp was one of the biggest software companies in the world and Oakstand pulled the levers of power within.

The man in the wheelchair was frailer than the one in those old pictures. So much so, Taylor felt a tender moment of contemplation pass over him. How fleeting life is. How transient its blessings.

"Let's cut to the chase," Oakstand said, interrupting Taylor's moment. "I think you understand my position in life, Mr. Albright. I have money. I have power. Enough of each to sustain the other indefinitely."

Taylor shifted, the notion unsettling him.

"Traditionally, neither of these things can out-balance the laws of nature. Money can't make you live forever, can it?"

Bewildered, Taylor shook his head in agreement.

A smile crossed Oakstand's lips. "What if I told you that chair was four hundred years old?"

Taylor ran his hand over the intricate carvings. "I believe it. Why are you telling me?"

"I'm the original owner of that chair."

A laugh jumped out of Taylor's throat.

"It's true. It was at a little shop in Vienna, the proprietor of which first introduced me to *Haut Tauschen.*"

A chill ran down Taylor's spine. Skin swapping? His German skills were pretty good, but he didn't want to be right about this. "What's that?"

"Well, *Herr* Sand hadn't really perfected it yet. He sold his services as something of a novelty. He'd trick a young lady into trading bodies with him for a while, and they'd strut around in each other's skin for the fun of it before trading back. I was the one who realized the implications."

The urge to run burst through Taylor's veins, but he assured himself Oakstand had become senile. "And what were those?" Taylor said, playing along. What could it hurt to humor someone so rich and powerful? Age happened to everyone, didn't it?

"I was wealthy then. Well-heeled, if you will. My father held a dukedom south of the city, and I was his rightful heir. I enjoyed what others couldn't: fine wines, plentiful food, art. There was little I couldn't have.

"My father took ill when I was fairly young—vomiting, fatigue—and he left this world much at the same time as I met my friend the furniture seller. Along with the dukedom, I inherited all its cares, many of which overwhelmed my young mind."

Taylor leaned forward, elbows on his knees. This story didn't reek of senility, and Taylor felt he was crazy to be drawn in. Still, he couldn't help himself. Oakstand had a way of speaking that intrigued Taylor.

"I began to contemplate life and my place in it. I remember thinking as the shopkeeper demonstrated his powers that wealth and power meant nothing in the face of death. The wealthy die every day. All the money and land in the world couldn't bring back my beloved father."

Oakstand leaned forward, the effort causing pain. "Then I realized what could be done with *Haut Tauschen*. If applied correctly, one would never have to die. One could simply trade to a younger body whenever the necessity arose and assure oneself as long a life as one wished."

The realization washed over Taylor. Was that what he'd been asked here for? Was that the reason for the physical?

Oakstand leaned back in his chair. "Don't worry, I won't make you do anything you don't want to do. I'm only here to make you an offer. I realized long ago the ethical questions this magic proposed. For instance, why is my life more important than another? Do I have more to offer than a young, smart man entering the prime of his life?

"I don't pretend I do. A wealthy life is not worth more than a poor one. Yet, here I am with all my wealth and yet another failing body. So, this is my offer."

Taylor stood up. "This is crazy. I'm sorry, sir, but this is beyond nuts." Taylor wondered where Oakstand's helper had gone. He needed to tell someone that the old man had gone off his rocker.

"Sit down, Mr. Albright. Like I said, you don't have to accept it. Nor do you have to believe it. Trust me, I can buy your silence if I need to. All I ask is for you to hear me out. You will be compensated."

Taylor took a deep breath and sat down. Regardless of how he felt, this was his boss. All his comfort and stability depended on this man, and money spoke louder than words in situations like these. "Okay," he said. "What's your proposal?"

"To put it bluntly, I want to swap bodies with you. Now," he said, raising his hand to calm Taylor before he could stand again. "I know what you're thinking. Why the hell would you want to trade bodies with me? You're young and virile and I'm old and decrepit. Like I said, money can't buy your health back, so why would you sell it?"

The question made Taylor nervous. Even if what he was saying was true, why would anyone agree to do it?

"You have a sister?"

"Yeah," Taylor said. "Cindy. Why?"

"You're close?"

Taylor smiled. "She's really the only family I have."

"And she's fallen on rough times."

Taylor squinted at the old, huddled mass in front of him. How did he know so much about Taylor? "Yeah."

"She and her son, your nephew, could really use something good in their lives. Her husband left her, and she's struggling to support her family on her meager paycheck."

"Look, I give them all I can. If Nathan needs school clothes, I take him shopping. If Cindy can't get her medicine, I pay for it." Taylor felt himself flush. How had his sister and nephew been dragged into this conversation?

"Yes. It's one of those situations where a little wealth could go a long way to making their lives better."

"You're not trying to convince me to ask her to swap bodies with you, are you?" Taylor couldn't believe these words were coming out of his mouth. They felt raw and uncouth on his tongue.

"No, no. Nothing of the sort. I am male in spirit and I wish to remain so. But imagine what you could do for her in my position."

The thought sat like a brick in the room. Taylor was all his sister had. Their parents never gave either of them a dime. After Keith walked out on her, things had gotten bleak. Taylor prayed every night for a way to help his sister.

"All I propose is a straight swap. I become you and you become me. I am Taylor Albright, software engineer, and you are Phineas Oakstand, wealthy oligarch. My fortune is yours to do with as you wish. I will pass no judgment."

The breath caught in Taylor's throat. Oakstand controlled an unimaginable empire. His fingers were in everything from philanthropy to world politics. Sure, CompCorp was still the center of this universe, but Oakstand represented something so much more. To become him would be to become a god, a giant among men. "I don't know what to say."

"I understand. It's a hard decision," Oakstand said, finally leaning back in his chair, his body exhausted by the effort. "For the first time, I may expire before I find someone to truly take the mantle from me."

Despite the appearance of Oakstand's frail body, thoughts

rushed through Taylor's head. Money, power, the ability to fix all life's ills and injustices. "You'd really give it all to me?"

"All except one thing. I will keep the chair you sit in."

Taylor looked down, aware of the ornate chair once again. "What's so special about the chair?"

"The chair is everything. Without it, I wouldn't be here."

It dawned on Taylor that the chair must hold the magic. Without it, *Haut Tauschen* wouldn't be possible. He scanned it for devices. Would it trap him? Would it peel his skin?

"Don't look so alarmed," Oakstand said with a grin. "It won't hurt. All I need to do is lay my hand on the back and the work will be done. I will be you and you will be me. But I won't do it without your consent."

Taylor nodded. "Can I sleep on it?"

"I would prefer a response before we leave this room today, but I can be patient as we sit. Do give a thought to your sister in your deliberations."

A notion struck Taylor. Hadn't Cindy told him she'd been praying for a miracle? How she couldn't keep going on like this; that the pressure of working three jobs and raising her kid was going to kill her.

"Let's do it," he said.

Oakstand's brow raised. "Are you certain?"

"It would be selfish not to. Cindy and Nathan deserve better. I could give them better if I were you."

"And what of you?"

Taylor leaned forward in the chair. "Is it even a choice? You question the value of wealth in the face of mortality. I question the value of life if I can't help those closest to me. What am I worth? What do I have that's so special?" Taylor refused to wipe the tears that streamed down his cheeks.

"As long as you're certain. I won't be giving your skin back."

Taylor hung his head. "Just do it."

Oakstand's hands went to the wheels of his chair, and he guided himself behind Taylor. Head still hanging, Taylor meditated on all the good he would be doing. Oakstand's empire would accomplish more than saving his sister from poverty, it could literally save the world.

The next moment, Taylor saw himself from behind. His body sat in an ornate chair, carved from some dark wood. The chair looked remarkably well cared for despite its age.

His body stood and turned to him. "Thank you," Oakstand said with Taylor's voice. He picked up the chair with seeming ease and crossed the room to the doors. Someone opened them for him, and he passed from sight.

Taylor looked down at his own shriveled form. His skin was thin and wrinkled as old paper, liver spots sprouting as though they were constellations. His legs would not move under his own command. Clenching his hand, Taylor realized how much his joints hurt. In a moment, he'd aged fifty years and the shock didn't wear off as Oakstand's helper approached.

"Finally got rid of that old chair I see," the man said.

"I suppose so," Taylor said with Oakstand's voice, an experience so odd, it left him in shock for a few moments.

"I always wondered why nobody was allowed to sit in it."

This made him grin. "Because it's magic."

The servant chuckled. "Sure it is. Are you ready for your lunch?"

Taylor nodded. "That would be nice. And tell me, how can

I give money to someone?"

Another chuckle. "You and your philanthropy. As though you've had trouble figuring out how to spend money. Which organization strikes your fancy today?"

"Not an organization, a person. I want to give money to the sister of that man who just left."

The servant rolled his eyes. "Okay, Mr. Oakstand."

"I'm serious. She needs help."

Taylor could tell by the servant's silence he thought Taylor to be senile.

Taylor tried to smile as he was rolled from the room. Regret surged through him. How many years did he have left in this body? What had he given up? What if he couldn't get the money to Cindy and Nathan? What if everyone thought he was going soft and took his control away?

Taylor tried to stand with Oakstand's shriveled legs. He wanted to chase after himself, get the chair back, return to his own body.

"Easy there, Mr. Oakstand," the helper said, restraining him with his hand. "You remember what happened last time you tried to get up."

Emotion burst forth. This body was feeble and weak. Taylor had been many things, but he'd never felt so fragile. "I need to find him. I need to give money to his sister."

"Sure, Mr. Oakstand. We'll take care of it, okay?" the man said, his voice patronizing. Taylor felt indignant. He wasn't a child. How could this man speak to him like this? "Now, what would you like to eat today?"

* * *

Discussion Questions

1. If you were in Taylor's shoes, would you accept the bargain? Why or why not?
2. Do you think Phineas was ethical in making the offer to switch bodies with someone younger? Can a freely made transaction between two parties ever be unethical?
3. If you could sell years from your life for money, how many years would you sell and for how much money?
4. If you were in Taylor's shoes and made the body switch, what would you do with your newfound wealth and limited time?
5. If you could, at the end of your life, go back to your younger years with nothing but the knowledge you possess, would you do it? Do you think you would be able to replicate, or improve on, the success you had in your first life?

M.I.N.D. Your Marriage

Kim Z. Dale

* * *

My car wouldn't start. That happened sometimes when there was a software update. I checked the versions, but everything was current. The battery had a full charge, so that wasn't the problem either. Nothing seemed to be wrong with the car except it wouldn't start. I called customer support. They said the vehicle had been remotely disabled by the owner.

"But I am the car's owner!"

The customer service person read the owner's name from their records.

"That's my husband."

"Then you need to talk to him."

I called my husband. He asked where I was.

"I'm parked in front of the coffee shop."

"Why are you at the coffee shop?"

"I was getting coffee."

"Who were you with?"

"No one."

"Don't lie to me."

"I'm not lying."

"So Ryan wasn't there?"

"Ryan? No. I mean, yes. I mean, he works there. I wasn't there with him. Do you know Ryan?"

"I only know him as the 'hot barista.' That's what you and your friends call him, right?"

"It's a joke. How do you know about that?"

"You feminists love to complain about men objectifying women, but when no one else is around you do the exact same thing."

"It was just something funny Brandy said once and it stuck."

"Of course. Brandy."

"Can you please reactivate the car so I can go home? I need to get started on dinner."

"Okay, fine. We'll talk about this later. Go straight home. I'll be checking on you."

* * *

"It was creepy," I told Brandy the next day. "How did he know we call Ryan the 'hot barista'? Do you think your husband told him?"

"Definitely not. My husband has no sense of humor about those sorts of things. I know jealousy is why he was so insistent on the M.I.N.D. implant in the first place. That's why any thoughts that could be misconstrued as potential infidelity get tucked safely away in my privacy vault. It sounds like you need one too."

"What's a privacy vault?"

"It encrypts a section of your brain so your husband can't

access the thoughts you put there. It's like having a diary with a lock on it but more secure."

"How would my husband access my thoughts at all?"

"Oh, honey. He didn't tell you? I hate it when guys do that. At least my Roger was open about it. He told me when we got engaged that we'd be getting a prenup and a M.I.N.D. implant. The prenup didn't bother me since I don't expect my Roger to get rich anytime soon, but the mindreading stuff is a bit icky. That's why I snuck out and got a privacy vault installed as soon as I could."

"What are you talking about? What is a M.I.N.D. implant?"

"Marital Intelligence Neural Device—it's a nanocomputer they attach to your brain so your husband can monitor your thoughts. Did you have any medical procedures recently?"

"I had a cyst removed two days ago."

"Did they put you under for it?"

"Yes."

"That must have been when they did it."

"Without telling me? That can't be legal."

"Unfortunately, it is. The Defense of Babies Act legalized monitoring pregnant people to ensure they don't do anything to harm their fetuses."

"But I'm not pregnant. I'm not even planning to get pregnant. I'm on birth control!"

"Sure, but unless you can prove permanent infertility you are considered 'pre-pregnant,' which—per the Supreme Court—means you can be subjected to monitoring to ensure you don't harm your ability to have a healthy pregnancy in the future. Of course, most of the guys who pay for M.I.N.D. implants aren't just checking to make sure their wives take their daily folic acid supplements!"

"Are you saying my husband knows everything I've been thinking since they gave me the implant?"

"Not everything. That's too much data to process, plus the monitoring takes time and energy on his part. He likely only pays attention when he's looking for something specific, or when he's bored."

"I feel sick."

"It'll be okay, Sherry. We just need to get you a privacy vault. We can go now, and you can be upgraded before your husband gets home from work. If we hurry, you can archive this entire conversation before he has the chance to see it. It's the only defense you have, but we have to act fast."

"Okay."

* * *

"Something is different," my husband said.

"It's a new recipe. Do you like it?"

"No. I mean, yes. I mean, I didn't mean the food. There is something different with you."

He closed his eyes, and I knew he was probing my thoughts using the M.I.N.D. thing, so I concentrated on dinner. It was advice Brandy gave me. She told me to think of a list, like the ingredients in a recipe (two tablespoons olive oil) to avoid having an errant thought (three cloves of garlic, minced). If I thought about getting the privacy vault (half a cup panko breadcrumbs) or anything else potentially controversial (salt and red pepper flakes to taste), my husband might discover it (one teaspoon fresh rosemary, minced) before I had chance to tuck it away into my vault (two tablespoons capers, drained). Since I'd only had the vault since the afternoon (one handful flatleaf parsley, chopped), I was still a bit clumsy with the memory transfer (one-third cup grated Pecorino Romano cheese), so deflection was my best option (three eggs, fried).

"Aha!" he said.

"What is it?" I replied (eight ounces dried spaghetti, prepared per package directions).

"Nothing!"

"Nothing?"

"Yes, you've never been able to keep your mind on one thing at a time before, yet the only thing you've been thinking about all evening is dinner."

"Do you like it?"

"I don't care about dinner. You installed a privacy vault, didn't you? Did that woman across the street put you up to this? Brandy? I knew she was a troublemaker. I'll be sure to talk to her husband."

"No! It was me. I did it. On my own. When I suspected I had a M.I.N.D. implant, it creeped me out, okay? I wanted something I could keep to myself. It's only human to need a little privacy."

"You don't need privacy if you have nothing to hide. What are you hiding from me?"

"Nothing!"

"You expect me to believe you modified you brain because of 'nothing'?"

"You modified my brain first! And you didn't even tell me!"

"I did that for us! The foundation of a good marriage is communication, but communication is difficult. Meanings can be easily misunderstood, which leads to distrust, which leads to disdain, which leads to divorce. I don't want that to happen to us, so I got you a M.I.N.D. implant. Because I love you, and I don't want to lose you."

"If you truly valued communication, you wouldn't have implanted something in my brain without even telling me."

"I feel bad about hiding it from you, but I only did it because I knew you'd be upset."

"Of course, I'm upset! You hacked into my brain!"

"I'm sorry I did it without telling you, but I truly thought it would strengthen our relationship. You did something behind my back too, but you did it to spite me."

"I didn't—"

"You weren't angry with me when you did it?"

"Yes, but—"

"Hey, babe, it's okay. I get it. You want something of your own. I understand."

"You do?"

"Yes. In a way. But I hope you realize this may take me a little while to get used to. It will take me some time to fully trust you again."

"I need to find a way to trust you too, you know."

"Of course. Of course. We can work through this. I know we can." He stood up and kissed me on the cheek. "Dinner was very good," he said as he walked away from the table after barely eating anything. He slept in the guest room that night. When I woke up in the morning, he had already gone to work.

* * *

The front door wouldn't open. The electronic lock wouldn't disengage. The backdoor was similarly locked. This time I didn't bother to call tech support. I called my husband.

"Did you do something to the security system? The doors won't unlock."

"After yesterday I thought you could use some time at home."

"You've trapped me here?'

"It's just a timeout."

"I'm not a child."

"I didn't say you were."

"You can't do this!"

"Yes, I can. It's for your protection."

"Protection from what?"

"From outside influences."

"I need protection from you!"

"I'm your husband."

"Precisely! I'm your wife! You can't just lock me up."

"Yes, I can, and after this privacy vault thing, we both need some time to reflect on what comes next. We will talk tonight. I have to get to work." Then, he hung up.

I tried the door again. It was still locked. I tried to call Brandy, but the call didn't go through. The same was true when I tried to call my mom, the police, and the fire department. My phone had been disabled. I tried my computer, but there was no network connection. I banged on the front door and yelled for help, but when I pressed my ear against it, straining to hear some sign that I was heard, there was nothing. I looked out the window. The sidewalk was empty.

The window! I realized I could climb out the window! I fumbled to work the latch, but just then the security shutters closed and locked like they knew what I was thinking, which—of course—the person who controlled them did.

My husband was watching my thoughts, but maybe he was watching more than my mind? Had he installed secret cameras the same way he installed a secret computer in my brain? I made obscene gestures toward every vent, electric outlet, and knick-knack that might be hiding a tiny surveillance device. I eyed every mirror and picture frame with suspicion.

I moved from room to room looking for a means of escape or an effective distraction. I told myself that there are worse things than having to stay at home all day, but I was having trouble breathing. The house felt hot and stuffy. I noticed the air conditioner was off. I was not surprised when I could not turn it on.

Eventually, I did the only thing left I could think of: I sat on the couch and cried. A few days ago, I was a happy newlywed. Now, I was trapped in my house because of a fight with my husband over my right to my own thoughts!

The rising temperature of the house told me the sun was reaching its noonday peak even though the shuttered windows kept my world eerily dusky. I placed a wet washcloth on my forehead and tried to think. It had only been a few hours, but I wondered if my husband was ever coming back to release me. I questioned if I wanted him to come back.

I flinched when I heard the door unlock and open that night. At first, my husband just stared at me. I knew I was a wreck. My hair clung to my face from a mixture of sweat and tears. My eyes were puffy from crying. My clothes were rumpled. My shoulders hung heavy with defeat as I cowered at the far end of the couch.

My husband walked over and put his arm around me. "I'm sorry," he said. "I overreacted. Can you forgive me?"

I didn't say anything because I wasn't sure I could forgive him.

"This is my fault," he said. "I should have never put that thing in your head without talking to you. It was a mistake. I want to undo that. To make it better. To start over. I talked to the M.I.N.D. people, and they said we can come in tomorrow and have the device removed."

"Really?"

"Yes."

"Thank you."

"I love you, Sherry."

I wasn't sure I believed him, but I smiled at him anyway.

* * *

My husband held my hand as we walked to the car the next morning. It felt like the damage of the past few days was already starting to be erased. There was just one more step to make it official, and we were on our way to our appointment at M.I.N.D., Inc. to have that taken care of.

As we reached the car, my husband said he forgot some paperwork for the procedure. While I waited for him to come back, I saw Brandy watering her flowers. I went over to tell her that I was getting my implant removed.

"Brandy!" She turned and waved as I approached, but her face seemed strange.

"Good morning."

"I have wonderful news!"

"I'm sorry. Should I know you?"

"Brandy, stop being silly. I have big news."

"I'm not being silly. I just don't... What's your name again?"

"It's Sherry."

"Sherry and Brandy?" she laughed. "You and me are a cocktail bar come to life!"

"That's what you said when we first met."

"Sounds like you have a case of déjà vu!"

"No. It's not—"

"Sherry! We have to go!" My husband honked the horn as he called to me.

When I got in the car, I said, "Something is wrong with Brandy."

"You can check in on her when we get back. We don't want to be late!"

The M.I.N.D., Inc. offices were in an inconspicuous white building that looked like any ordinary medical clinic. In the waiting room, half a dozen couples sat in uncomfortable chairs and looked at their phones or flipped through family-themed magazines while waiting for their names to be called. The room smelled faintly of disinfectant and was decorated in shades of beige. A wall-sized painting depicted the company logo: A glowing brain behind two wedding rings linked together like a chain.

When it was our turn, we followed a man in a white coat to a procedure room where they strapped me into a large contraption that I was told would keep me still while they used a long needle to remove the nanocomputer currently implanted at the base of my skull.

"Thank you," I said to my husband again before they put the mask on to deliver the general anesthetic. He beamed at me and squeezed my hand before turning his attention to the other man.

"I'm sorry the system didn't work out for you," said the man. "It's not right for every relationship."

"I appreciate you getting us in for the removal so quickly."

"Of course! Our ultimate goal is to make marriages better. If our product is getting in the way, we want to correct that as soon as possible. Did you bring your feedback survey?"

"Yes." My husband handed him a piece of paper.

"Excellent," said the man in the white coat as he reviewed the form. "I see you want to upgrade to a full cognitive replacement this time. I do think you'll be happier with that option. For one thing, it blocks the ability of the spouse or partner to install countermeasures like a digital vault."

My eyes darted back and forth between the men trying to convey my protest, but because of the straps and gas mask, I couldn't move or speak.

"Will she remember what happened before?"

"No, we'll remove all memories of the previous installation. It makes adaption to the new device go more smoothly."

I tried to pull out of my bonds, but the gas was overtaking me. As I was beginning to drift off, my husband said, "And when the new device is installed, I'll have the option to remove new memories and control her actions, right?"

"Within reason," said the other man.

"What's considered within reason?"

"Whatever you can afford to pay for!"

The last thing I heard was the men laughing.

* * *

Discussion Questions

1. Sherry's husband says, "You don't need privacy if you have nothing to hide." If the basis of a marriage is communication and trust, is he wrong? Can good marriages still have "something to hide?"

2. Police and government will review emails, text messages, GPS phone data, etc., arguing "You don't need privacy if you have nothing to hide." Is this different from the marriage example? If so, how?

3. Is there a version of the actions in this story you would support? For example, if Sherry gave her consent? Or if the couple agreed to mutually share each other's thoughts?

4. Is there any scenario where you believe the government would have a compelling interest to regulate and protect pre-pregnant women from certain choices?

5. Besides "I'm in love" and procreation, what is the purpose/function of having a spouse? What does Sherry's husband see as her purpose/function?

Understanding Ice Cream

Earl Smith

* * *

"Class dismissed," Professor Gault said. "Chapters five through nine next time."

As they filed out, the thoughts came. "Another unproductive session. They're graduate students. Years of education. And for what? They should be able to understand the dynamics of political polarization by now. Instead, they get caught in the web. An insect caught in the web is not the spider. By now they should be the spider." He smiled at the idiocy of the thought. "They fall into the trap so easily and get stuck. One side is wrong—misguided—ignorant. And they identify with the side they think holds the high moral ground. Foolishness. Where are the minds that can bridge the chasm?"

Those thoughts followed him out into the quadrangle. It was a pleasant spring afternoon. Mathew decided to forget about the class and the conundrum. He found a vacant bench under a broadly shading tree, sipped his coffee, and vowed to contemplate nature until the clouds cleared.

She entered the quadrangle from the opposite side. He noticed her immediately. Looked to be midsixties. Around five ten, black hair, tanned olive complexion, she walked a measured pace as if in deep contemplation. As that was also his manner, he felt an immediate kinship. "Maybe a visiting professor," he thought. "No, the clothes were wrong. Definitely not an American. There was a stylishness about her that American academic women mostly avoided. Faculty frumpy or freaky eccentric is what they opted for these days. He settled on the wife of a visiting donor and turned back to avoiding his conundrum. His miserably unsuccessful efforts to leave it behind were turning into a rout. It leered back at him from an impenetrable mist.

"You seem to be a man with a problem," she said. He hadn't noticed her approaching nor when she sat down at the opposite end of the bench. On closer inspection, her face was perfectly symmetrical. Her eyes were dark, almost black, matching the color of her hair. There was a presence about her that he found mildly disconcerting.

"I'm getting absent-minded," he said. "Or maybe it's the early stages of senility. I'm sorry. I didn't notice you sitting down. It's such a beautiful day. I've decided to play hooky from my..." He paused, not sure how to describe it. "I've not seen you around before. Are you new to the university?"

"You might say that," she said with a gentle smile. "My name is Anna. And it is a lovely day for playing hooky. But you do not seem to be fully enjoying it. I sense that something is troubling you. My father says that talking about such things to a stranger can sometimes clear the way. So, if you are willing to take a chance, tell me what is bothering you."

"Well, let's see if your father is right," he said with a smile. "You're correct. I'm teaching an advanced seminar on contemporary political dynamics. The participants are doctoral and master's students. So, they're not neophytes. They can't seem to think about polarization without getting caught in its snare. It's frustrating. I spend time muttering about spiders and webs. And end up getting nowhere."

"Well, dichotomies are a debilitating distraction dismembering much of what passes for human thought," she said with a sly grin. "What is your area of research?"

"Sociology and politics."

"So, you study the human condition from the perspective of sociology?" she asked.

"You could put it that way, yes. But I limit my focus to the human condition as it engages in politics. It's my calling. And my tormentor. If humans can't teach other humans about such things, then all of this," he said sweeping his hand around the quadrangle, "is just a kamikaze raid on a vacant lot."

"Clearly all of this, as you refer to it, has brought major benefits to humanity," Anna responded. "The question is, does any of it help you with your conundrum. Or is it a straitjacket that keeps you from a new understanding? What was the focus of the seminar?"

"The tabled question was, 'Why are we so polarized?' For two hours there were the standard ruminations on the subject, accompanied by hardening positions on opposite sides. They even got polarized about the definition of polarization."

"They were not polarized," she softly said.

Her statement barely registered. Polarization was the current filet mignon of political theory. Without it, nothing in the contemporary doctrines made any sense. "Not another amateur," he thought to himself.

"I am not the amateur you think I am," she said with a slight smile. He looked at her sharply. "Perhaps I can assist you in ways you might not anticipate. You see polarization as conflict. But let us posit that there are at least two flavors of conflict. One, to use a theological example, is between two who believe in God differently. Both have accepted the existence of a superior being but differ in the description and proscriptions of their deity. A second is between one who worships God and another who does not believe that such an entity exists. You might agree that the nature of these two conflicts is fundamentally different. Atheists are unlikely to attack believers simply because they believe, unless attacked first for nonbelieving. On the other hand, it is far more likely that believers will attack those who, through their heretical beliefs, either misinterpret or misrepresent their God."

Gault turned toward her. "I'll admit I was thinking you are an amateur, but this suddenly seems a conversation worth having. I'll posit there's a difference, but I'm not sure where that takes us. How can you say they were not polarized? It's so obvious that this entire society is polarized. Just look at the political situation. Left against right, men against women, liberals against progressives, conservatives against Trumpsters. Polarization is a defining characteristic of American society."

"Accurate as far as it goes," she replied. "But there is a problem with your analysis. It started with paragraph two.

Suppose for a moment that something more fundamental is the defining characteristic of American society."

"What the hell does that mean?" he replied. After a pause, he continued. "I apologize. I didn't mean to respond that way. It's a jarring suggestion. What am I missing?"

"You have ignored the possibility that what you call polarization is simply various manifestations of a defining underlying condition. That polarization is a collection of symptoms of a commonly shared, pervasive disease."

"Go on," he said.

"Do you like ice cream? Chocolate or vanilla?"

The questions stopped him for a bit. He decided to play along. "Yes, I do like ice cream. Almost everybody does. Of the two choices, I prefer vanilla."

"And your students, do they all prefer vanilla as well?"

"I seriously doubt it. They are likely as polarized on this question as they are on political matters. But you seem to be making my case rather than yours."

"So, which is the more defining question? What is the cause of the almost unanimous taste for ice cream, or why do people choose between alternative flavors?"

Gault paused. Then said slowly, "It depends on what part of the process you are focusing on."

"A fair response. But, if you do not answer the first question usefully, how edifying will your answer to the second one be? If you do not understand the conditions that support the urgency that underlies polarization, then how do you find meaning in its various manifestations?"

"You've lost me," Gault said.

"You said that almost everybody likes ice cream," Anna

continued. "So, you accept the possibility that, because of an allergy, lactose intolerance, or just a dislike of the taste or texture, there are people who do not get far enough along to make the choice between chocolate and vanilla. Are these the only nonpolarized ones when it comes to ice cream? And how many might suffer from one or more of these conditions and still crave the stuff? Or what of those who are indifferent when it comes to choosing? What does polarization mean within the broader context of preference or a lack thereof?"

Gault looked at her, smiled, and said, "I'm getting the feeling that either a psychiatrist or a philosopher might be handy about now."

"Perhaps," she replied with a playful grin. Gault scratched his chin in thought. Anna continued. "Preference is not prejudice, partisanship, or polarization. It is simply an indicator of a choice from among options. And the needs to make those choices are simply manifestations of the basic underlying condition of liking ice cream and the availability of a range of flavors to choose from."

"I think I'm catching up a bit," he said. "You're suggesting that the disposition toward ice cream is the underlying driver of the choice between flavors? I'll buy that. But aren't those voluntary choices based on individual preferences?"

"You need to go deeper into it," she said. "If you begin with the question, why does one person prefer vanilla over chocolate, without first focusing on the roots of the liking of ice cream, you end up studying the various symptoms of 'liking ice cream.' You are overlooking the underlying condition that makes choosing an imperative."

He started to say something, but Anna raised a hand. "Let

me finish the thought. The challenge is that foundational conditions provide a context within which choices are made. Without understanding that underlying context, choices can appear irrational and chaotic."

"Let's follow your reasoning," he said. "What is the underlying condition—the equivalent of liking ice cream—that is driving polarization?"

"Narcissism," she replied. "Intense self-involvement. Hubris. The determinative hegemony of ego. A population of narcissists will always become increasingly polarized as their condition deepens. It is inevitable."

"Are you suggesting that the defining characteristic of my students is a mental disorder?"

"I am suggesting that narcissism is *the* defining characteristic of American contemporary culture. It is the dynamic that is producing an increasingly dysfunctional society. That is because advancing narcissism causes a major internal conflict. Narcissism runs counter to a basic human need. Millions of years of evolution have produced extraordinarily successful social animals. But narcissism produces individuals who are self-definers of truth and fact. The so-called post-truth, post-fact generations. Their mantra is that every individual gets to define what they take to be true as true."

"But the individual isolated and bound within their own insistence on personal sovereignty still feels the need for social context. A truth that cannot be redefined away. The major cause of increasing polarization is the intensifying internal conflicts which arise because of the tensions between advancing narcissism and the echoing needs of an intensely social species."

"Then you are saying that we are all narcissists," came an

irritated grumble.

She sighed deeply, then continued, "Narcissism is one of three mental disorders widely seen as untreatable. The others being psychopathy and paranoia. You don't cure a narcissist. To misuse Kierkegaard, such a condition, once reached, is a sickness unto death. But the death of far more than the individual *being qua being*. Once narcissism flowers, the real world dies for the narcissist. A virtual world takes its place."

She turned toward him and said, "Narcissism involves extreme selfishness, a sense of entitlement, a lack of empathy, and a dominating need to be admired. The narcissist sees herself as the center of the universe. Indeed, its very reason for existence. Things such as truth, facts, virtues, and heresies are defined within her driving need to be the essence of every issue, circumstance, event, and thought. She has swallowed the lie that reality can be bent to her claim of omnipotence and omniscience. Her life becomes a fiction based on self-deception."

Anna smiled and asked, "So, what would a society of narcissists look like? How would they find a balance between their narcissistic tendencies and the need for social and cultural context? How would they balance the virtual understanding of their own sovereignty with their real needs for social connections?"

They sat in silence for a while. "Welcome to the void," Anna finally said. "Let us leap in. They would attempt to solve the dilemma by inverting the conditions. A narcissist redefines their virtual sovereignty as reality. Then creates a virtual social context which they also claim to be real. The hope being that these virtual associations will satisfy their need for human connections. But, as the old saying goes, only a fool attempts to warm herself before a picture of a fire."

He looked at her and, almost pleadingly, said, "As I understand it, you are suggesting that a culture of simplemindedness, of the undefined, of indefiniteness, is the only possible outcome in a population of narcissists. That's a..."

Anna interrupted him, smiling impishly, "You know, one of the greatest charlatans of all western philosophers was René Descartes. He famously wrote, *cogito ergo sum*. Roughly translated, 'I think, therefore I am.'"

Matthew grimaced and said, "You are going to suggest that he was wrong, aren't you?"

"Not so much wrong," she replied. "Descartes stopped short for lack of courage. Should he have had the courage, it would have been 'I think I think therefore I am.' And that would have become, 'I think I think therefore I think I am.' And on to, 'I think I think I think therefore I think I am. I think I think I think therefore I think I think I am. I think I think I think I think therefore I think I think I think I am.' And so on, right down the rabbit hole. He said nothing really. And the world found it profound. But he did lay the foundation for the evolution of a narcissism based on simple-minded self-definition. To think you think is to murder the very thing that is thinking. Its connotative substitute is really nothing but a hymn to self-glorification. But this is getting too heavy for such a nice spring afternoon. Let's get back to ice cream."

Gault frowned and shook his head slowly. "If I've followed you, you seem to be suggesting that the inevitable end product of the Age of Reason and the Enlightenment is a population of raving narcissists."

"You are envisioning wandering bands of rabid vampires," she said. "Reacting without reason. Changing identity on a whim. Drinking their own blood. But that is not what is happening. They are humans choosing virtual sides in a virtual world. Alone, isolated, disconnected except through their gossamer virtual imaginings. Unable to erase the manufactured self at the center of their manufactured universe. They live their lives inside video games in which they are the sole hero. The savior of mankind. If you are going to understand them, you need to muster the courage to step inside that game."

"I would be forever lost," Gault said. "I would cease to exist as the person that I have labored so many years to become. My knowledge is hard won. There is a core of my being that is substantial and real. I need to remain who I am. I've dedicated all my will and knowledge to educating new generations. I cannot do that as a figment of my own imagination."

"If you lack the courage to go further, dedication is a fine palliative. But, at minimum, you need to recognize that your students are doing the only thing that narcissists can do under their circumstances. Making choices that are trivial and claiming them to be foundational."

"They are self-virtualized prophets of their own imagined immortality," Gault said slowly and sadly.

Anna said sharply, "A population of narcissists, all of whom take themselves as prophets of the truth, constitute a legion of false prophets who are morbidly aware of their heresy and their corruption."

Gault felt a panic rush through him. "So, you are saying that a realization that salvation is not coming is driving the behavior of my students? Because they sit upon the throne of a god they have displaced and then denied. They know that it doesn't matter what is called true because they realize their own corruption is the very definition of who they are."

Anna nodded slowly. "Narcissism is a cold and lonely place. The God who has been overthrown cannot be recalled. The god enshrined in his place is a gossamer illusion. The narcissist fears the fate of a false prophet. He who follows the anti-Christ is forever banned from heaven. Condemned eternally to the pit. And the narcissist is both anti-Christ and ardent follower."

After a while, Mathew said. "I always thought I was the sane one, and they, my students, were deluded. But you seem to be suggesting that they are more creatures of their time and aware of their circumstances than I am. That they are the realists and I the... I don't know what I am in that."

"You are mostly irrelevant to them in their attempt to create sanity out of a completely insane situation," Anna said softly.

She reached out and touched his hand. "I am deeply sorry that our conversation has upset you. Please believe me that it was not my intention to spoil this beautiful spring afternoon. But, as jarring as the idea is, there is some merit in considering it."

"I'm not sure I understand what you are getting at, but I suspect I won't like it much if, and when, I do," Gault said.

"Who is the believer and who is the atheist?" she asked. "To you, they are the heretics. They defame your god of reason. Your urgency is to recall the fallen. But your students inhabit a different universe. In Virtual Land, they form armies, identify allies and enemies, assault those who misrepresent their god in battles beyond the stars."

"If my god is reason, what is theirs?" Gault asked.

"Themselves. Each themselves. Alone, isolated, like stars scattered across the void. Emptiness surrounds them and stands between them and any others. They strive to do what all stars must do. Burn brightly and then expire."

"But they don't burn brightly," Gault said. "There is little in them that speaks of brilliance or vision. Only a pedestrian, plodding mindlessness. How is that burning bright?"

"You are looking at it through your eyes," Anna responded. "Try it this way. Suppose you are a narcissist and the self-anointed creator of your world. But the hunger is inside you for social context—a hunger which requires you to recognize others as necessary to your wellbeing. And that thought has brought you to a despair that cannot be willed away. What would you do? How would you act? Would you not want desperately to be famous for even a few hours? Even if it means slaughtering a dozen children with an assault rifle. Or loudly proclaiming that the entire world is corrupt."

"Look at their world through their eyes? I'm not sure I can. The world you describe is so different from mine."

"Then let us focus on an inflection point. You begin to suspect that you are not in control. The arsenic of narcissism. You cannot build and maintain relationships with friends as equals. That path is closed off to you. So, what do you do? You lash out at the insanity of your situation. Rage at the darkness, to borrow a phrase. You manufacture a virtual reality in which you are supreme above all others. Even those who profess to believe all the virtual things you believe are inconveniences bordering on personal insults to your existence."

Anna settled back and then almost whispered, "But your actions cannot open you to yet another demonstration of your irrelevance and impotence. So, you choose to focus your rage where you are least likely to be proven wrong. What would be more appropriate than politics? You cannot be incorrect. You cannot be denied."

"Are you suggesting that they choose politics because whatever they profess to believe doesn't matter?"

"In a way. Because it allows both meaningless omnipotence and irrelevant omniscience. A narcissist's nirvana."

"You are suggesting that nothing that I am trying to accomplish matters."

Anna leaned forward. "There are impactful political actors. They shape, for better or worse, the arc of human history. But none of your students are likely to become members of that group. They like to think of themselves as the headlining performer at a global concert. But each is more likely to be the occupant of the cheap seat sold at a discount to fill the arena. Irrelevancy is the reality that a narcissist must most ardently deny."

She paused to let her last comment sink in. "Politics is the ideal focus for a narcissist," Anna said. "They can talk about big things without any risk. Nothing will ever come from their ruminations and gnashing of teeth in a world that they fervently avow does not exist—nor in the virtual one they ardently envision. They can strut about, loudly proclaiming their fierce independence. Posturing as the decider of things strategic. Pronouncing definitively. It does not matter which side they take. Vanilla or chocolate, their choice does not matter."

Anna paused, glanced at Gault, and then continued. "What is necessary for them is an impotent opposition to their claim of omnipotence. And this they decree without fear. They need others to shout, just as ardently and insubstantially, chocolate to their vanilla. Their desire is for an unending, and unresolvable, series of virtual battles beyond the stars against those who misrepresent their god. The legions of vanilla against the hordes of chocolate. Within the cocoon of their fantasies, they take the blue pill and settle into oblivion. To quote Morpheus, 'You take the blue pill... you wake up in your bed and believe whatever you want to believe.' Virtual empowerment. Virtually meaningless."

Anna looked directly into his eyes. "You see, Professor Gault, it really does not matter which side your students take. Chocolate or vanilla. It is all the same choice. Polarization is simply a ploy in a virtual game they play. A manifestation of advancing narcissism. A symptom of the underlying disease."

She glanced at her watch. "I need to be going. I have enjoyed our conversation and hope you have as well."

He shook his head. "Let me see if I understood you. Before there is ice cream, there is no choosing. But, once there is, choosing is only the result of the compelling need to choose. Narcissism compels a choice. In fact, it demands it if the narcissist is to maintain themselves at the center of their worldview. It's the act of choosing, not the actual choice, that is the symptom of the underlying disease. You said, vanilla or chocolate, it really doesn't matter. There is no logic. Only the imperative of choosing. If that is true, what is there for me to do? Have I nothing to contribute?"

"The delusion of pontificating definitively is the defining

currency of narcissism," Anna replied. "A narcissist can only maintain their claim to the throne of the overthrown God by self-certifying both omnipotence and omniscience."

"As for your question," Anna said softly, "do as you must. There is nothing more for you than that. Except perhaps a chance of a clearer understanding. There is no exit from your circle of beliefs. Nor any for your students from theirs. To quote an old Zen proverb, '*If you understand, things are just as they are. If you do not understand, things are just as they are.*'"

As she was walking away, Anna paused, glanced back, and said, "By the way, I have never tasted ice cream nor had to choose. Our talk has left me curious."

He watched her cross the quad and disappear through the arch.

* * *

Discussion Questions

1. How would you summarize the argument that Anna is making about the students, and do you agree with her?
2. Anna argues the underlying trait of the students driving their political debates is their narcissism. Do you agree? What is driving their narcissism?
3. Do you agree with the premise of the story, that narcissism is the foundational trait of political polarization, and that the polarization is the result, regardless whether you are liberal or conservative?
4. If, as Anna proposes, narcissists are fighting an "unending, and unresolvable, series of virtual battles beyond the stars against those who misrepresent their god," then how do you ever stop the cycle of polarization? Do you agree with Anna that once narcissism takes hold the imagined world can never be let go?
5. Do you agree with Anna's supposition that narcissists focus on politics because they want to "focus their rage where they are least likely to be proven wrong"? Are there counterarguments you would like to have made to Anna that the Mathew did not?

Glad All Over

Lee Dawkins

* * *

The C30 cassette concluded with a terminal thud, plunging the darkened room back into silence. The lounge of Angus's small, terraced house, in a neglected and unfashionable part of South East London, was familiar to me, even in the gloom. I had sat on this scruffy old sofa countless times chatting with him. Our discussions ranged from the prosaic to the profound; from soccer—and our shared love of an equally neglected and unfashionable South East London football team—to philosophy and the meaning of existence. But nothing in any of those conversations prepared me for this moment. As I reached for my phone to call the emergency services, I recalled the day I'd first met Angus, almost exactly a year ago.

It was one of those really warm afternoons you sometimes get on the opening day of a new football season, when the conditions are more suited to cricket than soccer. The players of Crystal Palace Football Club, the Eagles, entered Selhurst Park stadium, walking out to the sound of their anthem, "Glad All Over," blasting from the PA system. The Dave Clark Five were promising us truth, loyalty, and everlasting happiness. In response thousands of voices sang along, unanimously affirming that they were indeed feeling glad all over. A stout elderly man, his head topped with a froth of white curls, smiled as I wedged myself into the red plastic seat beside him. I was expecting a traditional South London greeting—a nod or maybe even an "All right, mate?"—so I was taken by surprise when, in an accent of a peculiar blend of Croydon and Glasgow, he said, "Epicurus taught that to enjoy a happy life, we should seek to avoid suffering." Holding out his hand he added, "I'm Angus, and I suspect we will be sharing more than a small amount of suffering, watching our beloved Eagles together this season."

It's always potluck who you end up sitting next to when you have a season ticket, but I immediately warmed to this fella. "It makes you wonder what we are doing here, doesn't it?" I replied.

Angus nodded thoughtfully. "I couldn't have put it better myself, son."

A few minutes into the game a quite unexpected thing happened; Crystal Palace took the lead. But it wasn't the goal that shocked me, it was my reaction to it. Instead of leaping to my feet in celebration as I would usually do, an unseen force pinned me to my seat. I was pleased we'd scored, but that was it, just pleased, nothing more. All around me people wildly punched the air. Complete strangers hugged each other. Few things in life invoke such raw emotion as soccer. Nothing else gets those neck veins bulging and nape hair bristling like this game. It's a truly unique feeling and one that has kept me coming back, season after season, for the last thirty-odd years. But that *feeling* had now suddenly deserted me. The passion vanished, its place taken by a strange sense of disconnection, a numb detachment. I was surrounded by thousands of jubilant fans but had never felt more alone. Something was wrong. Very wrong. Anxiety rose as my heart began to race. My immediate impulse was to get out of the ground. I stood to leave.

"Excuse me, Angus," I said as I began my attempt to seek the sanctuary of the gangway. But instead of standing aside to let me through, he seemed to intentionally block my way.

"You're not off already are you, son? Quitting while we're ahead, eh?" Laughing loudly, he slapped me firmly on the shoulder, folding me back into my seat. He then began to talk and didn't stop talking until the halftime whistle. If you asked me what he'd said, I wouldn't have been able to tell you, but I do know I found his words comforting, and the panic gradually subsided. The halftime break was the perfect opportunity for me to make my getaway, but instead of heading for the exit, I found myself offering to get Angus a cup of tea. We continued our conversation in the second half, and the Eagles were polite enough not to interrupt our discussions by scoring another goal.

I spent the next couple of weeks trying to work out what had caused my meltdown.

Perhaps I'd just fallen out of love with football. My wife had been telling me for years that it was a silly game—twenty-two overpaid men running around kicking a bag of wind. Maybe I had finally and belatedly grown up? But if it was that simple, why had my reaction been so intense? I decided to give my season ticket away and have a break from the game. I could look at taking up a different hobby. Gardening is cool these days, or I could try working out, before my body becomes totally irredeemable. However, as the next home match drew nearer, these plans faded. Bizarrely I found myself actually looking forward to going to the game. But I realized it wasn't the football attracting me, it was the thought of meeting up again with Angus.

Men are encouraged to be more open about our mental health these days, but baring your soul to a total stranger who just happens to sit next to you at a sporting event is still a tall order. Nevertheless, I felt surprisingly at ease when I confided in Angus at the following game. It didn't take him long to establish that this wasn't just a football thing, it reflected how I was feeling about life in general: work, family, everything. After hearing me out, he delivered his verdict; I was undergoing an existential crisis. I wasn't sure what it was, but it sounded a lot sexier than a boring old midlife crisis. Sensing my uncertainty, Angus ran through a checklist: Lack of purpose? Yes; Sense of isolation? Got it; Absence of meaning? 100 percent; Awareness of own mortality? You bet. I ticked every box. I was facing the classic paradox of someone who thinks life is important, while simultaneously believing it has no purpose. I must have looked worried, because Angus was quick to reassure me that my crisis was a perfectly natural response. We are hardwired to search for meaning, he explained, but everyday life gets in the way. Grappling with the technicalities of a 3-5-2 team formation over a midfield diamond is hard enough, without having to consider free will, the nature of the self, or proving the existence of an external world. But fundamental questions have a habit of bubbling to the surface in some of us, and when they do, they are impossible to ignore.

So, if that was the diagnosis, what was the cure? It was at an evening game against Manchester City when Angus told me about Antiphon the sophist and his "Shop of Consolation" in ancient Corinth. Above the door was the inscription, *"I can heal illness with words."* Angus revealed that he had suffered a crisis of his own many years ago and had found solace in words. His crisis had been precipitated by a heart-breaking tragedy—the death of his only child from viral meningitis at the age of just nine. Philosophy had saved Angus. He stumbled by chance on a story about the pre-Socratic Greek Anaxagoras. Legend has it that upon being told that his sons were dead, Anaxagoras calmly replied that he knew his children were born to die. These simple words gave Angus strength. They also inspired him to read the great philosophers and embark on a lifetime quest for understanding.

The wisdom he accumulated had recently been helping him through another devastating event, his wife's dementia. Ruth had introduced Angus to Crystal Palace shortly after he'd swapped Glasgow for London in the '60s. Until she became unwell, she accompanied him to every game. He refused to consign her to a care home, insisting on looking after her himself in their own house. He received very little assistance, but a kindly neighbor popped in to cover for him when needed. Fortunately for me, the neighbor thought it would do Angus good to continue going to football.

There is an old Buddhist proverb that says, *"When the student is ready, the master appears."* Angus offered to share his learning with me, and I jumped at the chance. I warned him that the closest I'd got to reading any philosophy was the *"Live.*

Laugh. Love." sign in our kitchen. Angus assured me that the only entry qualification to his impromptu course was an open mind.

So, match days became a symposium as Selhurst Park was transformed into my personal Lyceum. Each football game featured a masterclass on a different philosopher or school of thought. It was enthralling. Angus had a way of making difficult ideas seem simple. For the first time in my life, I enjoyed learning. The fixtures couldn't come quickly enough. Soon we were meeting for extra-curricular sessions over a pint of London Gold at Angus's local pub, the Crown and Sceptre, or a cuppa at his house. He was clear with me from the start that this wouldn't provide an off-the-peg blueprint for living the perfect life. He said if I wanted that, I should seek the ministrations of a priest. Nor did this learning come with a money-back guarantee that I'd find any answers. In fact, the most valuable lesson Angus taught me was that the questions themselves are as important as the answers. It's not just the destination, but the road you take. Even if life is ultimately unknowable, the quest for understanding, no matter how futile, is still an edifying one.

If you had asked me twelve months ago about Albert Camus, you would have been met with the blankest of stares. Thanks to Angus, I now know that Camus not only said some pretty profound things but was also a very decent goalkeeper—though whether he ever managed to perform both these feats at the same time, only his back four would know. Angus wanted to show me that philosophy was for everyone, not just intellectuals. It was as relevant for football fans as it was for academics. Camus combined playing the beautiful game with applying his beautiful mind to the purpose of life. Without meaning, Camus thought life was absurd. It's an absurdity that can ambush us anywhere: a street corner, a sun-blasted beach, a football match. And when it strikes, we must confront it, embrace it, live with it. Finding happiness then becomes a duty, a moral obligation. Angus said we should find happiness wherever we can: in art, in nature, in friendship, in love, and, yes, in sport.

After all, it was Camus himself who said, "What I know most surely about morality and obligations I owe to football."

Angus rattled off a list of things that gave him pleasure. It was an eclectic inventory, a mixtape of personal joys: country walks with Ruth, a traditional English fry-up, *The Hay Wain* by John Constable, a vinyl copy of *Kind of Blue*, quantum entanglement, the smell that follows a shower of rain, his battered edition of the *Nicomachean Ethics*, any film with Fred MacMurray, a decent pint of London Gold and, of course, cheering on the Palace as they walk out to "Glad All Over." These pleasures don't just add meaning—they are the meaning.

By the final game of the season my crash course in 2,500 years of western philosophy had taken me from the pre-Socratics of the ancient world to Plato, then on to the Cynics, the Stoics, the Skeptics, and the Epicureans. We had traveled through the medieval and Renaissance thinkers to Descartes and the modern age. There we met Schopenhauer, Nietzsche, Kierkegaard, and Sartre. Thanks to Angus, I am now familiar with epistemology, metaphysics, and empiricism. I know my Aristotle from my Hegel, my Berkeley from my Kant. Along the way, I was introduced to thought experiments involving evil demons, and cats that were simultaneously dead and alive. It was truly revelatory. Angus's love of knowledge and understanding was infectious; and while he'd been right to warn me it was no short-term fix, I was definitely feeling an awful lot better in myself. And Crystal Palace hadn't been playing too badly either.

I saw Angus regularly during the off-season. His mood was typically buoyant despite a worrying downturn in Ruth's condition. Whenever we met, he was as passionate as ever, always eager to introduce me to new ideas he thought I would enjoy.

Punctuality was one of Angus's many qualities, so when he didn't show up at the pub on time this evening, I suspected something was wrong. I walked the short distance to his house. The front door was open, and there was no sign of anyone inside. The lounge curtains were drawn, but once my eyes had adjusted to the dark, I saw an old-fashioned cassette recorder on the coffee table. Next to it was a note in Angus's distinctive script. It simply said, *"Play me."* I pressed the start button with trepidation. Nostalgic hisses and crackles filled the room as the magnetic tape started to revolve. Then Angus's voice was addressing me. He told me not to be alarmed—which immediately alarmed me—and warned me not to go upstairs. I sensed this was not going to end well. My worst fears were quickly confirmed when Angus broke the shocking news. He instructed me to inform the police that Ruth's body could be found in their bedroom. His own body, he added casually, would be lying next to hers. Surely this wasn't true. I wanted it to be an elaborate philosophical thought experiment that Angus had devised to demonstrate one of his ideas. If I went back to the Crown and Sceptre, I would be sure to find him there in his favorite chair sipping a pint of London Gold. The cassette continued to revolve, and Angus continued his monologue. I realized this was no experiment.

"What have you done Angus?" I shouted into the darkness with a mixture of anger and remorse. What right did he have to take Ruth's life? And how did it help by taking his own when he had so much more to give? He answered me by first explaining in cool and dispassionate terms exactly what he was about to do. He spoke without emotion, as if he was reading out the assembly instructions of a piece of flat-pack furniture. His tone changed when he turned to *why* he was doing it. Ruth had always been afraid of death. She was especially scared of dying alone. While the thought of death didn't bother Angus, he understood his wife's fear. Nothing he said ever gave her reassurance, so, many years ago, he promised that if she was ever facing death, then they would die together. Ruth took great comfort from his words, and although most of her memories had been erased in the fog of her disease, she had never forgotten that promise. Angus realized that her time was fast approaching, and if he was to honor his word, he would need to act now. When he told her what he was going to do, she smiled. It was a smile he knew so well, but which he had not seen in a very long time. And he knew when he saw it that he was doing the right thing. His voice was still calm, almost serene, but now with just an edge of emotion. It was not how I imagined a man who was about to take the life of his wife of nearly sixty years as well as his own would sound. There was no trace of doubt, no hint of any moral reservation. He was as certain he was doing what was right as any man could be.

Angus ended the recording with these words:

"Please do not mourn for me, son. I was born to die. I have lived my life to the full and found plenty of happiness along the way. I am now happy that it should end here. And happy too that my ending will bring comfort to the person I love the most as she passes. My epitaph will be the Epicurean epitaph: *Non fui; fui; non sum; non curo*—I was not; I was; I am not; I do not care."

The analog hiss of late twentieth-century technology resumed. I was about to press *eject* when suddenly I heard the familiar voices of The Dave Clark Five. They were promising a love that lasts for eternity. And they were feeling glad all over.

* * *

I have just finished scattering Angus's and Ruth's ashes on hallowed ground, at the hallowed ground. Just behind the Holmesdale Road stand at Selhurst Park is a little patch of grass reserved for the remains of Eagles fans who have gone to take their seat in the great stadium in the sky. Soccer is the closest thing Angus had to a religion, so I thought it was a fitting resting place. It's the first day of another new season and the sun is shining on cue. As I head to my usual seat, I still half expect to see those distinctive white curls greeting me. It feels strange to find an unfamiliar face sitting in his place. It makes Angus's passing feel more real. His substitute, a man in his twenties, sees me approaching and gives me a nod. "All right, mate?" he says as I sit down next to him.

I am tempted to shake his hand and offer a quote from Epicurus. I settle instead for a reciprocal, "All right?"

As the players take to the field Dave Clark and his four friends launch into "Glad All Over." I look at all the people standing around me. They are clapping and singing along; experiencing the simple pleasure of being part of something that transcends the individual self. For a few brief moments all their troubles, all their worries, all their frustrations are forgotten. They are happy. And in this instant, I see things with an exquisite clarity. I know that I too have every reason to be happy; to be feeling glad all over.

Five minutes into the game something quite unexpected happens—Crystal Palace take the lead. It isn't the goal itself that shocks me, but my reaction to it. A surge of excitement runs through my body, spontaneously propelling me out of my seat and onto my feet. I turn to the lad next to me and give him the biggest hug I've ever given any stranger at a football match. The noise is deafening, so he doesn't hear me shouting to Angus through my tears. "You were not; you were; you are not; I care."

* * *

Discussion Questions

1. Angus introduces himself by saying, "Epicurus taught that to enjoy a happy life we should seek to avoid suffering." What does this mean, and do you agree?
2. Later, Angus explains that "Without meaning, Camus thought life was absurd." What does this mean, and do you agree?
3. Angus defines an existential crisis as a (1) lack of purpose (2) sense of isolation (3) absence of meaning and (4) awareness of your own mortality. What is the difference (if any) between an existential crisis and a midlife crisis?
4. What would be your advice to a friend or family member suffering from an existential crisis?
5. Do you think Angus did the right thing by killing his wife and taking his own life? Once his wife was dead, why did Angus also decide to kill himself? Do you think any (*or all*) of this was the right choice?

Thorn

Erik Fatemi

* * *

Joseph was never anyone I had to worry about. Joseph was a nobody. He did his work, went home to his family. That's as far as his ambitions went. If you needed someone to build a door, fix a stone wall—odd jobs like that—and you didn't have much money, you hired Joseph. He had his regulars, but not enough to cut into my business. Most of the time, verily, I forgot he even existed. So, no, Joseph wasn't my problem. My problem was his boy. I just didn't see it coming.

The first sign came about ten years ago. I was walking through the market, and, lo, there was Philip, the son of Matthias, in his usual stall, chattering nonstop to everyone who passed by. The finest pottery in town! The lowest prices! But I wasn't interested in his bowls and platters. My eyes went straight to two new cedar stools that he'd set out for customers. The seats, rectangular and contoured, were unlike any I'd seen before in Sepphoris. I'd already taken over most of the labor in town, and none of my people were capable of such craftsmanship. This was Temple-quality work. Whoever built these stools wouldn't be selling to potters for long. He'd go where the money was, to a better clientele. My clientele. I'd seen it before. In fact, I'd done the same thing myself when I was breaking into the business.

I needed to find out who made these stools.

Philip fussed over me when he saw me coming, and I took a seat. I'm tall, nearly four cubits, and I eat well. Most stools would prefer a lighter load, but this one supported me easily. I picked up an oil lamp from among his wares and pretended to examine it.

"Martha will love it," Philip said. He listed its many virtues in great detail and quoted a price we both knew was too high. He also knew I'd pay it, because I could.

I considered the offer, then rapped my knuckles on the empty stool next to me. "Not bad. Where'd you get them?"

Philip stammered, nervous he was about to lose a sale. "You know I always buy from you, Timothy. But—"

I smiled and held up my hand. "Just curious."

When he said Joseph, the son of Jacob, I made him repeat it. Impossible. Where did Joseph learn how to make stools like this?

* * *

James arrived at my house early the next morning, as usual, to review my affairs for the day. Sepphoris was booming, and it was a good time to be in construction. I'd known James since school, but we were never what you'd call friends. Other boys mocked him and called him James the Lesser because he was the smallest of the three Jameses in our class and as meek as a lamb. But I tolerated him. He followed me around, hanging on my every word, and that came in handy sometimes—as was still true all these years later. I paid him well, but he lived in a simple home and dressed plainly. He wasn't married and seemed to have no interests other than serving as my steward and doing whatever I asked of him. Today, that meant visiting Joseph's workshop, an hour and a half's walk to the south, to see if he had hired anyone or was still working by himself.

When James returned that afternoon, he said Joseph was alone, except for his son.

"Was the boy doing anything?" I asked. "Or just watching?"

James checked his writing tablet before answering. He took notes on everything. "He hammered some nails, but that was all."

In hindsight, I should have put Joseph out of business then and there. It would have saved me a lot of trouble later. But I let it go. I was expanding into Cana at the time, so I was often on the road. And Martha was with child—John, my firstborn son—and I was building a new home (the one before where we now live). I had bigger things to think about than a few stools.

Years passed, and my business continued to flourish. The Romans hired me to build a stable in Capernaum, and that opened up a multitude of new opportunities for me—everything from crosses to courthouses. My laborers grumbled about working for Romans, but I had no interest in politics. Silver was silver.

Life was just as good at home. Martha gave birth to our daughter, Elizabeth, and my second son, Luke. I bought land on the highest hill in Sepphoris and built a mansion almost worthy of Solomon, with eight rooms, mosaic floors, and indoor baths. As James said, the greatest builder in Galilee should have the finest house. Same for the garden. I filled it with lilies and roses and all manner of fruits: figs, dates, pomegranates, apples. And olives, of course. I hired a servant to care for it full-time. Maybe my father used to tend a garden like mine. I would have enjoyed ordering him around.

So I had little reason to think about Joseph. I bumped into him occasionally if he had a job here in town, but we rarely spoke. Then James told me one morning that Joseph had died. He'd been sick for a long time—some sort of palsy.

I stopped listening. Construction on a wall I was building in Magdala was running behind schedule, and I couldn't afford any more delays.

"His son is taking over his shop," James said.

This made me pause. He was just one carpenter in a lowly village, but you could never be too careful. "Keep an eye on him," I said.

* * *

Then it came to pass that James said he needed to show me something at the synagogue. I hadn't stepped foot inside it in months and didn't plan on returning until the next high holiday. I'd suffered through enough services as a boy, thanks to my father. He earned practically nothing as a gardener, but every week he'd tithe a fifth of his wages—double what the scriptures required. Every night when we weren't at the synagogue, he'd read aloud from the Torah to my brothers and me while my mother mended holes in our threadbare tunics. So I'd had my fill of religion and the poverty that came with it. If my competitors wanted to waste their time at services, good for them. They'd be working for me soon anyway.

The synagogue was badly in need of repair; no doubt the priests were pocketing the tithes for themselves. The roof leaked, the benches wobbled, and the holy ark—a cabinet built into a recess in the wall that held the Torah scrolls—was on the verge of falling apart. Even a nonbeliever like myself found it embarrassing. If it had been up to me, I'd have torn the whole structure down and rebuilt it. But as soon as James brought me inside, I knew what he wanted me to see. The ark had been replaced, and the new one was astonishing.

It had two doors that opened from the center, like the old one, and was the same size as the original. But the craftsmanship was flawless. I reached out to touch it, then drew short. There was something strange about it—almost as if it had been there forever, and the synagogue constructed around it.

"Joseph's son," James said. "He donated it."

So that was my second sign. I knew then that I'd been right about Philip's stools: Joseph hadn't built them after all. But I never guessed it was his boy. Where'd he been hiding all these years? Waiting for Joseph to die? It didn't make sense. But whatever his reason for lying low in the past, he must have cast it aside. If you were an up-and-coming carpenter and wanted to show off your talent, the synagogue was the place to do it. I had to admit, it was a cunning move. I should have thought of it myself.

If I didn't act quickly, this boy could be a thorn in my side for many years to come.

* * *

With his short legs, James took three steps for every two of mine. "This way," he said, pointing left as we entered the village.

I'd been to Nazareth many times, most recently for a cousin's wedding. I could see why Joseph liked it here: nothing but average people, living unexceptional lives. Salt of the earth, the rabbis called them. The sooner I could leave, the better.

I smelled bread baking in an oven as we passed a communal kitchen. All these little villages had them; each one served several families. Near the entrance, an old blind man sat with his back to the trunk of an olive tree. When he heard us approaching, he started banging his cup with a stick, begging for money. We ignored him, and James turned right, proceeded about fifty cubits, then stopped in front of a modest workshop. Tools were arranged neatly on a bench. A table displayed a few items for sale: a small wooden box, a carved horse, some household utensils.

Joseph's son was unloading a cypress bough from a wagon when we arrived, so he didn't notice us at first. He was no more than thirty, medium build, and unremarkable in every way. Not ugly, but not handsome, either. His commonness disappointed me. This was the master carpenter? I wondered if James had directed me to the wrong man until, lo, he swung his axe into the limb and cleaved it in half. And I mean exactly in half. He laid the two pieces side by side; neither was a hair longer than the other.

"You have great talent," I said.

He looked up, and I had the feeling he already knew me. But then, most laborers in Galilee would have recognized Timothy the builder. He struck twice again with his axe, and now there were four pieces, all the same length. "My father taught me well," he said.

"No offense to Joseph. He was a diligent worker and a righteous man. But you're twice the carpenter that he ever was."

He set one of the four pieces on a table and, selecting an adze from his collection of tools, began stripping away the bark. He worked deliberately, but no motion was wasted.

"A man with your skill could do very well for himself if the right opportunity came along," I said. Again, no answer. My heart began to harden. If he truly recognized me, then he knew I deserved respect.

My thoughts were interrupted by two young men passing by. One grabbed his companion by the arm, and they stopped to talk. The first man said he'd been a good son. He worked hard and looked after his father—not like his older brother, who'd demanded his inheritance, squandered all his money on wine and whores, then came crawling back, begging for mercy.

Joseph's son paused to listen as the young man raised his voice. His father gave his brother a feast! He served him a fatted calf! Why should he have to settle for scraps while his good-for-nothing brother stuffed his belly?

The men moved on, and Joseph's son returned to his adze, but the story gave me an idea.

"Your father blessed you with something much greater than a calf," I said. "He taught you a trade. And now he'd want you to use that trade to care for your mother."

His pace slowed, just for an instant, then resumed. I had found his weakness. "Come work for me," I said. "You'll oversee all my laborers, in every village. You'll never have to lift an adze again, and your mother will have whatever she needs until the end of her days."

He was tempted, I could tell. But then he stood, stiff-necked, to face me. "I must carry on my father's business," he said.

James, behind me, drew in his breath sharply. Anger filled my heart. I had come to this young carpenter in a spirit of kindness, with an offer most men would die for, and this was how he repaid me? I was accustomed to such arrogance from physicians and lawyers, but I'd be damned if I took it from a common grain of salt.

I smiled at him coldly. "Then I wish you success."

As I turned to leave, I noticed the little box among his wares and picked it up. Oak and square, it was the length of my hand and half as deep. And light as a dove but so sturdy that I could have used it as a hammer. The lid slid along grooves—a simple design, but I'd never seen it wrought so skillfully in a box this small. If I could produce it in bulk, I'd make a tenfold profit off each one, and he'd never sell another again. "I've taken much of your time," I said. "Let me buy this as a token of my thanks."

"If you like it, please take it." He spoke to me as if I were a child.

I opened my bag of silver and removed two coins. "Trust me, I can afford to pay."

"Thank you, but I have no need of your money."

I dropped the entire bag on the table. "Everyone needs money." The bag contained more silver than he could earn in a year, but he refused even to glance at it.

"I know this manner of man," I told James on our way back to Sepphoris. "He's already in his house, where no one else can see, counting the coins one by one."

And he'd know: That money came from me.

* * *

When I returned home, Martha was sitting on a bench in the garden with a tunic in her lap, watching over the children. John dozed under a fig tree. Elizabeth marched a doll through an imaginary scene while Luke tossed pebbles in the air and counted how many he could catch. It was too peaceful to last. Sure enough, tiring of his game, Luke threw a pebble at the doll and knocked it over. Elizabeth punched him in the shoulder, and he whimpered.

If only Elizabeth were a boy. I couldn't imagine either son ever running my business.

Martha made room for me on the bench, and I sat next to her. She asked about my day, but before I could answer, Luke spotted the box in my hands and hurried over to inspect it. He had already forgotten about his shoulder.

"What do you think of it?" I asked.

He opened the lid, dropped his pebbles inside, and closed it up. The pebbles made a joyful noise when he shook the box, and he laughed. "Like a timbrel," he said. "Can I have it?"

Elizabeth grabbed the box out of his hands and dumped out the pebbles. Her doll fit inside it snugly. "This could be her bed!" she exclaimed. Even John roused himself and demanded to hold it.

Their reactions provoked me. I had built them this mansion with this beautiful garden, and the only thing that impressed them was a wooden box.

"It's lovely," Martha said. She, too, had fallen under its spell. "Did one of your workers make it?" She removed the doll and replaced it with a spool of thread that I hadn't noticed before. So that's why the tunic was on her lap; she'd been repairing it. I employed four maidservants, yet Martha did their work for them, as if she were married to a gardener.

I grabbed the spool from the box and held it in the air between us. "Don't we have servants?" I asked.

"I enjoy it. And what else would I do all day while you're traveling across Galilee?"

"I travel across Galilee so no one in my family will ever have to sew."

She made a sound between a laugh and a groan. "Right. I keep forgetting."

I was too vexed to argue with her. I took the box and went inside to a private room where I could be alone. Where had this carpenter gained such skill? Not from Joseph, verily. I slid the top of the box open and closed and open again, searching for its secret. I hadn't built anything with my own hands in many years. But even at my best, could I have matched it?

I pushed the question aside. I had chosen my path long ago, and I had no regrets. Anyone could be a carpenter, but I employed dozens of them. Tomorrow I would speak to James.

* * *

Three weeks went by. While I waited, I bought a vineyard near Tiberias. James found it for me. I was running out of ways to expand my construction business, and I already supplied other vineyards with barrels and presses. So it was a shrewd decision financially—not to mention something that no carpenter from Nazareth would ever accomplish.

Then it came to pass one morning that James placed four boxes on a table in the garden: the one from Joseph's son and, lined up in a row, three others of the same size. I put a few pebbles in the first one and shook it; the rattle was dull and somber, so I set it aside. The second box was too heavy; I didn't even open it.

The last was the most beautiful of the three. My hopes rose; this would be the one. But when I placed Elizabeth's doll inside, the box wouldn't close.

"These three were the best of them?" I asked.

"Yes," James said quietly.

All over Galilee, my carpenters were beginning their labors. They went wherever I commanded them to go and built whatever I commanded them to build. But not him. I felt like a shepherd with a hundred sheep until one wandered away. No matter where I searched or how loudly I called, it refused to come. The other ninety-nine meant nothing to me; all I wanted was the one I couldn't have.

Someone needed to suffer for this. If not Joseph's son, someone else. I swept the three boxes off the table.

James looked at me, his dark eyes full of sorrow. He leaned over to pick up the box closest to him, pinning it between his left arm and torso. When he tucked the second box next to it, both slipped through his grasp and dropped to the ground. Sighing, he gathered them and set them on the table. Then he retrieved the third one, returned it to the table, and stacked all three, topping them with his tablet. Lifting the stack from the bottom, he leaned it against his chest and secured it with his chin. His sandals scraped the ground as he slowly left my sight, afraid to lift his feet for fear of dropping the boxes all over again.

Alone now, I walked to the southern edge of the garden. Sepphoris lay below me. Wherever I looked, I saw my handiwork: houses, walls, gates, towers. I had built them to last for generations. And in the distance, beyond my vision, was Nazareth.

Everyone had a price. He was no different than anyone else.

* * *

This time, I traveled without James. I wanted to have this conversation alone.

The old blind man was under the same tree, still banging his cup. His sandals seemed new, but perhaps I had overlooked them on my earlier visit. Either way, he didn't need my charity.

When I arrived at the shop, the carpenter was speaking to a small group of men gathered in a half circle around him. I stood a few cubits apart, close enough to listen.

"There was a certain man who owned a vineyard," he said.

I gasped. Was he speaking about me? How did he know I'd bought one? But he continued his story; he meant someone else, of course. This man, he said, hired some workers early in the morning and offered to pay each one a denarius. Later, he hired more workers, and in the afternoon, still more. When the sun set, all received the same wage: a denarius.

The man nearest me interrupted. He had broad shoulders with a sunburned neck and looked as if he'd labored in his share of vineyards. "That's not fair," he said. "Those who worked longer should get more pay."

"Let's ask our visitor," the carpenter said. "What do you think, Timothy?"

The others turned toward me, and I felt the weight of their stares. Suddenly I was back in Torah school, a young boy again, struggling to name the twelve tribes of Israel while my classmates laughed at me behind their hands. I shook off the memory and spoke with a confidence I didn't feel.

"Did the owner pay each man the amount he agreed to

work for?"

"He did."

"Then the workers have no cause to complain."

He nodded at me and smiled. "Timothy is right," he said. "It's the owner's money. He can do with it what he will."

I felt a gladness in my heart that confounded me, and I chastised myself. Of course I had answered correctly. I didn't need this young carpenter's approval. When had he ever hired any workers? I was the only master here.

The others soon departed, leaving the two of us. Joseph's son turned his attention to a piece of limestone and prepared to cut it. I didn't know why he bothered; nothing would come of such a worthless stone.

"Have you reconsidered my offer?" I asked. He picked up a chisel but didn't answer. With no more customers around, his arrogance had returned. "You know I'm a wealthy man."

He smote the stone, and a piece fell to the ground. "Indeed," he said at last. "And my neighbors are grateful. Thanks to your silver, the hungry were fed, the homeless have shelter, the poor have new clothes."

A moment passed before I realized what he meant. "That money was for you," I said.

"Yes, but the owner can do whatever he wants with it, don't you agree?" He smiled as if pleased with himself. "You think I took the credit for helping those people? And then when they need a craftsman, they'll hire me instead of one of your workers?"

I wanted to deny it but could not. He chiseled off another piece of stone.

"I told them the money came from Timothy of

Sepphoris, the builder."

Was he possessed by devils? What would it gain him to praise a rival? Then, in an instant, I understood. He knew he could never equal what I had achieved. As hard as he labored, and even with his great skill, he would never be more than a common carpenter. So he pretended that he had no need of worldly possessions, that he was happier poor and unknown than I would ever be with my wealth and fame. That's why he rejected my offer to provide for his mother. That's why he gave away my silver. He was trying to turn the tables on me. To make me covet his way of life. But I was on to him now.

* * *

The next morning, I explained my plan to James. I would send my two best laborers to Nazareth. If Joseph's son charged six denarii to build a wall, they should charge three. They could even work for free. I'd make up the difference in their wages. Whatever it took to drive him out of business and out of my life. James wrote down my instructions in silence. If he disagreed with me, he knew better than to say so. Not after failing me with the boxes.

My laborers were soon busy in Nazareth while Joseph's son worked less and less. Within a week, James reported, no one was hiring him at all.

"What does he do all day while my workers are taking his wages?" I pointed to James's tablet. "Read it to me."

"He tells stories," James said. "People gather at his shop to listen." He read from his notes. "One was about a buried treasure. A certain man found it in a field, but he didn't want anyone to know about it. So he saved up all his money and—"

I cut him off. First vineyards, now buried treasures. I had

no patience for stories. "Does he try to sell them anything? Has he made any more boxes?"

"No," James said, "the people just asked him questions and he answered them. Or sometimes he asked them questions."

"He's up to something," I said. "Find out what it is."

The next morning, James reported that the crowd had grown. Entire families attended, even little children. "He stood on a table so everyone could hear him. He talked about a king who held a wedding banquet for his son and invited—"

I held up my hand. "Again, he did no work?"

"None."

"Does he ask anyone for money? Or food?"

James shook his head.

It made no sense. How long could he last without wages? Telling stories wouldn't feed his mother.

"If you wish," James said, "I could return to his workshop today and see."

He was facing the sun, so his eyes were narrowed and wrinkled at the corners. His tightly curled hair had turned gray, but he was still James the Lesser, still my faithful disciple. I wondered how long he would have waited until I answered. An hour? All morning? My heart was moved; I shouldn't have made him pick up those boxes.

"Yes," I said. "Go."

* * *

But, lo, James didn't return the next morning. This had never happened before. He was in good health and knew I was expecting a report. Was his head so filled with buried treasures and wedding banquets that he'd forgotten who he worked for?

Hours passed. I tried to occupy myself with other matters.

My vineyard was producing only half the yield that I'd been promised, and I should have summoned the steward to provide an account. But I couldn't stop thinking about Joseph's son. Why was he gathering customers to his shop if not to sell them goods? Did he have some other source of income? Then I remembered my bag of silver, and suddenly I understood. He hadn't given it all away—he'd only pretended to do so while hoarding the largest portion for himself. He was a hypocrite, no better than the priests at the synagogue! And oh, how he must be laughing at me, living like a king with my money.

I put on my cloak and set out to confront him face-to-face. I walked quickly, my anger burning hotter with each step. I would hear no more of his stories, no more clever words that troubled my heart. He would return my silver and depart from Galilee at once, or I would beat him until his dying breath.

But when I arrived at his shop, no one was there. The table was empty, and the tools had vanished.

An elderly man walked by, muttering to himself as if possessed. I called to him. "The carpenter—have you seen him?"

The man began laughing for no reason and pointing here and there. "I see the house, I see the tree, I see the sky, I see—"

I grabbed him roughly by the shoulders. "Joseph's son. Where is he?"

"I don't know." He was still laughing. "I saw him yesterday, but I don't see him today."

I shoved him aside, and the old man staggered away. Had I won? I wanted the carpenter of Nazareth to leave, and, lo, he had departed. But where was he now? Perhaps he had moved to another village to open a new shop. Yes, that must be it. He said he wanted to continue his father's business—he must have fled somewhere he thought he could escape me. If so, he was mistaken. Did he not know how far my reach extended? All my workers, in every village, would watch for him. Wherever the sheep wandered, I would track him down.

And if he continued to defy me? What would I do then? My thoughts turned violent as I pondered the price he would pay.

I wished then that I could speak with James. He had observed the carpenter many times; perhaps he could discern where he was hiding. Again, I wondered why he didn't come to my garden this morning. Could he have already begun the hunt? Of course! That was the only possible explanation. As soon as he'd discovered the carpenter was missing, he must have set out to look for him. He might be with him at this very moment.

Good man, James. No one was more loyal. A friend, even. I would discuss the matter with him tomorrow. He would surely return tomorrow.

* * *

Discussion Questions

1. Timothy the builder has a specific perspective and life focus. How would you describe it? Is he unique or wrong to have that perspective and life focus? What are the benefits and detriments of his life focus?
2. On several occasions, Timothy the builder incorrectly interprets the motivations of Joseph's son. Why is Timothy unable to understand the young carpenter's motivations?
3. What characteristic allows certain individuals to be better (*or worse*) at perspective shifting?
4. What could Timothy the builder have done to better understand and believe the motivations of Joseph's son rather than continuing to see them through his own perspective?
5. Is it wrong to simply want to work, become successful, and take care of your family as Timothy has done? Why is Timothy an unsympathetic character in this story?

Visions of Midwives

C.S. Griffel

* * *

The heavy groan sounded as though it were being dragged from inside the woman's body involuntarily. Her pregnant belly heaved as guttural sounds enveloped the tiny bedroom. Keery dabbed the sweat from the woman's forehead. The midwife, Luanne, examined the woman to check her dilation. A clock on the mantlepiece ticked away the minutes, piling them into hours.

"Illona, you're doing so well, darling. Your baby's head has engaged, and you're going to really start pushing."

Illona responded with only a nod and "uh-huh."

"Keery, come here, girl," Luanne ordered. Keery obeyed quickly. "Place your hand here. Feel that? That's how you can tell the baby's head is engaged. Illona, on your next contraction, you're going to push." Keery was nearing the end of her apprenticeship, so it was not the first time she had felt a baby's head engaged. Still, she obeyed. Each experience was building

Keery up, readying her for her practice.

The process went quickly. It was Illona's sixth baby. Within a few pushes, the baby's head was completely born.

"One more big push, Illona, and your baby will be born." Illona's contraction hit; she scrunched her face until it looked like a closed fist and pushed. Luanne's hands grabbed ahold of the baby as he was suspended in the space between being born and not yet born. The elderly midwife's eyes rolled back as a vision of the child's destiny encompassed her mind. The moment was over as quickly as it had come. The little boy was born. For the briefest moment, Keery saw that Luanne's features were grim. Before Illona could see her face, she wiped it clean of emotion.

"Is it a boy?" Illona asked, her voice breathy and rough from the effort of getting her child out into the world.

"Yes, it's a boy," was Luanne's dry reply.

Keery looked at the tiny baby. He looked perfect. He balled his little hands into fists and kicked with both his legs. She wondered what Luanne had seen. Keery had not yet experienced the second sight, but she knew she would when her turn came to be the attending midwife.

"Take care of Illona, Keery, while I take care of the mite."

Keery's job now was to wait for Illona's body to complete the process of birth. Soon the placenta would appear. Illona did not know that Luanne had seen her son's future. It was a secret long kept by the midwives of their people. The clock tower in the town square chimed out a quarter past one in the morning. Keery noted that the little boy had not yet cried. Illona noticed too.

"Is he all right?" Illona's voice, roughened from groaning,

broke the quiet. Luanne did not respond immediately. "Midwife, is he all right, I say?" At this, Luanne wrapped the boy in the soft blanket his mother had carefully knitted for him. Illona didn't have much in the way of wealth, but each of her babies at least got a new blanket, even if it was knitted from yarn carefully undone from his dad and grandad's old sweaters.

Luanne brought the little man to his mother, only his face visible in the mass of soft yarn, just yellow enough to not be white. The midwife handed the waiting mother her child. The mother's eyes were full of fear and love. She glanced at her baby's face, his closed eyes.

"He never drew the first breath of life," Luanne delivered the words gently, but they struck the mother like a fist to her gut. The woman gathered her baby to her, and a wail like the cold winter wind barreling through the high mountains grew out of the woman's belly and shattered the peaceful calm of deep night.

Keery wondered what had happened. She had seen the boy born. He had been kicking and balling up his tiny fists. She knew he had been alive. Confused, Keery glanced at the senior midwife. Luanne's face was a mask of stoic resolve. It was not the time or place to ask questions.

Upon hearing her mournful wail, Illona's husband rushed into the room. He climbed into the bed with his distraught wife and drew her and the baby to himself. He murmured into her ear that he loved her, would always love her, but he did not tell her to be quiet or that it would be okay. He simply allowed her to pour out her grief. Uncaring that they had an audience, the husband held his distraught wife, lest the pain take her away with her child.

Keery helped Luanne gather their things quickly. It was best at this point to leave the grieving family to their pain. It would be the father's job to care for the wee body now. Before they left, the father said, "Your payment is on the mantel, good wife." It was ill luck, even under the circumstances, to leave the midwife unpaid.

As they walked through the damp cold of the night, Keery struggled to put her question into words. What had happened to the child? She alone knew that the midwife had lied. That baby was alive when it was born.

"Luanne..." Keery began. Luanne anticipated the question.

"Child, you will understand when you birth your first baby. You will know when you see what the future has in store. That child was destined for great misery. 'Twas a mercy I done. It is a burden we midwives carry, the purpose of our gift." Her words were sharp and final. Keery knew she would answer no more questions. They parted company near the town square, Luanne to her snug, well-appointed home, Keery to the hovel where she still lived with her parents.

Keery did not sleep that night. She kept thinking of the tiny, perfect arms and legs, unused to the immense space outside the womb, making small, jerking movements, feeling for the boundaries of its new life.

The waning summer brought with it many births. The cold nights of December—all the harvest work done and winter settling in—brought with it many conceptions. Husbands, no longer exhausted from the hard labor of spring, summer, and fall, more frequently sought the affections of their wives.

August was the midwives' busiest month. It also brought an end to Keery's apprenticeship. "There are too many babies coming for me to hold yer hand any longer," Luanna told her as July closed. "We'll place you with the younger mothers who've already had a babe or two." These tended to be the easiest births. The mothers were young enough that the risk of complication was low but had already proven their ability to birth healthy babies.

Keery was summoned for her first birth on August 5th at one in the morning. It was, of course, a full moon. Luanne's errand girl, Peony, rapped loudly on the door, waking Keery and her parents. Keery would not be able to move into her own home until she had earned enough from attending births to purchase one. Her vocation as midwife meant that she would never have a husband. She did not mourn this fact. She had seen many women, married in the rush of youth's lusts, walk an unhappy path when passions cooled. She had also seen young couples wed soberly and advisedly and remain in love their whole lives. Her chances, she supposed, were as good as any to go either way. She simply knew that it was not her destiny to wed. It was part of the midwife's second sight.

"Mildred Connor has gone into labor and needs attendance," Peony said urgently. "Mistress Luanne is attending Morgrid's birth and cannot leave. It's not going well. She sent me to fetch you. She says you must attend Mildred on your own."

Keery nodded and grabbed her midwifery satchel. It had been a gift from the Midwives' Guild and still smelled and creaked like brand-new leather. "Tell Mistress Luanne I'm on my way." Peony scurried quickly into the darkness.

The walk to the Connor's home was about twenty minutes. Mildred's husband answered the door with a look of relief on his face. "It's going quickly," he said. Keery nodded in response and followed him to the back room where Mildred lay upon the bed, knees tucked back as far as they would go, sweat dripping gently down her forehead. As Keery walked in, Mildred was gripped with a contraction that made her push with all her might. Before Keery could reach her, Mildred's body reflexively pushed out a baby girl. Keery moved to check the baby was all right while Mildred took deep breaths, an automatic response to normalize her breathing. When Keery's hands touched the baby, she received no second sight. This child's destiny remained in the realm of the unknown and the unknowable. It happened often enough that a baby was born before a midwife could arrive, especially with healthy babies. It is only in the moment when the child is suspended between being born and not yet born, when the head has emerged, that midwives receive the sight. Frankly, Keery was relieved. The burden of knowing another person's destiny was frightening, and she was glad to put it off, if even for one more day.

Keery checked over the baby, who showed every sign of being quite healthy. After cleaning the baby, Keery handed her over to her mother, who cooed over her beautiful child in the way just birthed mothers do. "Hello, my darling," she purred into the child's ear, "aren't you pretty?" Mildred rained kisses upon the head of fine, raven black hair. Keery waited with Mildred until her placenta was born, checking that all was well. When mother, child, and happy family were well settled, she slipped into the bright midday sun, pleased with herself.

Coins jingled merrily in Keery's little purse as she strode through the village on her way home. It wasn't until Peony crossed her path that she noted the somber air of the village.

"Peony," she called, "how is Morgrid? Did her child fair well?" Morgrid and her husband had been childless for the first twenty-three years of their marriage. The couple had long since given up hope of ever having a child when Morgrid found she was finally pregnant at forty-two.

The child looked up at Keery, shaking her head, "No," she said. "Morgrid and her babe died."

It was common for there to be complications in birth for first-time mothers in their thirties or forties. Keery was saddened but not shocked at the outcome. This, too, was a part of midwifery, dealing with the loss of mothers in birth. The midwives did all they could to shepherd mother and baby safely through the process, but sometimes, there was nothing they could do. Death was fated.

It was three weeks later when Keery was summoned once again to attend the birth of a young, fourth-time mother. When Keery arrived, the woman's husband answered the door, drunk. "She's in there," the man said as he pointed to a room on the west side of the house, his stance unsteady. Three young children huddled together in a corner. The eldest sister, no more than eight, sat in between two little boys, looking to be about five and three years old, respectively. The sister's arms were protectively draped over the shoulders of her little brothers. She had a hardened look in her eye, something sad to see in one so young. The little girl made eye contact with Keery, and a little smile crossed the child's lips, a welcome for the young midwife. A groan came from the westward room, and the child's eyes darted back to her father as he shouted, "Quit yer yowlin! It's giving me a headache!" Hardness replaced the brief smile in the child's eyes.

"Why don't you step outside, sir, where your wife's cries won't bother you. She'll be fine now that I'm here. It looks like your girl there can look well after her brothers." The man nodded, stumbled out the door, and headed for the pub, Keery was sure. He looked like he had once been handsome, but drink and misery had twisted him into an ugly facsimile of his younger self.

The woman in the bed clung to the headboard rails like a drowning person might cling to driftwood in a raging river. Unlike her husband, prettiness still lingered on this woman's face. Love for her children kept her from total despair.

"You're Agnes, aren't you?" Keery inquired. The woman nodded in reply. "I'm Keery, the midwife. I want you to take some deep breaths." Agnes obeyed and breathed in deeply through her nose. Predictably, Agnes's labor went quickly. She seemed to relax with her husband gone and a midwife present.

No more than thirty minutes after Keery's arrival, the baby's head emerged from the birth canal. Keery placed her hands on the tiny head to support the child as its mother completed the birthing process. When the vision overtook her, the pain was so intense Keery thought she would explode into dust, down to the very last molecule. The sensation lasted only a moment, but within it, Keery felt what seemed an eternity pass. She knew now what Luanne had told her about. She knew this child would experience intense suffering. Yet, as she looked at the tiny, beautiful little girl, now fully born, she knew she could not do what Luanne had done. Keery didn't know if this meant she was cowardly or courageous. She only knew she could not extinguish the light of life burning in the milky blue eyes now blinking up at her.

Keery handed the child to her mother. "A lovely little girl," she said. And like all mothers, Agnes drew the child to herself, murmuring and cooing.

"Margery," Keery heard Agnes whisper. Whatever else may come in this child's life, she was loved and content in this moment with this mother.

Misery did come to the child. When Margery was just three years old, Agnes came to a sad end. A merchant in the marketplace allowed his eyes to linger upon her too long. Her husband, in a drunken and jealous rage, beat her to death, and he was hung the next morning, leaving their four children orphans. No one could afford to take in four children, and they were all separated. Within a few months, the families that had taken in the children woke to find their beds empty. The eldest sister had come in the night for her siblings, unwilling to be apart. What became of them after that, no one in the village knew. Keery surmised the child had gone to the city and taken up prostitution to keep her siblings under a roof and fed. There was appetite enough in the big city, even for very young girls, to keep body and soul together for the little orphans. Keery wondered if she was wrong not to have released Margery from this fate.

Most of Keery's visions portended a mixture of pain, sorrow, joy, and peace. All human lives have some of everything. Of course, there were lives that held more or less joy, more or less pain than others, but she had not yet again felt the pain that had been foretold for Margery. Keery, carefully saving every coin, now lived in a small cottage of her own. It was not ostentatious. In fact, it was small and lacked any luxury, but it was tidy and her own. Keery was now a well-loved midwife, popular with young mothers.

Keery awoke naturally in her own bed for the first time in three days. She had just overseen a first-time mother, and the labor had been slow. Even so, baby was well born, and mother was resting in the glow of new motherhood and the love of a proud husband. She looked at the clock on her mantelpiece. It read 10:00 a.m. Keery felt positively indulgent. She made herself a trencher of cheese and bread and poured a large glass of ale. Tucking in, she enjoyed a leisurely meal by the fire. No knock at the door disturbed her while she swept and dusted her little cottage. She even made it to evening mass. It wasn't until four the next morning that a knock disturbed her rest. Birgitta Hoskin was in labor. She and her husband, Tobias, lived in the manse, the largest home in town. Tobias was a merchant. Keery was lucky to have been chosen to be Birgitta's midwife. The fussy young mother required a lot of attention, which meant Keery was called to the manse for frequent visits. Each visit added more coins to her meager stash. Keery was not greedy by any means, yet she dreamed of delicate curtains adorning her little kitchen window, softening the glow of streaming sunlight.

Birgitta was buxom and well-built for childbearing. Though it was her first baby, her labor was rapid. Her body just seemed to know exactly what to do. It was ready to send baby number one into the world and prepare itself for birthing the next nine that would surely come. Birgitta's baby was crowning within an hour. When her hands touched the blood-stained head of the child, Keery felt something she had never felt before. The terror of a thousand souls ran through her in one split second. Another push from Birgitta and the child was born, and Keery's vision gone. The child would not suffer, she knew, but would cause great suffering. It was a boy lying limply in her hands with the umbilical cord wrapped around his neck. Keery's throat tightened. What should she do? The child had not yet drawn breath. She could let him expire. She could save many from suffering, were her vision to be trusted. It would be easy to say he had been born dead. He had the cord wrapped around his neck. Birgitta was anxiously peering at the midwife and baby through her spread knees.

"Is he all right?" Birgitta asked. Keery looked up at the question and saw in the mother's eyes fear and love for her baby. She looked back down at the limp body, bluish around the lips. He was a perfect baby otherwise. Sweet, like all newborn babies. Without further thought, Keery loosened the cord and coaxed breath into the baby's lungs. Soon, he let out a mighty wail. Keery handed him over to his waiting mother. Stoically, Keery finished the rest of her duties, waiting for the placenta, cleaning and clearing things away, and packing her bag. She left a happy mother with a nursing child as she slipped out of the manse.

Once again, Keery was plagued by the fear that she had done the wrong thing by letting a child live. When she arrived home, she did not unpack her things for her customary cleaning. Instead, she knelt before the little altar in her living room. The statue of the Virgin Mother, wearing robes of robin's egg blue and a gilt crown, had been her one indulgence. It had made a deep gouge in her savings. She prayed to it now, her heart pouring out her fears before the saintly young mother depicted in wood. Was she wrong to allow such suffering into the world if she could stop it? Was Luanne right? Was the purpose of the gift of sight for snuffing out suffering? She looked up at the statue, its beatific eyes staring perpetually up to the heavens. She would get no answer here. Keery looked at her hands. They had helped usher many lives into the world already. She wouldn't use them to usher it out. Perhaps she would answer for it one day. She prayed the virginal lady would speak up for her when the time came. A knock at the door caught her attention. She sighed and stood. It was Peony.

"Astrid's water broke," the young woman told her.

"Tell her I'll be right there."

* * *

Discussion Questions

1. Would you be willing to work as a midwife if it meant seeing the future of the child being born?

2. Should any baby be put to death under any foreseeable future? Is there any situation where killing the newborn is the right choice?

3. In the story, Keery hesitates in her decision to allow the birth of a child who will live to cause misery for others. More so than when she decided to allow a child to be born into experiencing a lifetime of misery. Do you agree with this distinction?

4. Would it be better to tell the parents of the child's future so they could choose whether the child lives or dies? What are the pros and cons of this approach?

5. What, if anything, is a practical distinction between killing a child in the story and terminating a pregnancy in modern society when a severe genetic defect is found?

What We Talk About When We Talk About Reincarnation

Edward Daschle

* * *

My boyfriend, Mike, was talking, just really going on like he was delivering a lecture in one of his economics classes. He's twice my age, so he thinks that gives him the right.

Our friends call us Michael squared when they think they're being cute, but we're safe around Jaime and Amy since their names rhyme. Amy was my friend, and Jaime was Mike's, and it was the two of them who'd introduced the two of us, though not with any intention that we'd begin dating. We were just two guests at the same party they'd been hosting. Sometimes I felt this, more than anything else, was what kept us all as a set. There was little else we really had in common. Mike and I only drink wine, but since Jaime and Amy brought the drinks, what we had was beer. The bottles we'd already emptied crowded the table under the light, and I was trying to decide if they were amber or just brown while Mike got himself worked up over the history of reincarnation. He'd made his way through literature and metaphysics and ended up in a cul-de-sac of science fiction. He doesn't believe in anything he calls woo-woo or what anyone else would call spiritual, though there is a little Buddha nestled between a few books in the living room.

The apartment is Mike's, and his furnishings are to die for. I don't remember what we ate or drank the first time he invited me over, but I do remember the mid-century modern Danish chairs, futon, and cabinet, the tastefully minimalist, queer paintings, and the small statement sculptures on his shelves and the coffee table. His, I recognized in this first glimpse, was a life well-organized and not one spent on anyone else. He had constructed himself, too, in a way, through daily workouts and tight shirts, a neatly trimmed beard to deemphasize his age, and the gold-rimmed glasses he preferred over contacts. When we officialized our relationship by telling our friends and touching each other delicately in public the way couples do, he became my safety net, a personification of the concept of security. Already, I'd been thinking of him as something of a template for who I'd like to become. I'd decided, not so explicitly at first, though certainly it was a decision, once I reach his age, once he's passed and I have my own apartment overlooking the water and a boyfriend half my age, I will shorten my name to Mike and carry on his legacy of good taste.

"Hey, who do you think you were in a past life?" Jaime asked.

It took all of Jaime's burly force to interrupt Mike. Jaime was built like a Tolkienesque dwarf, looking as though nobody would ever be able to push him over. He'd transitioned only recently. Sometimes I guiltily felt that talking to him was a pronoun minefield, though on the couple occasions I slipped up, he said nothing. For a brief period when I was younger, I thought I might like to be a girl. I'd never told anyone this, and it didn't matter, because I did not feel that I was trans or at least not that I could live as a trans woman. It was just an idle thought, and I figured if there were an afterlife where I could choose how I would turn out in my next life, I would probably not choose to be a boy again. Biologically anyways. I wondered if it was fucked up to think along these lines, if this reinforced the notion of who was a real woman and who wasn't, but I wasn't about to have that conversation here, not now. It wasn't a beer conversation, something so delicate. Maybe it was a conversation I could only have with a therapist since Mike would condescend, not cruelly, but only out of years of experience in entertaining fruitless hypotheticals and out of his own misgivings over the complexities of gender identity.

Jaime said that in a past life, he figured he was nobody special. He'd never won any awards growing up—the only statistically unusual thing about him being the fact that he was a trans man. He'd probably worked, ate, shit, and then died of something stupid like a toothache.

"Though considering I have you now, I must've done something right in my last life," Jaime said to Amy in a voice that sounded like he was talking to a dog. Though I hadn't yet said it aloud, I did love Mike, but I would hate to hear my own voice dribble so mushily from my mouth.

"I think in a past life, I was Galileo," Amy said.

"Galileo?" Jaime asked.

"I just think I have a connection to him; I did a report on him in first grade."

"What?"

"On Galileo, Michael, you remember, right? We had to choose a scientist, and then our teacher was fired for spreading secular beliefs."

I laughed.

"No, I don't remember any of that," I said, "but that's kind of hilarious. I can't believe they fired, what was her name—Ms. Miller, right?—over something like that."

"You can't?" Mike asked. "I can believe it completely."

"You know what I mean. Sure, it was a Catholic school, but seriously, besides the uniform, it was more or less normal, I think," I said. "And I don't know, things like that... they just always seem to happen somewhere else."

I looked around at the others. Amy shrugged.

"But why Galileo?" Jaime asked. "I mean there's more to it than a report, isn't there?"

"It's stupid, but I guess he just always sort of stuck with me. He's like my own personal inspirational quote. Like 'hang in there, Amy, at least you aren't imprisoned,'" she said.

I laughed again, but Jaime, I could see, looked thoughtful.

"But you were imprisoned in a way," Jaime said. "You had to hide yourself. I basically had to break down that closet door with an axe."

"And I'm glad you did," Amy said, tilting her head gently so that it touched Jaime's. "But I don't want to blame my parents for that. I mean, they gave me everything and they loved me, even if I couldn't always, you know, say everything to them."

Jaime wrapped an arm tightly around Amy's shoulders,

pulling her into his side.

Amy's parents adopted her when she was old enough to be grateful but young enough not to be bitter about the whole system. We've had conversations about what that means to her. Once, she told me how she had this feeling that if she wasn't perfect, they'd get buyer's remorse and question her adoptee warranty. It was why she'd taken longer than I had to renounce the faith in which we'd both been raised. She still considered herself to be a spiritual person, and sometimes her social media posts made me wonder if she didn't need something to fill the space the church had left behind.

"You are perfect. Anyone who could reject you just doesn't know you," Jaime said.

Mike, I could tell, wanted to say something. Maybe how that wasn't true. How there were plenty of people who would reject you because they knew you, but I reached across and squeezed his thigh gently to shut him up. He set his warm hand on mine.

"All right, Mike, let's hear it," Jaime said smugly and resignedly, ready it seemed for something longwinded. He was leaning back again, the thin-armed chair looking entirely too delicate to contain his swagger, the empty beer bottles before him forming a crenulated parapet. "And I don't want to hear any sort of theory or anything like that. Just pretend, for a moment, that reincarnation exists in the way most people understand that it does."

"Fine, fine," Mike said, in that fake exhausted voice he sometimes uses, the voice I hate because it reminds me how much older he is, how in the wrong light he looks like my dad. "Actually, my first boyfriend totally bought into all that spiritual bullshit. This was back in the early '80s when things like psychics were on their way out, barely holding onto the market share they'd scratched out for themselves in the '60s and '70s. I was a skeptic, but I was also smitten, just over the moon for him. He was so brave and out there and sexy too. I'm not ashamed to say he was my first love, and first love really makes you do crazy things. I was practically a different person from the bitter old faggot you see before you now. What I mean is, I was willing to believe anything he believed in, no matter how crazy I really thought it was.

"So he had this psychic he went to, and one time he took me to see her. She had on all this eye makeup and loads of shawls and things. At the time, I thought she was really old, though now I think that was just the effect she was going for—you know, to make herself seem wiser and more mysterious—she probably wasn't much over forty at the time." Mike lifted his beer to his lips, but didn't take a drink, just held it there before his face almost as though he'd been petrified, the Medusa gaze of memory holding him fast. I held my own second beer, though I'd already decided I wouldn't finish it, not with all those empty calories. I couldn't afford them, not if Mike was going to think about an old boyfriend. I didn't like the look he had in his eyes. Or maybe I was just jealous he wasn't looking that way at me.

He blinked, took a drink, and then set the beer back on the table.

"He asked her to tell us about our past lives, if we'd been lovers then like we were at the time. Apparently, this was the main service she provided. Anyway, she told us that she saw something—she put on this misty voice—and for his sake, I really tried to let myself buy into it. Later though, after the first time we broke up, I promised I'd never pretend to believe in bullshit for a guy again, no matter how hot he was. I did, I believed in a lot of bullshit, but I got more suspicious each time. She said why yes, the two of us were, but things ended tragically.

Maybe she knew fags loved melodrama, or maybe she was picking up on something else, but that really got him, and me too by proxy. She said we'd been in boarding school together in the 1910s. We had a clandestine relationship. He'd had to put off the girls his parents tried to set him up with, and I was always finding new ways to sneak into his room when his roommate was out. Very *Maurice* and *A Separate Peace*. But then the war started, and there we were, me English and him German—it could've been the other way around, but I guess she noticed a sort of Teutonic intensity in him, which is probably why she was in the business she was in, the way she picked up on things like that. We fought on opposite sides of the war, memories of each other were all that kept us alive in the trenches. But then, when in the heat of battle, we didn't recognize each other, all covered in trench mud and wearing our uniforms, we fought, and I killed him. Only as he lay dying in my arms did I realize who he was. I died not long after from sepsis or something else ugly and painful.

"That's what she told us, anyway."

"I'm going to have to talk to that psychic," Jaime said. "Do you think she's still alive?"

"I don't know," Mike said. "But Harvey died seven years after that."

We could hear the rush hour traffic on the street far below, but that was all we could hear. I kept expecting someone to break the silence before realizing it had to be me. "How did he die? You've never talked about him before."

I felt so impotent. I was always thinking about how even if our relationship ended with Mike's death of old age, barring unreasonable longevity, we would be together for less than half his life. It's disconcerting, sometimes, to think how long I'll be left alone.

"How do you think?" Mike asked, but the gruffness was only playacting. It was a bad actor's attempt at putting on the anger the script asked for. It was well-worn and cliché.

"So, it was AIDS," Jaime said, and I could see Amy tense up beside him. "That fucking sucks. It's always fucking AIDS. You know, my uncle died of AIDS. I was young when he passed; this was in the early '90s. I just remember him being all thin, pale, and wrung-out looking. His lips were dry and looked like the Salt Flats in Utah near where my grandparents lived. I was certain he'd been cursed since I was really into mummies at the time."

"It's always fucking AIDS," Mike agreed. "He died in '89. I don't really want to get into everything, but it was just as terrible as you're imagining. I wasn't there as much as I know I should've been, but I was young, and all he was doing was dying. He didn't have any family with him either; they'd decided to forget him before we even met. When I did visit, he just kept repeating that bullshit story the psychic told us. I think that's why I still remember it. There were times when I was certain he couldn't tell the difference between what was real and what was the story. He didn't just believe that he'd lived that past life; he believed he was living it out in that hospital. He even tried to speak German a few times. But he didn't know German, so he just muttered a few made-up phrases in the worst fake accent I've ever heard. I had to work so hard not to laugh, even with all those men dying around him."

The sky began to orange and then purple, blooming like a flower or like a bruise, considering the topic of the conversation. Mike's furniture cast spidery shadows across the floor, and just for a moment, before Jaime shifted, the light caught in the empty bottles on the table, refilling them.

"What month did he die?" I asked.

"What month...?" Mike asked, still smiling off the end of his sad laughter. "It would've been... August? Yeah, fucking terrible month. He thought he was freezing to death, but I was boiling in that shitty apartment we used to share."

"I was born in September that year," I said. I was speaking quietly because even as I spoke, I knew I probably shouldn't be saying what I was saying. But I couldn't help it; the topic of the evening had caught hold of me. "You know how that psychic was talking about lovers in past lives? Maybe he was my past life, and that's why we're..."

Mike stared at me, eyes seeming to reach right to the edges of his gold-rimmed glasses.

"You know, I just thought there would be something magical about that, and considering the coincidence," I said, "of when he died and I was born... it just fits, I guess."

We stopped breathing, all of us. Amy and Jaime were still; Mike stony beside me.

"It's all bullshit," Mike said finally without force. "The psychic, reincarnation, all of it. And I hate the idea of soulmates. The world's too big for soulmates and any of that bullshit. You shouldn't need to believe someone is your only choice to fall in love with them. You should just be able to love or lust or whatever else. I mean, Jesus Christ, none of that is necessary. It's just about compatibility and making it work. Fighting to make it work if you have to."

I set my hand back on Mike's knee, and though his body was warm, all I felt was coldness when he didn't set his hand on mine.

"Soulmates scare me," Amy said.

"How do you mean?" Jaime asked.

"It just seems so easy for two people to never meet and then your souls would never be fulfilled. I mean, sorry Michael, but Mike is twice your age. I don't think you ever expected to end up with him. And what if there are rules to soulmates we don't know?"

"Jesus," Mike muttered. He was done with the conversation.

"But maybe that's what reincarnation is all about," Jaime said. "Correcting mistakes made by another you in another life. Maybe we just keep coming back until we find our soulmates."

"Or maybe it doesn't mean anything at all, and it's just something our ancestors made up because their lives were shit, their world was shit, and every day they were starving and depressed," Mike said.

The cats screamed just then from the bedroom.

"Oh, shit, forgot to feed the bastards," Mike said and went to let them out. We always keep them in the bedroom whenever we have guests over, even, or maybe especially, guests who like cats. It's not that we're concerned about the cats being a nuisance, they are nice enough as far as cats go, but guests are always making a nuisance out of themselves around cats. Some people are allergic to cats, but the real issue is how the cats derail conversations. They come into the room, and there we go spending an evening talking about cats instead of whatever it was we were talking about before the cats entered the picture.

And in they came, mewing up at each of us. Jaime nabbed the orange one we called Marmalade when we weren't calling him Stinker, and though Amy wiggled her fingers at Alfredo, he sauntered off into the kitchen after Mike, more interested in food than attention for the time being.

"You know, cats have nine lives," I said.

"So they say," Jaime said while he scratched behind Marmalade's ears. "Hey, can we get...?"

"Hey, Mike? Can you grab a few more beers? So, is it reincarnation," I asked, "when a cat dies, and they use another life? Or is it more like Mario, and they just get to try again?"

"I hadn't really thought of it that way, but now that you mention it, I guess I would probably say it's more like Mario," Amy said.

"But what if it were reincarnation?" I asked. "How many cats are actually running about in the world? I mean, how many have there ever been?"

"Nine times fewer than we think, I guess," Jaime said.

"No, but seriously," I said, "what if reincarnation doesn't obey the laws of space and time, you know? I mean if we're going spiritual anyways, there's no reason to believe that a cat with nine lives has to live those lives back-to-back like dominoes. Oops, got ran over, there's one down. Oops, got eaten by a coyote, there's another—"

"Michael," Mike warned as he returned to us with what would turn out to be the last round of beers. He's sensitive to talk about the cats dying. He grew up in California, where his family had practically been feeding the coyotes with the cats they brought home from the shelter.

"So, Mike's—our—two cats might actually be the same cat reincarnated into the same place and time in two different bodies," I continued. "In a few years, when one... passes... it will go on to the great kitty beyond and then get its next life and reincarnate a few years before now as the second cat. Just like that. Or maybe one cat is the first life, and the other is the seventh or something. So maybe the sixth life experienced the end of the world or was a sabretooth tiger."

Marmalade leapt from Jaime's lap to join his brother in the kitchen.

"You know, I kind of lied earlier." Amy admitted.

"What about?"

"About who I thought I was in a past life. I mean, about why I thought I was who I was," she said. "I did do a report on Galileo and all, but actually it has more to do with that Indigo Girls song. I went to one of their concerts with an ex—sorry honey—and I felt like I was experiencing destiny. Like I did a report on Galileo, and there they were singing about him."

"Oh fuck, major lesbian credentials alert!" Jaime said, jabbing the air repeatedly with his index fingers like an insistent sign pointing Amy out.

"Destiny and reincarnation? I feel like there's something there," I said.

"Actually, hey, I have a theory. My theory is that having a child is the closest thing we have to reincarnation," Jaime said. I noticed he and Amy exchanged a meaningful look.

"Really? Come on," Mike said. "That's so hetero. It's such

a straight belief to think that having children is anything like reincarnation. It's completely toxic. My parents had that sort of feeling about me and then hated when I didn't turn out just like them."

"You know I actually don't disagree with you there?" Jaime said, and Amy nodded. "Like it's fucked, yeah, but I was thinking more biologically speaking. There's genetic memory and all that shit. I read something about how stress can be passed down through generations."

"Plus, you're talking about expectations, right? Not really reincarnation," Amy said. "My parents aren't my biological parents, but they had expectations."

"Sure, fine," Mike said. "But it's still fucking hetero to think of your child as any sort of extension of you. They aren't beholden to you. Like do you think you owe your past lives anything? I mean, obviously not because reincarnation isn't real, but it's the same with children. Just let them be their own person. Maybe we should just stop having kids for a bit, like as a society, until we get our messed-up shit sorted out."

"You're going to hate this then, but Amy and I have something kind of big to tell you."

Jaime loves saying he has something big to tell you. Those were the same words he used to come out as trans, and likely how he'd announced he was a lesbian in a previous life, years before he and Amy started dating. But, though occasionally he chases this phrase with truly momentous news, mostly it's exaggeration, and we all get to roll our eyes at his idea of scope.

"We're planning to get pregnant," he said.

Mike and I didn't have to exchange looks, though in a sitcom, we would have, very urgently and dramatically. We'd both been blindsided, and neither one of us knew quite what to say about this.

"Congratulations!" I said.

"Living that hetero fantasy!" Mike said. "Fantastic!"

"That's not—" Amy said.

"As a queer couple, anything we decide to do is inherently queer," Jaime said. "Anyways, I'm the one getting pregnant."

"Yeah, okay, okay," Mike said. "Oh, wait, hold on, back it up. How's that?"

"I've always wanted to be a mom," Amy said, tone halfway between apologetic and staunch, "but getting pregnant, going through all that, and then the time I'd have to take off from work... it just doesn't appeal to me. But you know, before Jaime came out, we weren't considering having a kid at all. It wasn't even on our radar."

"It's because I wasn't being who I am yet, if that's not chronologically confusing," Jaime said. "I had to kill whoever that bitch was—"

"Honey," Amy said lightly. She'd fallen for that bitch after all.

"Sorry, but I mean, going back to reincarnation again," Jaime said, picking up his empty bottle, not remembering he'd already emptied it. "I couldn't even conceive of being a parent in that past life because being a parent meant being a mother. But now, my soul and mind are aligned, and I can be the father I was always meant to be."

"Soul and mind," Mike repeated with a hint of derision, whether over the spirituality of the sentiment or over the absence of "body" in the equation. "But you're a man now, right?"

"I've always been a man," Jaime said. "It just took me some time to figure myself out."

"Hmmm," Mike said and finished off his third beer.

"What?" Jaime asked.

"It's just you were a lesbian, and now you're planning to have a kid, so was it really always?" Mike asked. They'd had this sort of discussion before to varying degrees. When Jaime came out as trans, Mike had had any number of questions, only a few of which he'd asked Jaime and a few more he'd ranted about to me later. He was from a different generation, I'd explained to Amy, the two of us acting as wartime negotiators when our partners argued over identity.

"Don't give me that bullshit," Jaime said. Amy's fingers jolted in a warning caress across Jaime's shoulders. "Look, identity's fluid, and we're all always just trying to figure ourselves out. I mean, come on, dude, no need to be transphobic."

"Transphobic? What the hell," Mike said. He never raises his voice just increases the pressure. "I'm the fag who lived through the AIDS epidemic here. Look, I'm just saying you can't have it both ways. You can't expect people to think of you as a man if you plan to get pregnant. And hey, this isn't really about you. I'm just tired of people making up new identities now because they want to be special. We didn't live through all that bullshit so that the next generation of dykes and fags could find new ways to be discriminated against. Jesus Christ. You can be a masculine lesbian without being trans. Identity doesn't have to be so binary as—"

"Fucking binary? I'm a man, and I'm having a baby! Fuck!" Jaime shouted, though he was still leaning back in his chair.

"How would you define a man then?" Mike asked. "Can you even define a woman anymore?"

"If I started to define *woman*, you'd just pull out a plucked chicken and say 'behold, a woman!'"

I laughed. Somehow, I was laughing. As much as I didn't want to push on Mike's ego or test the already strained flex of the evening, I was laughing, imagining a woman-sized plucked chicken, taking calls in an office, walking about in heels, wearing lipstick. As though heels and lipstick were what anyone might use to define a woman.

"Sorry," I said. "I was just imagining..."

They were all looking at me, and for a moment, I wondered if this would be enough. Mike always apologized in the end when he went too far—he was always taking things as far as he could. But even so, I wondered when the end would be too late, when Jaime or Amy would decide to put the story down before they got there, and if too late might've just passed us by.

"Jesus," Mike whispered. And then looked back up at Jaime, earnestness in his eyes. "Hey, congratulations on the whole baby thing. Forget I said anything. So how are you doing it? Are you going to bust out the old turkey baster?"

He'd toted out that old gag, the clumsiness itself an attempt at an apology.

"You know, it's getting late," Jaime said. "We should get out of here."

"Oh, come on," Mike said. "It's still rush hour. Stay a bit."

"I have this great aged cheese I found at the market. We could have some of that while we wait for traffic to calm down," I said.

Maybe if I were worried about karma, I'd have tried

harder to mend the rupture before our guests left respectively angry and disappointed. But I didn't have any expectation that I'd be able to change Mike's perspective on the concept of gender identity, certainly not in a single evening after many beers. And like Mike, I don't believe in all that woo-woo stuff, in karma.

"I'm just tired," Jaime said tensely, already standing.

We clumped ourselves in the hall while our guests put on their things, and I waved to Amy as she walked beside Jaime down the breezeway to the stairs.

Mike stood behind me as we watched them go and massaged my shoulders. I could hear the sound his thumbs made against the cloth of my shirt, a soft scratching hush. And though I strained to hear something more, the coalescing human noises of the whole world from beyond the apartment, all I could hear was Mike. His thumbs, his stomach, his pulse, all that kept him alive behind me.

* * *

Discussion Questions

1. The first half of the story discusses reincarnation. Do you believe in reincarnation or a form of reincarnation? If so, what (*if anything*) is the purpose of reincarnation?

2. The story also talks about soulmates. Do you believe in soulmates or some variation of soulmates?

3. The third part of the story talks about sexual orientation, gender identity, and gender fluidity. Do you believe that sometimes people are born the wrong gender or that people can be both gay and born the wrong gender (i.e., a gay man that was born into a woman's body)?

4. In the cases of questions 1, 2, and 3, what are the scientific, religious, experiential, or value-based constructs we overlay that cause us to come to our own conclusions for each question?

5. In the story, Jaime was born a biological woman, transitioned to a man, but is going to have a baby. Mike questions how to define a man (*or a woman?*) if not by the ability to have children. What would be your answer to this question?

The Draft

Jan McCleery

* * *

Throngs of people entered the fifteen-story building crowned by the gold sign reading, *Center for the RTL Headquarters*. Most had no idea what *RTL* stood for.

Valets were running back and forth in front of the building, taking the next expensive car in the long line that circled the block before entering the curved driveway. Men in tuxedos and women in cocktail dresses emerged from their cars. Servers passed out champagne to those in the long line waiting to enter the building. Once inside, they entered a massive conference room with huge screens on several walls displaying the words *Center for the RTL*. A live five-piece orchestra played chamber music. Servers with trays of up-scale appetizers circulated the room as the attendees milled about, greeting business associates. Empty champagne glasses were promptly replaced.

Congressman Mitch Mitchell and his wife, Gloria, were a handsome couple in their early fifties. Mitch had been swept into his seat in Congress in the 2022 midterms when he was only thirty, running on a strict pro-life platform. As they stood talking to a billionaire contributor and his wife, the lights dimmed. A deep male voice reverberated from above: "Welcome to the grand opening of the Centers for the RTL. Now... here is the Founder and CEO, Dr. Celeste Rivers."

A trim woman with intelligent green eyes and short dark hair framing her pixie face eagerly took the stage and walked into the spotlight. The screens around the room projected her image. Smiling. Beaming. Charismatic. She doubted anyone knew she was thinking about how needing a hysterectomy all those years ago in college had been such an unexpected blessing, leaving her free to pursue a Stanford PhD in engineering and accomplish what had become her life's goal: to give all women in America a choice whether or not to bear a child. Now it had become a reality. Her heart beat in her chest with a combination of pride and excitement.

"Thank you all for coming," she said, her voice strong and clear. "What you will see and hear today will amaze and thrill you. It is the beginning of an era of new freedom for all women! The letters R-T-L stand for 'Right to Life.' As of today, all women can embrace the right to life without relinquishing the right to control their bodies."

The women involved with the project for the past ten years started applauding wildly. Others clapped politely but looked confused.

Celeste continued, "Today, we have the technology to allow a fetus to grow safely and healthily, from embryo to a fully developed newborn, without using a woman's body." She paused. "Behold, the incubators."

The screens displayed pictures of the center's incubation rooms. Dimly lit, each room was filled with hundreds and hundreds of incubators: some pods contained small fetuses with enlarged heads and small limbs curled into a C-shape; others held nearly full-grown babies. It was like an eerie scene from a science fiction movie.

The mood in the conference room quickly changed; some gasped. Celeste was prepared, and the screens quickly changed to a series of beautiful babies wrapped in blankets and held by their beaming mothers.

"Babies who are gestated in our incubators are healthier. No more preemies born too early due to their mother's medical issues. No more crack babies or those addicted to alcohol. Healthy babies who will bond with their mothers. Gretchen, model your baby cord for us, please."

A beautiful, tall, young, Germanic woman, all in red from her hair to her luscious lips and down to her bikini and spiky heels, mounted the stairs to join Celeste on the stage, towering over her. Low on her waist hung a gossamer silky string.

"What is that I see you wearing?" Celeste asked mischievously.

"My red bikini?" Gretchen answered her rehearsed line, spoken with a heavy German accent while flashing a smile.

Celeste winked at the audience. "She knows." People laughed, men nervously because they couldn't help staring at the striking woman on the stage.

"You mean this?" Gretchen pointed to the gossamer string. "It's my 'baby cord.' It's letting me feel what my baby is doing, just as if he was right here in my tummy." She patted her flat, bare stomach.

"Do you mind if a few of our guests feel what you do?"

"I don't mind. My husband is fascinated by it."

Celeste motioned to the audience. "Come toward the stage." She didn't need to urge. Men were pushing to get forward. Gretchen knelt, and Celeste leaned down and held a mic as the stunning woman let a few people take turns placing their hands on her stomach.

Every monitor had gone to split screen, half showing the beautiful Gretchen letting men feel her bare stomach; the other half displayed an image of her baby in the incubator, kicking and squirming.

In turn, each exclaimed, "Wow!" "I felt it kick!" "That's amazing!"

Celeste laughed. "Thank you, Gretchen."

The tall redhead stood, smiled sweetly at the men, and left the stage.

"We've placed one thousand RTL Clinics at prior Planned Parenthood sites plus added hundreds more in rural areas. Any woman can easily get to one of our clinics, where her fetus will be removed and whisked to the nearest center to be placed in an incubator. Near the end of term, the mother will be notified and given an appointment date."

On the screens, a swaddled baby is taken to a seated mother, who immediately puts her newborn to her breast to nurse. Her husband sits by her side, his arm lovingly around her. In the next view, the couple stands up with their baby, is handed a "New Baby Gift Bag," and walks out the front door.

Celeste added, "Better than the stork!"

Laughter and excitement filled the room.

"Now, are there any questions?"

A woman reporter was the first to raise her hand. When Celeste pointed to her, she pushed her horn-rimmed glasses further up her nose. "Judith Baker, *Today's Times Magazine*." She pursed her thin lips. "Are you playing God here?"

Everyone quieted. A few gasped at the implications.

"Believe me," Celeste responded, "we wrestled with difficult questions. Think of it. We could eliminate babies with gene defects. Alter survival rates based on sex, race, or other traits. Create a master race." Her voice had gotten louder as she raised her eyebrows, a look she knew made her appear sinister, and she looked around the audience. Not everyone was smiling. In fact, some looked shocked.

"But that would be playing God, wouldn't it?" Celeste chastised. "That would be altering the natural balance and plan. We said 'No!' Rest assured. We are not playing God. We are providing an alternate womb for women. Plain and simple."

Some people nodded approvingly. Celeste pointed at another reporter.

"Annie Walker, *World News*," the woman said. "What if the mother didn't want a baby?"

"Good question. After her fetus is extracted, she has up until the time of full gestation to decide whether, at the end, she wants to claim the baby or put it up for adoption. Same as the current US law. Next?"

A male reporter raised his hand. "Gerald Cross, ALT Cable News," he opened. "Won't this result in significantly more babies born per year? We all know many women buy smuggled contraceptives and abortion pills, and there are ways for women to obtain illegal abortions. Now women and their doctors will have no reason to take that risk. Won't we end up with millions of babies without mothers?"

Celeste shrugged her shoulders and didn't answer.

Gerald countered, "But what's the plan? Won't all these extra babies overwhelm the system?"

Celeste smiled sweetly. "That's an excellent question. Why don't you answer it for us? For the past few decades, the political party your station supports has pushed for every fertilized egg to result in a baby. They have outlawed contraception and all abortions. So, if there is now a problem of too many babies, it is up to your party to solve it. Next question?" And with that, she looked away from Gerald.

* * *

The Women's Revolution

Soon, all women were taking advantage of the free service. The gossamer strings became a sign of motherhood, like a rounded, protruding belly had in years past. No longer having to deal with stretch marks and bulging stomachs, expectant mothers wore bikinis at the beach to show off their baby cords.

Released from the need to use their bodies to grow babies, women used their newfound freedom to pursue higher education, and the number of women in better-paying jobs increased. More women entered the government and formed a new political party, "The Women's Right to Life" party, and soon women were in control of the country: Congress, the White House, and most state governments.

As Gerald from ALT News had predicted, before long, the availability of babies had overwhelmed adoption agencies and foster system.

The government created the "Office of Equality and Fairness" (OEF) to resolve the problem and established "The

Draft" system. According to Draft rules, all males between the ages of sixteen and fifty must be entered into a lottery to determine which among them would, under penalty of law, take the unclaimed babies.

Of course, men fought back, whining it wasn't fair to select only males to take unwanted babies. The OEF's answer came first in the form of questions: Who, for centuries, were forced to subject their bodies to the strain of growing unwanted babies? And who were often left to raise those children with no support from anyone, no matter how many children they already had? Who had to leave school—sometimes as young as sixteen years of age—and despair of ever being able to secure a better future? The answer: Women. "Well," the OEF argued, "now is the time for men to step up, take their turn, and accept responsibility."

The Draft Rules were solidified, and men realized the law would not be changed, not in the near future.

On January 13, 2050, "The Draft" went into effect.

* * *

January 13, 2067

Tim Mitchell woke up when four-year-old Curt jumped on him and pummeled him in the face. Tim grabbed Curt's hands and held him firmly, trying to quiet his aggression.

The sun was barely up. Having reached the age of fifty, Tim knew this was his last year; after this, he would no longer be eligible for the Draft. He had ducked it for the first sixteen years after it was established, but for the last four years in a row, he had been a big loser and was now raising four children under the age of five.

Curt, his first child, was born with a rare genetic disability that left him with cognitive learning problems as well as anger issues. He barely spoke and still had to be spoon-fed and diapered. Tim had to quit his job to raise Curt.

When Curt was diagnosed, Tim's fury was directed at his father, former Congressman Mitch Mitchell, who had been a fervent advocate to end all forms of birth control and abortion.

Tim had called his father and screamed, "What were you guys thinking? What did you imagine would happen if abortions and contraception were outlawed?" But Tim knew his father was tired of being blamed. Tim's mother still blamed Mitch for Lizzy's death. Tim's sister had committed suicide when she found herself pregnant in college. She was Congressman Mitchell's daughter, and abortion was not an option. Now Mitch's son had joined the blame game. Mitch hung up on him.

Max and Lucy, ages two and three, heard the commotion and padded into Tim's bedroom in their one-piece PJs. Tim carried screaming Curt into the kitchen. Max and Lucy followed him. Tim left Roger, less than one year old, in his crib.

The three were eating their cereal—well Max and Lucy were, Curt was throwing his—but Tim couldn't wait any longer. He turned on the TV. He'd missed the standard opening, the pomp and ceremony, but it was always the same.

The President greets the emcee, who comes on stage with a great deal of fanfare, clapping, and music. "Elmer Greco," the President says, smiling. "Are we ready for this year's excitement?"

Elmer is a flamboyant man. His hair is waved up too high in front, and his white teeth gleam. He's got on too much makeup, even by TV standards.

When Tim turned on the TV this year, Elmer was seated by the large wheel, beaming. Tim checked the board for his best friend George's birthday, May 17th. Number 279. "Lucky bastard," Tim muttered under his breath. "He's ducked it again." Tim and George had worked together at the ad agency until Tim's first unlucky draw. Men with numbers higher than two hundred rarely ended up with a baby at their doorstep.

Tim's birthday, July 19th, had not yet been called.

Now Elmer spun for July 15th. "The lucky number is..." The huge roulette wheel spun, click-clack-click, then stopped at 330.

"Aw, 330!" exclaimed Elmer, disappointed. "That's a high number. Better luck next year."

It annoyed Tim to no end that a high number could be bad. That everyone could be so cheery, so upbeat about low numbers. Changing men's lives forever. It was atrocious!

Curt's yelling distracted Tim for a moment. Then Elmer called out "July 19th." Tim stared at the TV, shaking.

Time stopped. The world slowed down as the wheel clicked, making its way around the large circle. Then it decelerated. All motion stopped. Everything around Tim stopped. The kids stopped yelling. Roger in his crib stopped crying. There was nothing. Nothing. Except... the number... "5."

His heart sank. It couldn't be! "Five! *Five?*"

Tim could barely function. He picked up the phone. "Cindy! Can you come over and cover me here?"

"Sure, Tim." His next-door neighbor was compassionate. She, too, had been watching the Draft, worrying about Tim, fearing he couldn't handle yet another child. She knew he was already on the edge.

Through his mind fog, Tim grabbed a warm coat, put it over his pajamas, and rushed out in his slippers as Cindy came in, facing four screaming kids.

Tim exited the apartment building into the chill of the morning. Standing in the street, he didn't hear a taxi honking as it roared by. "Just run me over," Tim muttered. The next cab stopped, and he jumped in. He gave the driver the address for the agency he'd worked for until the unlucky year when he'd lost the Draft for the first time.

He jumped out of the cab, ran into the building, and took the elevator to the tenth floor. He walked right by Millie, the receptionist.

"Tim? Tim. You can't go in there."

He ignored her and burst into George's office. George, who had never lost the Draft, looked up from his desk. Lucky bastard.

"Did you see? Did you see?" Tim stammered.

"The Draft? I watched until they called my number, then got a phone call and had to get to work. Lucky, huh?" Suddenly, George seemed to become aware of Tim's expression. "Oh... my... God, Tim. What number did you get?"

"Five! Five! I fucking got five! I'm dead, man. I can't do it. I've got Curt driving me crazy. Roger's still in his crib. Number five? Why is there no sense to it? No limits? I called the Center last year after they dropped Roger on my doorstep and screamed at them. 'How can you do this to me?' Do you know what they said? 'Men made the laws that said all fertilized eggs must become babies. These are your rules.'"

"They aren't *my* rules," sobbed Tim. "They're my dad's rules. Not *my* rules."

George looked at Tim with anguish but had no words. All men were powerless in America now.

* * *

February 28, 2067

On February 28, it happened. There was a knock on Tim's door. He felt dread, not expecting any visitors except one, the Center for the RTL.

He opened the door reluctantly. A woman stood in the hallway, smiling, accompanied by two others, each holding a bundle.

"You're so lucky! You've got twins!"

Six weeks later, Tim was exhausted. The way he'd been every day since Curt arrived. But he was more than exhausted: drained, shattered, incoherent. He'd spent another day trying to rock the twins and get them to eat. Curt screamed at the top of his lungs. Lucy and Max demanded attention. Roger, Curt, and Max still in diapers in addition to the twins. Finally, Lucy, Max, and Roger were in their beds.

Tim watched the twins, asleep in his arms. He couldn't believe how beautiful they were. It made him so sad. Holding one in each arm, he tiptoed into the bedroom to check that Lucy and Max were asleep. He smiled at Lucy's sweet face, at Max's cuteness. As he entered the babies' room, Roger was asleep in his crib, but when the floor creaked, he awoke. Now all three were crying.

He put the twins down, then went from one crib to the other, trying to soothe them, rubbing their backs. They were still fussing, but Tim, completely beat, left and shut the door to the room, ignoring their cries. Curt was watching TV. Tim knew the boy would either crash in front of the TV for the night or scream around midnight for his dad to get up and take him into their bed. Curt had never been able to sleep in a bed alone.

Tim crept by softly so as not to attract Curt's attention, unlocked the front door, and then headed quietly to the bathroom. He shut the door and telephoned Cindy. "I need your help."

"Sorry, Tim, but it's late. Maybe tomorrow."

"No," he said it quietly, but even he could hear the despair in his tone. "The kids need your help... now. Tomorrow will be too late."

"What's wrong, Tim?"

But Tim couldn't answer. He had slashed his wrists and was bleeding to death on the bathroom floor.

* * *

Becoming a Grandparent

"Mr. Mitchell?" the policeman on the porch asked.

"Yes?" Mitch Mitchell felt a sense of dread; whatever it was, he knew it wasn't going to be good.

"We are sorry to inform you that your son, Tim, passed away last night."

Mitch was stunned, but he remained stoic. "How?"

"I'm sorry, sir. He committed suicide."

Mitch just stood, shocked. They hadn't been close since Tim drew his first unlucky number in the Draft. His wife, Gloria, had passed away a year after Tim first lost the Draft. She'd never gotten over blaming Mitch for Lizzy's death. Then seeing Tim with a problem child had broken her heart.

Mitch didn't know what to feel. He simply thanked the policeman, who turned and left.

As soon as he was alone, Mitch's phone rang.

"Mr. Mitchell?"

"Yes."

"This is Director Martin from the Center for the Right to Life." The woman's authoritative voice was irritating. "Don't go anywhere. We have paperwork we need you to sign."

"What's this about?"

"Please don't leave, sir. That would cause you legal difficulty. We will be right there."

Click.

Ten minutes later, when he responded to the knock on his door, he saw two black cars parked in front of his Maryland residence. A tall woman with a "Center for the RTL" patch stood on his porch. Mitch looked at her warily. Her nametag said, *Martin*.

"This shouldn't take long, sir. Is there a place we can sit down and review the paperwork?"

"What paperwork?"

"Please, sir, the explanation is in the paperwork. Where can we sit and review it?"

He motioned her to sit on the couch, and he took a chair.

She sat, put her binder down on the coffee table between them, and opened it to the first page.

Mitchell Adoption, it read in large bold letters. Suddenly realizing the implications, Mitch felt his eyes grow wide. "I can't... what? What is this?"

"Obviously, sir, your son's unfortunate demise means he can no longer fulfill his obligations to the government to care for his six children."

"Six?" Mitch stammered, then he remembered about the twins.

"Since Tim never legally assigned a godparent, the responsibility falls to you, his father, the children's grandfather."

"No, what? I'm seventy-five years old. I can't take on six children, twin babies."

"Legally, they are your responsibility."

"Take them back to the Center!" he directed.

"That wouldn't be legal," Director Martin answered coldly. She paused, and her voice softened a bit. "I understand this is happening suddenly, but there are no other options. The responsibility is yours and yours alone."

She turned to the signature page in the binder and held out a pen. "Sign," she directed. He looked at the doorway and saw two guards, armed, standing there at attention. He understood. *Take the children or go to jail.* He signed.

She rose and left six folders on the coffee table, each labeled with one of the children's names. The last name on each was Mitchell. "I am sure you will be a good grandparent to the children. But, of course, there are significant fines and legal issues for men who shirk their duty. Oh, and I suggest you identify a godparent. You're getting up there in age." He could see a slight smirk on her face. Then her face softened. "We will bring the children in now. Please greet them warmly. They have been through a lot."

She turned and went to the door. Mitch sat, shocked. He couldn't think straight. Then Lucy and Max ran in with tears in their eyes and hugged him. "Oh, Grandpa. Daddy's gone," little Lucy sobbed. They had only seen their grandfather a few times at Christmas, but they remembered him. Kids do.

Curt walked up and kicked him in the shin.

The children's clothes, toys, diapers, a week's supply of food and formula, and multiple car seats were carried in and set down on the floor. Finally, the twins came, pushed in a double baby carriage.

"This is Inge," Director Martin introduced the tall, gray-haired, Swedish woman, helping Roger toddle in. "She will assist you in making a smooth transition with the children today. It's a new service we offer for the children's sake. She can lend a hand as you prepare lists of how to care and feed them and make school plans. She can stay until the children are in bed tonight and can return during the day tomorrow if you still need her and then offer phone consultations for a week."

He nodded, relieved that he wasn't going to just suddenly be left with them all. "Yes, please."

Inge held Max's and Lucy's hands while Mitch carried a squirming Curt and showed the children their rooms. A staff member set up two cribs, and another staffer carried Roger to one of them and then went back for the twins. Inge began moving their belongings into their rooms.

Director Martin said, "Could I have one more word with you, sir? Alone."

Inge picked up Curt and carried him into the den where Max and Lucy were watching TV, leaving only Director Martin and Mitch in the living room.

"You know, during your time as Congressman, women didn't *want* to make the choice between bearing an unwanted child or having an abortion. Young girls still in high school, women who were raped or with too many children already, women just feeling they had no control over their bodies and their lives. I think men in America now understand how the loss of control feels when the government makes the decisions about your life. I really hope this will work out for you and your grandchildren. They need you. And I am sorry for your loss, sir."

She left and shut the door softly behind her. A tear rolled down his cheek.

* * *

Discussion Questions

1. What do you think would happen if women could easily and cheaply have a newly conceived child removed and grown outside of their body? How do you think society would change?
2. Would you support a law that required men to have a 50/50 chance of being the primary caregiver for the children of all unplanned pregnancies?
3. Assuming there were far more children placed in adoption than those looking to adopt, would you support a "Draft" like the one in the story? Why or why not? Do you have an alternative?
4. Given the choice between easy and inexpensive access to incubated babies, like in the story, and easy and inexpensive access to contraception and abortion, which would you prefer and why?
5. Does the government have a responsibility to provide excellent care for unwanted children? What societal advantages/disadvantages exist in pushing that responsibility onto individuals through a system like the story's "Draft"?

Final Determination

Lea Pounds

* * *

This is not a morality tale. It's simply a story.

Living people get a lot wrong about the After Life. It isn't binary Heaven or Hell but a spectrum where most people end up somewhere better than their Earthly life. There's also a state of Abeyance where you stay if you have unfinished business. For the worst of the worst, there is Eternal Damnation which is like permanent solitary confinement.

Time and space don't have much meaning in the After Life. However, being in Abeyance includes the ability to experience time and space if it helps with the process. There's a kind of holo-deck like in a sci-fi show. The first time I tried it, I imagined being at Sunday dinner with my paternal grandparents. I come from a big family. I have an older brother and sister and two younger brothers, plus tons of cousins on both sides. Everybody on my dad's side lives within driving distance of my grandparents, so at least once a month, we all show up on Sunday after church. Instead of being comforted, I got overwhelmed with sadness and anger. Knowing that I would never experience family gatherings again, and that they would never be the same for the people I love, was too much.

Now I stick with imagining places without people, like the pasture next to our house on the farm. I like to see the field through changing seasons. In the spring and summer, the pasture is sprinkled with wildflowers. In the fall, the switch grass grows to my waist. There's a giant cottonwood tree that's fallen and made a bridge across the creek that runs behind our house. The root end forms a kind of seat where I can lean back and look at the sky. Sometimes I imagine the pasture on a clear night and look at the stars. My dad taught me the names of the constellations when I was little, and I try to remember them now. I loved being on the farm, loved being outside.

I was active in school. Mom calls me—called me—her social butterfly. I got involved in every activity at my rural consolidated high school that I could: cheerleading, track, choir, drama, anything that looked interesting. During the summer, I worked at the local Dairy Cream drive-in to save money for college. I wanted to get a degree in wildlife biology so I could work on habitat preservation and restoration. They had my memorial service at the high school gym because so many people attended. Based on news reports, the place was packed. My death was big news in my small corner of the world.

Right after high school, my best friend and I moved to the city. It seems cliché, naive farm girl goes to the big city. It was only around thirty thousand people, not even the biggest city in my state, but home to one of the state university campuses. It was a new world to me. During the day, I took courses at the community college. At night and most weekends, I waited tables at a truck stop. I took on all the extra shifts I could to save up so I could transfer to the university. I made good tips too. I guess my wholesome farm girl vibe resonated with the customers. It didn't hurt that I've always been the kind of person that makes friends easily; never met a stranger, my dad always said.

I had an array of exhilarating possibilities in front of me. Every opportunity was a new adventure. My friends warned me to be more cautious, but I was high on life. That attitude helped put me here. I should have found a balance between common sense and my giddy belief in possibilities.

I don't know much about the algorithm the Divine uses to make placement decisions for ordinary people. For murderers, there's a Council that reviews the case with the victims. The goal is to look at every aspect of the killer's life and the crime from different points of view, so the victim understands the full context of the situation. There's a lot of information like lawyers' emails and phone calls, the perpetrator's criminal history, psychiatric evaluations, juvenile records, and other stuff that the jurors and public don't always see. When I look at my case, I bring my tablet to the field because it's less horrifying when I'm in a familiar place.

Joshua Allen Wiznisky is the name of the guy that killed me. He worked at the truck stop doing mostly janitorial work. At the time, I figured from what people said and the way he acted that he'd had a hard life. We were close to the same age. I sometimes felt guilty that I had so much hope for the future while he seemed like he'd already given up. The court-ordered evaluation before his trial said that even though his IQ was at the bottom end of normal, he was competent. So I guess he was smart enough to understand right from wrong.

Even though everything was caught on the security camera, and there were witnesses to some of it, Josh pled not guilty. His court-appointed attorney played up his childhood trauma. The trial was ghastly. The prosecution spent hours asking detailed questions about the crime scene and autopsy results. They put blown-up photos on easels at the front of the courtroom and left them there. Still, my family came every day.

The defense's play for sympathy didn't work. Josh was found guilty. During the sentencing phase, my sister read a victim impact statement. She talked about how the weekend before my death, she and I had gone shopping for bridesmaid dresses for her wedding that summer. Since I couldn't be her maid of honor in person, she put a picture of me on an easel where I would have stood. My dad wanted to give a statement but was crying so hard he couldn't talk. The judge let the court clerk read it into the record. The three-judge panel that handled sentencing could have given Josh life without parole, but they all agreed on death.

I learned from the investigation during the mandatory appeal process just how bad his life had been. His parents were alcoholics and addicts that couldn't take care of their kids. His father used to pimp Josh out in exchange for drugs. His mother beat him all the time with whatever she had in her hand: an iron, a frying pan, or whatever. He was in and out of foster homes and juvenile detention facilities most of his life. By the time he was sixteen, he was living on the street doing whatever he needed to survive. Because I was so happy, I tried to be extra nice to him. In retrospect, that wasn't such a good idea. It never occurred to me that he'd interpret my friendliness as anything more than common civility.

Despite all the discussion and all the information, I'm still not sure what Josh's final determination should be. The last step is an in-person interview once he's in Abeyance.

The head of the Council comes across the field. "He's waiting."

Through the glass walls of the conference room, I can see Josh sitting with his head bowed and his hands folded on the table. He's wearing jeans and a short-sleeved blue shirt with DOC stenciled on the front. A piece of medical tape hangs on the inside of his left arm. He's been in prison for twenty-five years. His hair is gray and thinning. He looks gaunt like his skin is a size too small. He has more tattoos than I remember.

I sit at the opposite end of the table. The Council members are behind me, but he can't see them. Not yet. He looks up.

"Hey, Alli." He picks at the tape. "I finally got the needle."

What's the appropriate response to that? I don't know. I want to be sure he understands what's going on. "Do you know where you are? Why you're here?"

He looks around. "Heaven, right?"

His assumption that he'd be welcome in Heaven startles me. "What makes you think that?"

"Well, you're here, and you went to Heaven, right? Besides, I repented, and God forgives me."

"Oh? That gets you off the hook?" My voice trembles, and I feel the Council's energy behind me.

"No. A few years ago, I accepted Jesus as my Lord and Savior. After a lot of reading the Bible and praying, I came to terms with what I've done." He straightens. "I am sorry, Alli. I didn't mean to hurt you like that."

"Hurt me like that? What does that mean? Did you intend to hurt me in a different way?" Now that I'm face-to-face with him, I'm angry. I want to hurt him the way he hurt me, but that's not possible.

"I didn't intend to hurt you."

"I don't believe that. Anyway, we're not in Heaven. We're in Abeyance."

"Obey-what?"

"Abeyance. As your victim, I get a say in where you end up."

Josh looked doubtful, but he sat up straighter and changed the subject. "You look good."

He's aged. I look the same as I did the day I died. I'm stunned to see my name tattooed on the inside of his right forearm. There's a little heart in place of the "o." For a second, I'm scared. I feel the hot pain of his knife jabbing into my chest. I look down, half expecting to see blood soaking into my waitress uniform. I'm reassured to see the white tunic everyone here wears when they take on visual form.

"Did you want to see the stab wounds?" I emphasize *want*. Maybe he wants to see the bloody mess he created. When I first got here, I looked at those wounds a lot because I couldn't believe that really happened to me. After a while, they faded. Now I only see them if I think about it. They're not exactly healed scars, but they're not gaping wounds anymore.

"Not really." Expressionless, he stares at me. Maybe he can't believe what he did, either.

"Did you get counseling in prison?"

"Yeah, it was mandatory that I see a shrink and do some

group therapy. I know what I did was wrong, but I'm not crazy. I was really high that night."

"Are you saying that you're not responsible because the drugs made you do it?"

"I am responsible, but I've repented. God forgives me." The pupils of his eyes are black voids focused on me. His voice is flat. The words sound rehearsed, like he's saying something he's memorized without understanding the meaning.

There's a touch screen in front of me containing all the case information. I stall for time by flipping through the files. I had a long list of questions I wanted to ask. Now that I'm face-to-face with him, I can't remember them. When I come to the crime scene photos, only one thing comes to mind. "Why?"

Josh looks confused. "What?"

I'm looking at a picture of me lying in the dirt by the dumpsters behind the restaurant. My blouse and bra are ripped, exposing my left breast. One of my shoes is off. I barely recognize my face. "Why did you do this to me?"

Josh keeps staring at me and shrugs. "Like I said, I was doing a lot of drugs that day."

The shrug dismisses the whole thing as inconsequential. The strength of the Council radiates behind me, holding me up. "That's an excuse not an explanation."

Josh lowers his head for a second, then looks at me blankly. "I said I'm sorry. Doesn't that count for anything?"

"Only if you're truly remorseful, and I don't think you are."

"I didn't set out to hurt you, Alli."

"Why?" I ask again.

He sighs and stares at his folded hands. "My whole life,

nobody cared about me. My parents didn't want me. All the foster parents and case workers thought I was garbage. You were the only person who was ever nice to me without wanting anything in return."

He rubs his hands across his face. "I started drinking and doing drugs when I was ten or eleven. Numbing out like that was the only way I could cope."

"I know you had a tough life." The difference between my childhood and his makes me feel like he's owed something. Does he deserve a spot in Heaven, even on the lower end of the spectrum? I don't know. His taking my life and all the pain inflicted on my family has to count for something, too.

"You remember when I told you I was going to rehab?"

"Yes." I remember thinking that having hope might turn his life around.

"Remember you hugged me? Nobody ever hugged me like that before. You felt so soft in my arms. Your hair smelled like flowers. You said you were happy for me. I thought about that the whole time I was in rehab. It was hard, but thinking about you got me through."

He stares at the table while I flip through more pictures. The blood and dirt obscure the pale blue color of my uniform. There's one of those L-shaped police rulers marking a knife by the dumpster. My hair band is lying in a pool of blood with a numbered yellow cone beside it. The crime scene photos are right after pictures and news clippings from my memorial service. The contrast between the two sets of pictures reinforces everything I've lost. Josh had twenty-five more years of life. Sure, he was in prison, but at least he was alive. I've missed out on everything: holidays, birthdays, weddings, family dinners, reunions, even funerals. Everything. Anger clogs my throat. For a moment, I struggle to breathe.

Josh clears his throat. "Anyway, after I got out of rehab, I wanted to tell you how I felt; how much I loved you. I figured I'd catch you at work. To pass the time, I hooked up with some buddies. I smoked a little weed to calm my nerves. One thing led to another, and before I knew it, I'd done some meth, too. I probably should have sobered up before I came to see you."

My reaction would have been the same. He'd surprised me when I was taking out the trash. He stepped out of the shadows, and I could see right away that he was high. He was so incoherent that, at first, I didn't understand. If I had just gone straight back into the building the minute I saw him, I'd probably still be alive. But I felt sorry for him. A month in rehab, and he gets high the minute he gets out. That's so hopeless, so pathetic.

He had kept going on about how much he loved me. He even got down on one knee and asked me to marry him. I said no. Maybe if I'd gone along with him, I'd still be alive. I could have straightened things out once he sobered up.

He attacked me when I started to go back into the building. He was trying to hug and kiss me. My clothes ripped when I tried to get away. When I screamed, he grabbed me by the hair and smashed my face into the side of the dumpster. At first, I was so stunned that I didn't realize he was stabbing me.

"I thought you loved me, Alli. I thought if I went through rehab, you'd see that I wasn't garbage and want to be with me. Me showing up high and all was dumb. I understand that scared you. But you saying no without giving me a chance made me look stupid. I guess I just snapped." Josh sniffs and rubs the back of his hand against his nose. "I just wanted you to love me, Alli. Just one time to have someone love me."

Looking at Josh now, I still feel sorry for him. I can't imagine living your whole life being so starved for affection that you think someone being nice to you is the same thing as love. Thinking that a quick hug would lead to marriage is twisted. I was kind to him because I'm a decent person, but it wasn't my responsibility to make him feel loved. The people who were supposed to take care of him as a kid let him down. That clearly skewed his view of the world. He had a right to be angry about that, I suppose.

"Did you ever think about my family, what my murder did to them?" His miserable family life didn't justify inflicting pain on mine. His thinking made no sense to me.

Josh shrugged again. "I guess. I mean, I heard what they said at sentencing."

"Did you ever think about them afterward?"

"Yeah. After I became a Christian, I tried to send them a letter through my attorney. They sent it back unopened."

"They're not obligated to forgive you just because you said you're sorry. You didn't just kill me; you hurt them too. Do you understand that? Do you get how many people you hurt just because you were angry?"

"I wouldn't have been angry if I'd have had a decent shot at life." There's an edge to his voice, and he leans across the table.

"You had a terrible childhood that set you up to have a difficult life. But I didn't cause any of that. I'm not responsible for the choices you made as an adult."

He stares at me with those vacant eyes for a long minute before leaning back. "I spent twenty-five years on death row and then died by having poison put in my arm. What more do you want from me, Allison?"

He says he's sorry, but there's nothing behind the words. I'm not sure he's capable of true remorse. "You can't give me what I want."

"What? Just tell me what you want to hear, and I'll say it." Josh throws his arms out. "Well?"

For a second, my fear of him stops my voice. "I want the twenty-five years I didn't have. I want to have a career and make a difference in the world. I want to be there for my aging parents, to be the cool auntie to my nieces and nephews. I want to fall in love and have kids. I want to grow old and die in my sleep."

The head of the Council takes form beside me. Josh's eyes pop, and his jaw drops.

"It's time to make a decision, Allison. Time to move on," they say softly.

Josh hangs his head and whimpers.

I've reached the last item in the file. It's a form titled "Final Determination" with two boxes. One marked *redemption* and one marked *eternal damnation*.

* * *

Discussion Questions

1. If you were in Alli's shoes in the story, how would you sentence Josh, and why?

2. Does everyone (*even a person like Josh*) deserve forgiveness after committing horrible actions? What factors would you use to determine if you forgive them?

3. Do you believe Josh is truly repentant for what he has done? What, if any, additional questions would you ask him to make that determination?

4. Does anyone, for any action, deserve an eternity of pain for a moment (*or series of moments*) of wrongdoing?

5. Should Alli's primary goal be to punish Josh or to find peace with her trauma? How might her primary goal change her decision regarding Josh's afterlife? What is Alli's "unfinished business" that has kept her in Abeyance?

More

Julia Edinger

* * *

Jacob was finishing his cup of coffee, which he didn't really need with his nerves already shaking him, when his wife, Dina, walked over with the coffee pot.

"More?" She inquired sweetly, but he shook his head. He had enough coffee. He had enough in every sense, he realized, as he looked around the dining room. His older son, Michael, sat at the table, reading the back of a cereal box while he ate. Michael was in third grade and already labeled gifted. Jacob's other son, Elijah, had not yet woken. He had only been born six months ago, but Jacob already had an unbreakable bond with him. The boys were close with Dina, too, but never lit up around her the way they did when Jacob got home. Perhaps it was because Jacob was almost never home, between work and other matters. It wasn't that family wasn't a priority for Jacob. He simply didn't have the time to spare.

With that thought, Jacob checked his watch and noticed

he had to leave now if he wanted to have time to stop for a cup of coffee before work. Jacob wasn't looking forward to the coffee, but the woman he was meeting there. He grabbed his jacket and briefcase and kissed Michael on the top of his head.

"Have a good day, Michael," Jacob smiled, then leaned in to kiss his wife, adding, "Love you both." Jacob truly did love his family. They were the most important people in his life. Yet, somehow, he heard his wife's question, "More?" repeating in his mind, and wondered why he still felt he needed more.

As Jacob made his way down the block, he imagined what his wife was doing. She was always caring for somebody. She was probably busy packing lunch for Michael or waking up Elijah. Dina wasn't the kind of woman who liked to stand in place. But at the same time, Jacob thought, she was never willing to change. There was no spontaneity, no excitement, and no longer any passion. They were comfortable together, and though that should have been enough, Jacob felt he deserved more. He craved that passion.

As he walked into the coffee shop and found a seat, he refused to look up at the faces around him. Instead, he grabbed a napkin to scribble down his thoughts. His final masterpiece was a list of rationalizations for his behavior, and the only bullet point he could come up with said "more."

Jacob worked hard to support his wife, who he had proposed to the moment she found out she was pregnant with Michael. Jacob had a great job offer in New York City, but Dina had convinced him it was nowhere to raise a family, and she had talked him into settling for a smaller place and a lower-paying job. Less, less, less. Jacob believed that, for once, he deserved more.

"Jacob!" A smooth, luscious voice exclaimed from across the room. Sasha. She shot Jacob a wicked smile, and he reveled in it. She took off her barista apron, revealing a blouse with just enough buttons undone to invoke Jacob's curiosity. She began walking over to Jacob, and he crumpled up the napkin. He tossed it in the nearest trash can and abandoned all thoughts of his home and his family. Had he continued to think of them, it would have been harder to go through with what he planned to do. But knowing that, he made the active choice to block them out of his mind and push the guilt down for a later time. Jacob would rather feel regret than guilt because at least regret meant he would get to touch Sasha's soft skin.

"You look beautiful," Jacob grinned, pulling Sasha into him and smelling the vanilla wafting from her long brown hair. She smelled sweet and sensual, a stark difference from his wife's floral fragrance. How lucky was he, he thought, to have two women at the same time.

"Enough sweet talk," Sasha demanded firmly, "You know my break is only an hour, and if we aren't quick, we'll both be late." Her voice was smooth, despite her strict tone, causing Jacob's hair to stand on end. Dina would never talk to him in that tone; she was completely submissive. Perhaps he should have appreciated it more, but he would rather have a woman who was strong enough to stand up for herself.

Once they got into Sasha's red convertible Sebring, his hands were all over her. He touched her thigh immediately, trying to breathe steadily while his heartbeat sped up. She looked over at him with sharp eyes, signaling him to wait. But he couldn't wait. He began kissing her hand over and over, repeatedly telling her how beautiful she was. Seeing in his eyes and pants that he could no longer control his wanting, she pulled over at a desolate overlook to the north side of the river; his home was on the south side.

Home. He thought for a fleeting moment about Dina, Michael, and Elijah. At the recognition of his conscience, he immediately pushed the memory to the back of his mind, focusing on what he was doing, who he was touching: Sasha.

Sasha's hands were touching Jacob all over his body, grasping desperately. He could taste the hunger in her kisses and feel the yearning in her fingertips. He had no idea why she was so impressed with him, and that may have been part of what enticed him. Whatever it was, she had a thirst for this relationship in the same way he did. He thought about what it was about her that made her so irresistible to him. Was it her age, her eyes, or simply that she was forbidden fruit? Whatever it was, he liked how she made him feel: free.

It was a harmless crime in Jacob's mind—like taking a candy bar from a convenience store or glancing at the closest paper during a test. What Dina didn't know wouldn't hurt her. He kissed Sasha, trying to get out of his head. He kept his eyes closed the whole time, but it felt different from what he was used to. Her lips were fuller, and her tongue was colder. She was new. It was a change. He wanted more, more, more...

* * *

Sasha brushed down her hair while Jacob pulled on his shirt and buttoned the top buttons. His arm wrapped around her slim shoulders, and her face was glowing, youthful. Jacob began to think about how youthful she really was and frowned. She was much younger than him, and Dina would never forgive him if she found out. He touched his wedding ring at the bottom of his pocket and flipped it over with his fingers.

"That was fun," Sasha grinned, lighting up a cigarette. He envied her free will, lacking any ideas of consequences. She was simple, young, naive.

"Sure was," he smiled and thought for a moment about Dina and what she would say after they made love. She always told him she loved him, and even though it was cliché, he found comfort in that.

But Jacob knew that this was not making love. That was the only reason he could continue this. He loved this, but he didn't love Sasha; he did love Dina. Jacob was sure that Dina would never know, so he would never have to worry about it. He was very careful. He always made sure to lock his phone when he went home, and he kept his displays of affection discreet. Sasha and Dina didn't have any mutual friends, so there was no way Dina would ever find out, nor would Sasha find out about Dina. The silence was making him overthink, and if Dina smelled cigarette smoke on him later, he would never hear the end of it, so he decided to step away from the car.

"I've got to take a leak," he mumbled, getting out of the car and walking to the patch of trees by the water. He looked out at the pure, clean water as he did his business, trying to clear his mind. He zipped his pants and patted his pockets to find his phone. Anxiously, he realized he must have left it on the seat, without making sure he locked it. When he got back into the car, his phone was sitting face-down on the seat. He breathed a sigh of relief, his secrets still just that. He smiled at Sasha, only to see her glaring at him in return.

"You have a wife?" Sasha scowled, but she spoke softly. "This is over."

Jacob's world began to spin. He looked at his phone in his hands and then back at Sasha.

"Wait," Jacob interrupted, "I can explain." His voice was frantic, and his palms were sweaty. He felt his whole body taken over by a wave of heat, and he could feel the flushed scarlet color rising in his cheeks.

"No," she said sternly. "There is nothing to explain. Not to me."

"Please," Jacob begged. His heart was beating faster in his chest, and he could hear it all around him. It sounded to Jacob like the ticking of a bomb, and he knew it was inevitably going to explode. He had lied to her about his wife and family, and she had found out. He had thought he was being so smart, locking his phone at home. His double life involved living in a constantly growing entanglement of lies and stories, and he had fallen into his own web. He was trapped. Still, there had to be more.

"You disgust me." She spoke softly and grimly, while keeping her focus straight ahead. She was driving fast, too fast. Jacob realized he was holding his breath when she pulled over to a bus stop to let him out of the car.

He started to catch his breath, remembering that Dina didn't know. He had a solid, concrete thing with a woman he loved. He started to imagine a new life, one in which he did not hide things from Dina. He thought about honesty and not having to remember what he said. He thought about his children and not having to feel guilty when he thought of them.

"Okay," Sasha sighed, finally turning to face Jacob. "This is what's going to happen. You'll tell your wife what you've done. You'll be honest. You'll be gentle. If she's ignorant enough to stay with you, that's her own fault, but my conscience will not be cleared until she knows. You have until I get off work at 4 o'clock, and if you haven't told her, she will find out from me."

Jacob felt his heart sink into his stomach, and it fell so hard it hurt. Dina was his rock, and he couldn't imagine living without her. She was so pure, so chaste, so honest. He was none of those things. He was the opposite of her, filled with lust, sin, and lies. He had manipulated both women, and now Sasha was turning the tables. He wanted more time. There was no more.

"Okay," he sighed, accepting his inevitable defeat. "I'll tell her. Please, let me be the one to tell her." He shifted his feet back and forth and fiddled with the ring in his pocket. He looked at Sasha, who looked more infuriated than heartbroken, and took the final moments in the car to give her what he knew he owed her. "I'm sorry, Sasha. I really am."

"Goodbye, Jacob," she sighed, reaching over him. For a short second, he thought she was reaching to touch him once more. Her hand passed right over him and connected with the car door handle, which she opened and gestured for him to leave. Jacob got out of the car and stared longingly at Sasha once more. He longed not for her but for the ability to erase the entire relationship. She held up four fingers, emphasizing that he had until 4 o'clock to tell Dina about his affair, and then she turned from him and drove off.

As Sasha's tires screeched in the distance, Jacob realized he didn't have a choice. He had given that up when he met Sasha. Now he had to tell Dina.

Jacob took his phone out, the dreaded device that began his downfall, and called his office to claim a family emergency would keep him from work. For once, he didn't feel like he was lying. Dina was the pulsing blood in his veins, and Sasha was only the goosebumps on his skin. He would go to Dina, tell her the truth, and pray to God she would give him another chance. He knew if she heard from Sasha first, he would have no hope for redemption.

Walking briskly toward home, Jacob tried to prepare his speech; his thoughts bounced through his head recklessly with no direction or flow.

Dina, my love. There is something you must know. She was a temptress, a lapse in judgment. You are the one who has my heart. I'm sorry. I'm sorry. I'm sorry.

He planned promises of his fidelity; he would swear it was a one-time thing that would never happen again. He swore up and down to himself that if she were to take him back, he would be content. He would never stray, never even glance at another woman. He would be completely honest with her about everything that happened between him and Sasha. He would tell her what they did, what he said to her. He would tell her how much he regretted it.

I was going to end it. It will never happen again. I'm sorry.

As he walked, he saw many beautiful women but immediately turned his gaze at the moment of recognition. He felt like a new person, a better man. He hoped that when Dina saw how sincere he was, that he truly wanted to change for her, she might forgive him.

I will be a better man. I will go to church, to therapy, to the moon for you. I'm sorry.

Jacob arrived at the stairs of his front porch. It had never looked so large and daunting. It almost looked like the windows were eyes, looking into him and mocking him. He shook his head, and the image disappeared.

Jacob knew forgiveness only came with confession, and he had every intention to do just that. How could he have ever imagined not telling her what he had done? She deserved to know. She needed to know. As he reached the final stair, Jacob couldn't help wishing there had been more.

Jacob let himself in the front door, and the sight of his home both lifted his spirits and crushed them all at once. Pictures of his family lined the walls, his children's toys lay scattered across the floor, and his wife beamed at him from the couch where she had been sitting and folding laundry. She smiled with a tenderness that Jacob feared he might destroy. The guilt bubbled in his stomach, and he felt it would poison him from the inside out if he did not confess his sins. He kissed her passionately, knowing it may be the last time she let him do that once he came clean.

"Well, hello! You're home early." She pulled apart to smile, only to be alerted by the sound of the baby monitor. "Hold that thought," she said and made her way toward the hall. Jacob wandered to the couch and looked at the news playing on the screen. He fumbled for the remote to put on something lighter, hoping to ease the mood, when a headline caught his attention. **Woman Dies on Impact in Car Accident.** The car on the screen was a red convertible Sebring. He sat frozen with the remote in hand.

"Sasha Sanders, 26, was pronounced dead at the scene," the TV finally said, and Jacob thought he might pass out. He was anxious, shocked, and guilty, but the feeling that triumphed the rest was relief.

Dina would never have to know what he had done with

this woman. His heart still thumped rapidly in his chest, and he feared Dina would see it moving as she walked back into the room, holding Elijah in her arms.

"Now, how was your day?" She smiled, rocking Elijah gently. "Did anything eventful happen?" She was the portrait of innocence. If Jacob told her the truth, it would only break her heart. And besides, he would never see Sasha again.

"Not a thing," he shrugged nonchalantly, looking down at his feet.

"Just another day in paradise?" she teased, wrapping her arms around his neck, and Jacob genuinely believed in that moment that he was making the right decision.

"Couldn't ask for anything more," he smiled sincerely, and they sat down beside one another in the bliss of ignorance, and together, finished watching the news.

* * *

Discussion Questions

1. Given that Sasha is dead, do you think Jacob should still tell Dina about the affair? Why or why not?

2. Why do you think Jacob was cheating on Dina in the first place? Was it simply a failing in Jacob? If so, what is the source of that failing?

3. Do you think Jacob will cheat on Dina again, or do you think he has learned his lesson? What leads you to this conclusion? What causes a cheater (*Jacob*) to give someone so much power (*Sasha*) over their marriage and future?

4. Do you think Sasha has any culpability in this story? Is there anything she should have done differently? Does Dina bear any responsibility for Jacob's cheating?

5. How do you know if someone is truly repentant or only repentant because they got caught? Is there any question or test you can give them to know which is which?

Hard Metal

Porter McKoy

* * *

When Raúl gave me his security job for August, he told me not to see anything. You don't see nothin', he said, because we both know I get curious. Sometimes the other guys think I'm soft, the way I get lost in my head. My girlfriend says it's trauma, but that's her answer to everything these days. After my schnauzer bit her leg, and she yelled, I told her it was probably his separation anxiety, but she scrunched her eyes in a mean way, and I knew something was broken. She said she was going to Cape May with her sister, and I said I'd rather be in church than that shithole town. Still, she packed up her fancy shampoos and left. So when Raúl asked me to fill in a stretch at the federal courthouse, I said yes.

He said August would be easy, with most judges and lawyers off in the Hamptons or Europe, and me escorting folks around a mostly deserted building, a granite trapezoid spanning three city blocks in downtown Manhattan. Thanks to Raúl, I cleared the background check without pissing in a cup and got my cap and uniform the next day. The job was dull at first, with lots of folks forgetting to empty their pockets before they left home, meaning I confiscated penknives, scissors, corkscrews, lighter fluid, box cutters, and even an inert grenade some dumbass was using as a keychain. Same folks who, high or stupid, let the cops search their cars and got hauled in. Or maybe they held up a deli for quick cash or got caught using a coat hanger on an ATM. Folks too poor to save.

The day the cameras and newscasters showed up, I admit, I muscled my way into the throng, thinking my ex would see me in my uniform and fall in love again. But everyone was too busy swarming the accused, a pudgy white guy whose nose looked like a melted candle. What he'd done to a little girl, the way he killed her, was so bad they had to try him in the off-season. Raúl called me from the Dominican Republic that night, mad that I was on the Shastovich trial, sucking his teeth in envy. He said I owed him half my overtime pay. Half my ass, I told him and hung up. Then my supervisor called, told me to get in at 6:00 a.m. for my new assignment—escorting the dead girl's mom.

Running late, I ignored the people clustered on the sidewalk around the pretty news lady and headed toward the back entrance. Alarms were going off as I went down the stairs, past the tarnished brass mail chutes that cobwebbed the building, past the goddess of justice's white marble tits. Sure enough, I saw a tall woman with shiny black hair and yoga pants standing near the metal detectors. On the conveyor belt, the guts of her macrame sack spilled out like a slaughtered pig. She was yelling at the security guard who was confiscating her knitting needles. What, she said, I'm going to stab him from across the courtroom?

I got her, I got her, I told the onlookers, taking her by the elbow. She was shaking like a dog on the Fourth of July. I walked her down the linoleum hallway toward the old wooden elevators, feeling sweaty and irritable. The basement was humid with a moldy smell I couldn't wash off. No surprise, the municipal government doesn't air condition the place.

We got on the elevator. I pressed 14. Nobody joined us.

Don't yell at Louis, I said as the doors closed. That's his job.

She pressed her lips together, wanting to argue, then sagged.

I don't want to be here, she said.

So go home, I said. The curly numbers winked higher.

I need to watch.

Why? I said.

She didn't answer.

I said, if you think knitting and crying in the courtroom is going to make him feel bad for what he did, then you're tripping. If I was you, I'd leave the country, let the judge handle it. You can't do anything anyway.

The elevator stopped and the doors creaked open.

I let her stew. Any luck, she'd head back upstate.

She followed me into our break room. Clean with a high ceiling, it had a nice view of the treetops out the window. The lower panes were open, and an overhead fan blurred out the traffic noise.

I nodded toward the wall of lockers, told her to pick one and memorize her four-digit code. Something told me she was going to use her daughter's birthday, but I pushed the thought away. Over the water cooler, a flatscreen showed the courtroom down the hall. The jury hadn't filed in yet, the bailiffs cracking on each other and straightening the chairs.

Ready, she said.

* * *

After that, Veronika would text me when she was on her way, and we'd meet up under the goddess of justice. I'd wait for her to clear security, and we'd go to 14. She'd fish the previous day's knitting from her locker, swapping out balls of yarn and plastic needles from her macrame bag and filling her pockets with gum and Altoids before I'd take her down the hall to Courtroom B. Mostly, I drank my coffee and checked my phone. When friends and family came, she'd bring them to the break room. Those days, I'd put my AirPods in so I wouldn't hear anything. Other times, she'd be alone, and I'd bring us lunch from the cafeteria: cheeseburgers and fries for me, chopped salad and chocolate pudding for her. Afternoons, she'd pull out a yoga mat and do intricate combinations: downward dog, cobra, pigeon, warrior, corpse. My stomach would flutter in a funny way when she'd dab lavender oil on my forehead and tell me to inhale, exhale, inhale. As if I could forget.

* * *

You were absolutely right, she said in the elevator the night before the verdict.

Come again?

He's unrepentant. You think he'll die in jail?

Sooner or later, I said.

A Dutch criminologist wants to interview him, wants to feature him in a book.

Who told you that? I said. No way she was talking to

defense counsel.

The *New Yorker*.

Our elevator arrived in the basement.

He's got fanboys on Reddit, she continued as we walked down the hall toward the exit. I wanted to bolt into the twilight but held myself back. Veronika nodded to Louis, and he gave her a smile.

Forget that dirtbag, I said. After tomorrow, he disappears.

She laughed the way a ghoul coughs.

Ain't that the truth, she said as we reached the sidewalk. She patted my arm, then dug through that monstrous bag for her phone, shiny hair swinging as she ordered a car.

I loped west on Foley Street, but funnily enough, I found my feet circling back toward the main entrance. I sprung up the forty-odd marble steps, spooky in the lengthening shadows, my thighs throbbing with exertion as I reached the big columns at the top.

Everything okay, asked the guard, nodding at my uniform as I scanned myself in.

Forgot something, I said.

* * *

By the time I got to the break room, it was pitch black. I clicked the switch and a sodium bulb buzzed like a mosquito, flooding the room with yellow light. I unlocked the safe, located the master keys and opened Veronika's locker. The bottom half was taken up with her yoga mats, purple and blue, snug as a pair of sausages. Her knitting was tucked in the upper shelf, a quiet drool of yarn spilling out between the denture-pink needles. I reached behind and pulled out a skein of fishing wire hooked to a heavy red pouch. Clever. She breached the perimeter.

I put the whole mess on the table. Believe me, I used a napkin to pull out the loaded gun. I took a picture with my phone and did a reverse image lookup. A Saturday night special, it said. Small-caliber handgun, likely a Röhm RG-14. Accurate at point-blank range.

My mind drifted back to a lunch last week. The prosecution had gone hard at the accused, using words like *amputation* and *unforgivable*. I could see Veronika was rattled, and over sandwiches, I said, hey, you're still a mother. I'll always be a mother, she nodded, and it felt good to be gentle with her pain. What I miss, she added, chewing slowly, is being a mom.

I thought about Veronika sitting in her Airbnb in Brooklyn. Lately, she'd been raving about the cheesecake from Junior's, and I pictured her in a soft robe on her couch, drowsy in the lamplight, savoring forkful after forkful. I thought about Shastovich farting in his jail cell, cold and miserable, tormented by murders he couldn't commit. And I thought about Raúl. You don't see nothin'.

I put the gun in the bag. I pushed the bag toward the back of the locker and arranged the knitting in front. I closed it and put the keys back in the safe. I turned off the light and took the old wooden elevator down and went home.

* * *

My alarm rang at 5:01 a.m.

I left my supervisor a voicemail saying I was throwing up and went back to sleep.

I awoke around nine to a bright sun, a hungry schnauzer, and a stream of texts from Veronika. The last one said, Heard you're ill, feel better soon with a kiss. I went into my kitchen and poured myself half a box of Kellogg's Frosted Mini-Wheats. I brewed a pot of coffee. I fed the dog and wondered what my ex-girlfriend would say. I lit a joint. I clicked on my flatscreen and tuned in to Court TV. Then I pulled up my chair and waited.

* * *

Discussion Questions

1. Should the narrator have done something after finding the hidden gun? If so, what should he have done? What would you have done if you were in his place?
2. All we know from the story is Shastovich brutally murdered Veronika's daughter. Would knowing more details about the murder change your answer to the first question? What details, or new information, might change your opinion?
3. Is parental/vigilante justice never appropriate in a country with civil society and a just legal system? If Shastovich was found not guilty, would vigilante justice then be justified?
4. Do you think Veronika made the right choice by attending the trial? What would you do in her situation and why?
5. Do you think Veronika killing Shastovich will lessen the pain she feels from the loss of her daughter? Is there anything Shastovich or Veronika could do to lessen Veronika's pain?

The Things We Give

Allison Padron

* * *

The Collection Specialist at LifeCorp has no softness to her. Everything about her is a razor's edge—her sleek black ponytail, needlepoint stilettos, bony elbows, and long fingers. She smiles without any real kindness as she sits across from the woman in the ratty sweater and dirty sneakers.

"Can I have your full name, ma'am?" The specialist's fingers sweep across the thin white keyboard in front of her.

"Martha Johnson."

"Thank you." The woman's blue eyes drop to peer through the glass table, watching Martha's left leg bounce. "Now, Ms. Johnson, before we approve you for the procedure, I need to ask you a few questions. Is that alright with you?"

Martha's brow lifts slightly. Then she nods, brown eyes flicking from side to side as she takes in the room again. Gleaming white walls, a floor so polished she can see her reflection. It's all perfect, sterile, unfeeling.

The specialist smiles again, revealing prominent incisors. "Fantastic. What's your occupation?"

"I'm a waitress. Over at The Golden Biscuit."

The keys make tiny clicks as the woman types, the only sound in the windowless room. "What's your estimated annual salary? Tips included."

"I reckon that's my fucking business."

The specialist stops moving. She looks back to Martha. Her eyes never seem to blink. "Of course, you're welcome to keep it confidential, Ms. Johnson, but we can't proceed without that information."

Martha clenches and unclenches her jaw before she speaks. "About $25,000."

"Thank you, Ms. Jo—"

"Jesus, quit doing that. Just call me Martha."

The specialist finally blinks before smiling. It's a patronizing smile like she's speaking to an insolent child. "Of course, Martha. My apologies. So, $25,000 a year. Do you drink or smoke?"

"All of the above."

"How frequently?"

"A pack a day and a few beers at night."

"Do you exercise?"

"No."

"Any children?"

"No."

"Do you travel?"

"No. Unless you count commuting."

The specialist finishes typing. "Thank you, Martha. That's all the personal information we'll need—though we will require you to verify your income before we proceed." The soulless smile returns. "We should discuss the procedure and your preferred method of compensation. How many years were you interested in selling?"

"I was thinking just one."

"Just one." The specialist nods, glancing over at her computer screen. "For one year, we can give you $20,000. Would you like us to—"

"Wait—wait just a fucking minute, lady. $20,000? Are you fucking with me?"

Bemused eyes meet Martha's, and for a second, the other woman seems unsure how to react. "I don't understand your question, Ms. Johnson."

"My friend's husband got $500,000 for one year. That's the whole reason I came in here—to sell a year and be set!"

"What does your friend's husband do for a living?"

"He's a surgeon. Heart or brain or something like that."

The specialist smiles. "Oh! I see. This is just a simple misunderstanding, Ms. Johnson."

"Martha."

"Right. You see, there's not a flat price per year. It varies from person to person based on salary and various additional life factors."

Martha's leg bounces even faster. "That doesn't make any damn sense. A year's a year, isn't it? The billionaires are getting the same number of days no matter the source."

That insufferable smile grows even wider, ever more patient. "We aren't paying for the year, per se, but instead reimbursing you for giving up a year of *your* life. Therefore, we take all factors into consideration to determine what one year in your life is worth, and then we compensate every person fairly."

Martha's eye twitches, her fingers drumming against her stationary leg. It takes her a few moments to compose herself before she speaks. "That won't work. I need... well, I need $350,000."

"In that case, you can sell eighteen years and have money to spare."

A choked sound erupts from Martha's throat. "*Eighteen* years?"

"If you want $350,000."

She stands suddenly, knocking the chair back a few inches. "I can't do this."

The specialist stands as well, frowning for the first time. "Of course, it's your choice, Martha. If you change your mind, you know where to find us."

The squeak of Martha's dirty sneakers on the shining floor is her only response.

* * *

Her shift that afternoon is dogshit. It ends with twenty in cash and an insulting lack of tips. She blows the cash at the bar down the street and is lucky enough to score a few free beers off a man in a leather jacket.

That night she calls Benito.

"Can you believe it, Benny? $20,000 for a year of my life? Is that all I'm worth?" Martha steadies herself on the concrete wall outside the bar, her words slurring together.

"I can believe it, babe. You're hardly the Queen of England."

"Shut up, asshole." The world around her spins, a bad sign. She leans forward a little, and the nausea overtakes her, spilling vomit onto the pavement at her feet.

A group of college boys are walking out of the bar at that moment. She can hear their laughter. "Go home, you old coot," one of them calls, and the rest snicker.

Benny clears his throat, and the reception crackles. "I told you not to go to LifeCorp. They're a bunch of soul suckers."

Martha rubs her throbbing forehead. "I don't think I have much of a choice anymore."

"You gotta do what you think is best. Hey—are you out? You should come over."

"You only want me to come over when I'm drunk."

"You only bother to call me when you've been drinking."

"Touché." With the taste of vomit lingering on her tongue, she looks up at the fluorescent lights of the corner store. "Fine. I'm coming. Just let me grab a bottle of water first." Martha hangs up without waiting for a response.

* * *

The next week, Martha walks through the front door of LifeCorp again, hands stuffed in her sweatshirt pocket. The blade-thin specialist smiles at her from behind the desk. "Ms. John—Martha. It's good to see you. I saw that you submitted the tax forms. Have you—"

"Let's just get this over with," Martha snaps, pushing past her into the hallway. The click of heels from behind grates on her nerves, but she keeps her composure. Barely.

The specialist sinks into the chair behind the desk. "Would you still like to sell one year?"

"I'll do eighteen." Martha's leg starts bouncing again, and she instinctively reaches for the cigarette pack in her pocket before realizing they probably don't allow smoking in here.

Figures.

That smile grows wider, sharper, and the keyboard clicks as she types. "Eighteen years. That'll be $360,000. Do you prefer electronic transfer or check?"

"A check is fine."

With a nod and a few more clicks, the specialist ends the pre-procedure meeting. Martha is escorted down the hallway to a dim room with an exam chair in the middle of the barren space. The specialist tells her to sit, and then she starts pulling out needles and tubes from the drawers below the computer.

"You're going to stick me?" Martha asks, feeling like a caged animal.

The woman smiles again, her blue eyes locking onto Martha's brown ones. "Only in a few spots. And the needles are so thin that you won't feel a thing."

"How long have you been doing this, anyway?" Martha shifts in the seat, trying to get comfortable. The specialist is right—she can't feel the first needle even when it slides into her wrist.

The specialist moves to the other wrist, then both her ankles. "Since LifeCorp opened their first public clinic. So... nearly ten years. I've seen countless patients, so don't worry. You're in good hands."

A faint glow from the screen next to the chair illuminates the specialist's face as she puts the final needle in the base of Martha's throat.

Martha closes her eyes, inhaling deeply. "Will this hurt?"

A few clicks and a mechanical humming sound. Martha hears the specialist drumming on the keyboard again. "Don't worry about that. You won't even know it's happening." The specialist is right. Martha doesn't feel any different when she leaves a half hour later, check in hand.

* * *

The first place Martha goes is the bank. After that, she goes back to the bar. She's got an extra $10,000 to do with as she pleases, and she wants to get obliterated.

The next morning, nursing a hangover, she writes out checks and mails them. Then she drives to the nursing home. The receptionist greets her with an overly warm smile. "Martha! Miss Betty is in her room. I'm sure she'll be glad to see you."

"Thanks, Anita," Martha says, taking two peppermints from the jar on the desk and heading down the familiar corridors.

Betty is sitting in the chair by the window, watching the birds at the garden feeder. Her roommate isn't there, which Martha is grateful for; the woman has a staring problem.

"Hey, Mom," Martha says gently, settling into the chair on the other side of the table. "I brought you a peppermint."

Betty glances between her daughter and the candy, smiling slowly as she takes it from her hand. "What a nice girl you are. Would you like to stay for dinner?"

Martha forces a smile, resting her chin on her hand. "No, thank you. It's a little early for dinner, and I have work at four."

Betty purses her lips, then looks out the window again, hand clenched tightly around the plastic wrapper. Martha reaches over, takes the peppermint back, and opens the packaging. "Mom, you need to actually put it in your mouth to eat it."

"A nice, nice girl," Betty responds, popping the peppermint in her mouth. It rattles between her teeth for a while. Martha puts her own candy in her mouth and watches the sparrows.

After a bit, she clears her throat. "I want you to know I sent in the money for Dad's bills. All of them—hospital and funeral. So you don't have to worry."

Martha keeps staring out the window. She can feel her mother's blank gaze on her cheek, but she can't bear to meet it. They sit like that for several moments before Betty smiles. "Would you like some dinner?"

A soft exhale escapes Martha's mouth, and she buries her face in her hands. After a moment, she stands, pushing away from the table. "I'll be back in a few days, Mom. Don't forget to take your medication." It's a useless parting phrase, but she says it every time, like a bad habit.

Martha has already closed the door behind her, ignoring Betty's cheerful "Goodbye!", when the nurse places a gentle hand on her arm.

"I was about to bring her lunch in, and I couldn't help but overhear... It's a great thing you've done, but it's no use telling her about it. It might upset her, you know, to remember her husband. Even for a few seconds. Her memory is getting pretty short these days."

The muscles in Martha's jaw clench. "Yeah, I gathered that. Thanks." She wrenches her arm away and heads back out to her car, wiping the moisture from her eyes with a rough hand.

* * *

That night, Martha chain smokes. Then she calls Benito.

* * *

Life goes on. For a while, everything is fine. Back to normal. She makes enough to pay for rent and gas and a shit ton of beer. Sometimes she goes to Benny's.

Until those two pink lines divide her world in half.

Martha has to smoke through most of a cigarette pack before she can think about that little white test. She'd chug a handle of vodka if she could to help make sense of it. The only thing she can think to do is call Benito.

He hangs up on her. Martha throws her phone at the wall and lies face down on the couch until her doorbell rings. When she answers the door, Benito is standing there. He pulls her into his arms, catching her off guard. She sobs against his chest for the better part of an hour.

When she's calmed down, he orders Chinese food, and they sit on the rickety balcony.

"I don't have any savings, Benny. I can barely afford rent." She whispers into the twilight haze, her eyes still throbbing from her tears.

He stares down at his fried rice. "We'll move in together. Then we have two jobs and only one rent payment."

"Will it be enough?"

Benito is silent for a long moment, and Martha's leg starts to bounce. Then he clears his throat. "We could each give a year. I wager I'm worth about $30,000—together, that's $50,000. That's a good start, right?"

Martha buries her head in her hands. "Okay," she whispers, heart in her throat. That would be nineteen years gone. Leaving her with, what, fifteen years or so? It's bleak, but Martha's used to bleak. Besides, they're out of options.

But she's used to that, too.

* * *

They go in together, but Martha has to sit in the waiting

room while Benito goes with the specialist. After twenty minutes, he reemerges, giving her a weak smile. "$35,000. Better than we expected."

He sits in the chair while she heads to the back. They skip the meeting this time since the company already has all her information. The needles slide in, one at a time. Martha watches the shadows on the ceiling in the half-light.

"Another year this time, Martha?" The specialist's black ponytail sways as she stands up and moves to the computer.

"Yeah."

There are a few clicks, a whir, and then a beep. The specialist blinks at the computer, then at Martha. "Can you confirm your age for me?"

"I'm thirty-seven." Martha sits up slightly, frowning at the back of the monitor. "Why?"

A smile. "Let me just check something in the program." A few clicks, a whir, and a beep again.

The specialist lets out an exhale, walking back to Martha's side and pulling out the needles. "I'm sorry, Ms. Johnson, but you're no longer eligible for this procedure," she says pleasantly.

Martha stares at her. "Why? Is it because I'm pregnant?"

"No."

"Then why?"

The woman clears her throat delicately. "You're attempting to donate more time than is left in your lifespan."

Martha's heart stutters a *one-two* in her chest. It feels like it stops.

It was just one year. A single year. She doesn't even have a year left? Her hands curl in and out of fists, and her mouth goes painfully dry. "That can't be right."

"I assure you the program has never had an error."

"Well, it must have had one now. Check again."

The specialist sighs. "I'm sorry, Ms. Johnson. I checked multiple times. You have my deepest condolen—"

Something inside of Martha snaps. She leaps out of the chair, wrapping her hands around the specialist's throat and slamming her into the wall. "Check again!" She spits, hysteria crawling through her chest. "That can't be right! You're lying. *You're making shit up!*"

"Get your hands off of me." The specialist's expression has soured, her lip curling in disgust.

"You stole *eighteen* years of my life!" Martha screams, shaking her. The specialist knees her in the groin and steps aside as Martha folds in half. She presses a button on the wall and turns back to the weeping woman.

"You sold us those years of your own volition," the specialist says coldly, dusting off the front of her dress. "It's not our fault if you smoked and drank your lifespan down beforehand."

Martha straightens and lunges, but she's intercepted. A large man has come in through the doorway, summoned by the call of the button. He tucks her arms behind her back, holding her still as she thrashes.

"Take her out through the back," the specialist says, reaching up to readjust her ponytail. "I have another client coming in the front soon."

The man starts toward the back of the room, and Martha sobs. "Wait—please, wait!" The specialist signals, and the man stops. Martha takes a few hitched breaths, bent over the man's large forearm. Her blurred gaze turns to the specialist, pleading with her. "What... What am I supposed to do? What do I do now?"

The specialist smiles broadly and tilts her head. "If you want my professional opinion, Ms. Johnson, I'd suggest booking a pregnancy termination. There's a great clinic just down the street. After that, you can spend your final few months the way you spent the rest of your life—drunk and useless."

Martha breaks down. She's still sobbing when the back door is locked behind her.

* * *

Discussion Questions

1. If you could sell years off the end of your life, would you? If so, how many years would you sell and for what price?

2. Do you agree with Martha selling eighteen years off the end of her life to pay for her dead father's bills and her mother's care? Should she simply have left her parents to financially fend for themselves?

3. At the end of the story, the specialist tells Martha she is "drunk and useless." While this is certainly a cruel thing to tell someone, is it inaccurate as well? Is Martha drunk and useless to society?

4. Is there a difference between selling years of your life for money versus selling years of your life to a job for money? What, if anything, is the difference in the time for money exchanges?

5. Is there anything inherently wrong with spending your life drinking, socializing, and generally being unfocused on future goals? Is this an accurate description of Martha, or is there something else going on?

Three Blocks

Kathryn LeMon

* * *

I lock my car and shove my keys into the pocket of my big coat. The parking garage is nearly full this morning, so I have to use the elevator to get down to the exit. The moment the doors slide open, there is a woman waiting for me. She is wearing my face.

I watch my expression contort in surprise and then settle into relief. My makeup, I note with some pleasure, is impeccable today. "Please," she says, thrusting a fistful of flyers at me, "can you help me?"

* * *

I lock my car and shove my keys into the pocket of my big coat. Outside the parking garage, the three-block walk to the office building where I work is plastered with flyers of a lost corgi. Across the street, standing at the corner of a busy intersection, an old man is handing out long-stem pink roses from a paper bag. I check my watch and decide to stop in at the corner coffee shop.

"I'm sorry to bother you, miss, but if it's not too much trouble, could you get me a black coffee? Just a black coffee, miss." The person who has taken my face today speaks nothing like me. I am huddled just outside the entrance, hands deep in the pockets of my big coat. I wonder how long I have been there like that, asking strangers for a little warmth. I give myself a nod and push open the door, letting in a little of the lingering winter.

At the counter, I order a cappuccino, a black coffee, and two blueberry muffins.

"Quinn!"

The card reader beeps for me to remove my credit card. I scribble a signature and accept the pastries.

"Quinn, hey!"

It's my newest coworker, Ajmal. He got the job with the environmental nonprofit Green Resource Initiative, fresh off a Fulbright scholarship two months ago. He's still full of energy for a job that sucks most people dry in a decade.

"Hey, Ajmal."

"This is for you," he says and extends a pink rose to me.

I clutch the pastries closer to my body. "Oh, no, thank you."

"I mean, that man across the street gave it to me, but I want you to have it."

"That's sweet, but no."

"Oh." The rose in Ajmal's hand falters in the direction of the ground. "Okay."

I like Ajmal, but he is six years younger than me, and we're all too swamped with work for any real romance. He'll learn soon enough that there's a reason none of us date each other. *Sorry, Ajmal,* I think to myself as I pick up my cappuccino and the coffee for the me that's waiting outside.

"I'll walk with you to the office?" The pink rose has disappeared since I turned my back, and Ajmal's voice is all uncertainty.

"Of course!" I reassure him, trying to convey pep and friendliness.

Outside of the coffee shop, Ajmal's dark eyebrows knit together when I stop and hand the person with my face the coffee and a pastry. I don't know what Ajmal sees, except that it is not two Quinns in the same winter coat.

I watch as the other me breathes in the scent of the coffee. "It's a blueberry muffin," I tell her when she lifts it to the light to inspect it.

"Bless your soul," she says.

When we are almost to our building, Ajmal asks, "Do you know that man?"

I shrug and ignore how he holds the door open for me. "No more than anyone knows anyone."

* * *

I have refused to help the other Quinns who approach me every morning in the three blocks between the parking garage and the office. It was the sane thing, I thought. The sanest thing I could do without checking myself into a mental hospital. It never ended well.

The first time, the person who took my face asked for help looking for a lost wallet. I kept my gaze straight ahead and walked faster. The next day, another me approached when I was running late to ask for my help shoveling and salting the sidewalk. I refused to acknowledge her. On my way back to my car, I slipped and sprained my ankle.

I started building an extra fifteen minutes into my commute. I started saying yes when I came face to face with myself. Yes, I will help you look for your earring. Yes, I will give you directions. Yes, I will take a photo of you and your boyfriend.

Yes, yes, yes, I will help.

* * *

I had to go back for my umbrella, so I am running five minutes late, today. I lock my car and shove my keys into the pocket of my raincoat, emerging into the cold downpour a second before my umbrella springs to life above me. I try to ignore the woman whose grocery bag has gone soggy and spilled all over the sidewalk. If I do not look too closely, I will not be able to tell if *she* is actually *me*.

I make it halfway to the office before I turn around. The water is a sloshing mess in the gutters beside her. She is making an admirable effort to gather her fruits and vegetables and boxes of macaroni, but she has nothing to carry them in. I shove my wallet and tablet inside my jacket and root around in my tote bag for any other personals. I have packed lightly today. This tote bag was a birthday present that I got for myself. It cost two hundred dollars.

I squat beside her and start putting the things into my bag.

"Hey!" she says. Then she meets my eyes, and I see how my mascara has been running from more than just the rain. My heart softens. I have to believe she sees this happen because she stands up and wipes her hand down her face. A small shudder runs through her body. I pretend not to see it. I hate when people see me crying.

"Here," I say, and I see how hesitation plays out across my

features before they finally settle into acceptance.

"Thanks," she says.

She has no umbrella, so I hand her mine. For all I know, she has to walk all the way home. For all I know, she's parked right beside me. "We've got to help each other out, right?" I check my phone. I have a missed call from Ajmal, and I'm late. Very late. "Stay dry," I say, uselessly since she is already soaked, and splash away down the street.

She calls out after me, but the sound of rain on the pavement is too loud to catch her words.

* * *

I am standing on the corner of a busy intersection handing out flowers, and so I cross the street to meet myself. I have never been able to identify so specifically the person who wears my face on any given day, but I can see the old man if I squint. The roses are red. I/he holds out the rose and winks. Ridiculously, I feel myself blush as I accept. I walk on. Today, this is all that is required of me.

Back in the office, Ajmal asks who gave me the rose.

"An admirer," I say and laugh self-consciously, remembering how my fingers brushed against my fingers as I took hold of the stem. I touch the back of my neck. I cannot meet Ajmal's gaze.

"The old man gave it to you," Ajmal says, his voice almost accusatory. Then, softer, more amused: "He is a great admirer of life, isn't he? He sees the beauty in everything. Whenever I see him, you know, I think about you and that poor man who asked for coffee."

"Oh?"

"He asked me for coffee, too, but I ignored him. When I

saw your kindness, I felt ashamed. You are a great admirer of life like the old man. You see the beauty, and I—" He stops short and hums, looking out the big windows and down over the busy streets below.

Ajmal is not wearing my face. I did not meet him during my three-block walk, and yet...

I hold the rose out to Ajmal. "I got this for you," I say.

"You did not," he says, but his hand reaches out to accept.

* * *

Ajmal lives in the neighborhood and always walks to work. He walked me to my car for two weeks before I learned he lives in the opposite direction. By that point, it was too late to change his mind. I don't want to change his mind. I am thinking less about the fact that he is six years younger than me.

We are almost to the parking garage when a car pulls to a screeching halt beside us. Ajmal pushes me behind him. I do not recognize the woman who rolls down the passenger side window. "Hey!" she says, a frantic look in her eye. "It's you! I have your bag!"

"Do you know this woman?" Ajmal asks, his body still tensed in front of me.

"I think so." I approach the car. The woman is rooting around behind her seat. When her head pops back into view, her expression is triumphant. She is holding my tote bag.

"It's a damn nice bag," she says. "You shouldn't be giving it out to strangers, though I'm grateful you did. You—" She shakes her head. "You saved my ass, but damn, girl! Next time, give me your number."

I reach through the window and take the bag. "I was running late."

"Yeah. So was I."

I stand there like that, clutching my bag. We are just staring at each other, she and I. I am drinking in her face, the curve of her nose and lines around her eyes so different from mine. I do not know what she is seeing.

"Well," she says, "I've got places to be. You take care of yourself, now."

I nod. She rolls the window up and drives away, and I remember that Ajmal is here.

"Are you a saint?" he asks me.

"I'm just a person," I say.

"You're a blessing."

I laugh and sling my bag over my shoulder. "Do you want to get a drink sometime?"

* * *

It is 2:00 a.m. on a Tuesday when I leave Ajmal's apartment complex. It's just one block down from our office, but the streets look new to me with the taste of red wine on my tongue. An early-spring frost clings to the brick buildings and glimmers in the street lights. My laugh, when I let it loose, hangs in a mist around me, and I walk back to the parking garage slowly, lingering in the wonder of my happiness. I reach into the pocket of my big coat for my keys. They aren't there.

I text Ajmal, humorously at first, and then more urgently when he doesn't reply. I have no family in this city, and the few friends I've made are sure to be asleep. It's freezing outside. The clouds of my breath come faster.

I exit the parking garage and stand on the sidewalk. I stare at the icy pavement. I consider my options. To my left, I hear the sound of someone's shoes crunching against a thin layer of snow, and when I look up, I see that she is wearing my face.

"Goddamn," I say, and she notices me.

For a moment, she hesitates, and then, inevitably—invariably—I approach myself.

"Can I help you?" I ask, hearing the brittle snap in my voice.

She laughs and gives me a once-over. "Are you sure you're not the one who needs help, honey?"

"I'm fine."

"Oh yeah? Normally when this thing happens," she gestures between her face and my own, "someone needs something from me."

* * *

In the morning, the woman who serves me chocolate chip toaster waffles alongside her two children is a stranger. She tries to act unconcerned, but I catch her staring at my face when she thinks I'm not looking.

Ajmal calls when I'm halfway through my mug of coffee.

"I'm so sorry! I fell asleep. Are you alright? Quinn, I'm so—"

"I'm alright," I say, laughter warming my voice. "I found a place to stay for the night. Or, a place found me." I glance at the woman whose name I still don't know, but she is elbow deep in the sink.

"I have your keys. I'll bring them to work. Unless—should I come to you?"

"No, work is great. I'll see you soon."

* * *

Sylvia works at a bar just down the street from my office building. The face-stealing started happening to her almost a year ago, and it normally occurs on her way home from work.

"Face-stealing?" she scoffed when she heard my word for it.

"Well, what do you call it?"

"A cry for help. What else?"

Sylvia drops me off at the coffee shop, where I get a cappuccino for myself and a café miel for Ajmal. I set off for the office, tired but warmed by the realization that I am not alone in this madness.

I am almost at the office door when a woman approaches me. She is wearing my face.

* * *

Discussion Questions

1. Do you think you would be more likely to help others in need if they were "wearing your face"? Why do you think some people, metaphorically, see their face on others, and some do not?

2. What is it about physically seeing (*rather than metaphorically seeing*) our face on another person that might make us more empathetic to helping?

3. What do you think are reasonable and unreasonable motives for ignoring the plight of others? How does "wearing our face" adjust those motivations?

4. Ajmal calls the narrator a saint. Do you agree? Or is she simply responding with the exact same level of goodness in her choices but simply being exposed to different input data?

5. Some argue that giving food or money to street beggars/homeless only enables their behavior. Is it possible for a person to see their face in others and refuse to help? How would you reconcile this issue?

Euthanasia

Kelly Piner

* * *

On a frigid December morning, Hank Sanders stomped the caked mud off his worn boots and entered Discount Hardware. He couldn't shake his cousin's remarks. *Put her down*, he'd said. The words had rolled so effortlessly off his lips, as if her life meant nothing at all, as if, simply by being old, she'd become too much trouble.

Hank marched up one aisle and down another, searching for a new blade for his knife. When had the shelves become so barren? It hadn't looked like this the last time he'd shopped there. But with the fuel shortages and the lack of truckers, was it any wonder? And where was everyone? He hadn't seen any other customer or any staff. With no one to help him find the blade or even care if he made a purchase, he returned to his old pickup, trash crunching under his boots.

He drove south, thirty miles along the Ohio River, where sheets of fog hovered over the water and worn concrete road. As he squinted and leaned into the wheel, he choked down his sense of loss for his nation. Once an abundant land of plenty, it now resembled a third-world nation with food and energy shortages. Little by little, residents were adjusting to lack and uncertainty. Incredible, he thought, how easily people could be conditioned to accept less and less.

At the fenced compound, he punched the access code into the keyboard, and a gate slid open, exposing a comforting wrought-iron sign that read: *House of Hope: Where Your Suffering Ends*. That sign had greeted him for as long as he could remember. In stark contrast, the massive gray government structure stood cold and uninviting just beyond the gate.

He drove to the back entrance and mentally prepared for another twelve-hour day. When he climbed from his truck, he avoided looking at the blurry mounds spread out on the grass. Through the darkness, he spotted a new shipment of crates that had been delivered during the night. It never ended.

Inside, he said, "Hi, girl," and bent over to pet the blue point Siamese that greeted him.

He'd often felt that Ling Ling had the gift of second sight, the way she seemed to sense the fear and dying spirits of those about to be put down and did her best to comfort them.

Hank flipped on the overhead fluorescent lights, and they made a hissing sound like that of a final breath being expelled. The sterile, concrete warehouse had no windows on the main floor. The only windows were in Hank's office on the second floor, facing the large cemetery out back. Some days, when he'd been outside digging holes for the smaller creatures, he could have sworn that he'd felt dead eyes staring at him. Just how many had he put down over the years? He refused to count. So many that the cemetery was full.

He checked his clipboard. Forty to dispose of today. He'd never gotten used to it, the death and misery he'd witnessed during his ten years running House of Hope, but he didn't want to think about that. Instead, he steeled himself and went about doing his morning inspection, going from one cell to another.

He donned a mask and entered the ice locker where the deceased rested, awaiting processing. It, too, was so full that now he arranged the overflow bodies on the ground by the cemetery. He checked his calendar. The eighteen-wheeler had last collected the corpses over two weeks ago. The crew had used a conveyor belt to move the dead bodies inside the trailer where they were stacked. What happened to them afterward, he didn't want to know.

In Euthanasia Cell Block No. 1, twenty dogs awaited euthanasia. However much he disinfected the cages between each use, they still smelled of death, and the animals all yelped for his help. He reached down and handfed a chicken-flavored treat to a toy poodle. Did the dogs understand that their owners had elected to put them down? And how many were really suffering, as opposed to having worn out their welcome through aging? No longer adorable puppies, many now required ongoing care as elderly pets.

And of course, the pet food shortage didn't help. Owners had grown tired of the weekly search all over town for dog food. Even here, the government refused to pay for pet food. The animals were being put down anyway, so why throw money away? But Hank refused to let the creatures suffer, so he purchased food out of his own pocket. He didn't mind the extra running around.

A chocolate Labrador, beautiful and bouncy, stuck his

paw outside his cage and cried. Hank opened the cage and petted the dog's head. "Who'd put you down?" he asked the distraught animal. He passed each cage and spoke kindly to every dog. It was the least he could do.

Put her down, played over in Hank's head like an endless tape loop. The knot in his chest tightened when he entered Cell Block No. 2, the feline room. He'd had a special fondness for cats ever since his mother had given him a marmalade kitten for his fourth birthday, and Hank had slept with Dylan every night of the cat's life. Now, a newly arrived marmalade, just like Dylan, whined when Hank approached, and he scratched the cat's neck. "It'll be okay, boy. I'd take you home if I could." He put the cat onto the floor, and Ling Ling rushed over and washed his ears.

In the beginning, Hank's dad had built a welcoming barn for the creatures they would take home. He'd even installed heat to keep them comfortable during the frigid mid-Western winters. But that had ended years ago with the government's No Removal Laws, forbidding euthanasia contractors from rescuing animals. Too many lives were unaccounted for, the government had said. Oversight was necessary for the welfare of the community. So now they kept strict inventory, and a hefty euthanasia tax paid for the centers.

His father had been the first operator hired by the government over twenty years ago. A soft-hearted man, his passion had been to humanely lay all forms of life to rest, however big or small. His dying wish had been that Hank would carry on the business.

Unlike his father, Hank didn't remember a time when the private medical sector handled these matters in their small practices. Still, when he had accompanied his dad to work, families hadn't simply dropped off a loved one to be euthanatized. They had delivered them kindly, with tearful goodbyes. But new laws had banished families from the compound. To make the whole process less personal, Hank figured, so families could more easily walk away.

He sometimes wished he could walk away too, but if he did, he'd have no way of knowing how the new operator would treat the "inventory." Most days, he wondered if he served any valuable function at all, beyond showing a bit of kindness to every poor soul brought to the facility.

Outside, he cranked up the forklift and moved first one crate and then another into the warehouse. When he'd moved the last one, he used a crowbar to open the first crate, smaller than the others. Inside lay a hodgepodge of tiny rabbits, guinea pigs, and lizards, all shivering from being left outside overnight. At least their owners hadn't just abandoned them on the side of the road, as millions of others were abandoned each year.

Hank rolled a heat lamp over to warm them. He saw no reason they shouldn't be kept comfortable during their final moments. He lifted a trembling bunny and wrapped her in a soft fleece blanket. In the past, he had occasionally broken the rules and had taken an animal home, despite the risk. If he'd gotten caught, he would have faced not only stiff fines but criminal charges, and he would have lost his license as operator of House of Hope. Since the enactment of the government's surveillance program, his every move was filmed, making it impossible to rescue defenseless creatures, so instead, he moved the menagerie into Cell Block No. 3.

As he had done for the past ten years, he prepared the supplies to euthanize the first group. As always, he avoided eye contact as he lifted a trembling dachshund from her cage and inserted the intravenous catheter into her leg. "I'm here with you, girl. It'll be okay," he said softly. Next, he injected a sedative to relax her. "Our Father who art in heaven," he recited before he inserted the death serum into her vein.

One by one, Hank moved down the line, avoiding eye contact as he inserted the death serum. He ended the procession with the Labrador, which he cradled in his arms as the dog gasped his last breath. Then, he moved the corpses outside onto the grass, where the cold temperatures would preserve their bodies until pickup later. He ran his gaze over the expansive grounds, where no fewer than five hundred creatures lay as if sleeping.

He hadn't known it would be this way when his dad had trained him as the next operator. The loneliness and isolation. But his father had pounded a strong work ethic into him, and Hank often worked seven days a week, carrying out his father's last wishes. He had never married. It wouldn't have been fair, being away from home so much. Ling Ling was his only constant companion during the endless days and nights when he elected to sleep on his cot.

"Ling Ling," he called, and the Siamese rushed up, meowing. "Come inside with Daddy." His hand trembled when he placed it on the knob of the main euthanasia room, Cell Block No. 4. He had unloaded four crates into the room earlier, and he took a deep breath before using the crowbar to remove the first lid under the watchful gaze of the blue electronic eye in the ceiling. It was always the same, the shock.

Inside lay an emaciated man, identified as Subject No. 36, age seventy-five. The old man's lips trembled as he struggled to speak. Hank leaned down, but no words of comfort would come. Did he have an incurable disease, or was the family just tired of caring for him? He'd never know, so he focused on inserting the catheter into the man's frail arm. He avoided looking into the elderly man's eyes, lest he be identified as the bad guy, the executioner.

It had once been an honorable institution, the euthanasia centers, after the new right-to-die laws were passed. No more lingering for months in cancer wards or in unsanitary nursing homes, barely remembering one's name. Finally, the sick could choose to end their suffering. In the beginning, patients and families met with a trusted physician, and together they made the best decision. But as with most well-intentioned programs, greed and corruption eventually got their fingers into the pot. Little by little, the dignities were chipped away until one day—he couldn't remember how it had happened—the trucks started delivering flimsy wooden containers. Supply chain shortages, the government had said. Crates, inhumane and barbaric, were plentiful and cheap, and no need to tie up limited emergency vehicles transporting those who would only be put down anyway. With too few resources and too many souls on the planet eating up limited supplies, especially the infirm and old, a single family member could elect to put someone down with only one federal physician required to sign off on the procedure. Now the sick and helpless were being shipped out like expired produce. How much worse it could get? He was afraid to guess.

Tears rolled down the old guy's face as Hank recited the Lord's Prayer for him. It was the least he could do to send the old man off with a little dignity.

In the next crate, a sixty-nine-year-old woman barely had a pulse. Her legs had already been amputated. Diabetes, Hank thought. He inserted the catheter and injected the death serum. He saw this as a blessing, ending her suffering. Maybe she had loved ones waiting for her on the other side. He could hope.

Hank removed the lid from the third crate. "Granny!" he shrieked.

Inside, his eighty-five-year-old grandmother, wrapped in only a flimsy white sheet, was identified as Subject No. 78. So much adrenaline shot through him, he could barely feel his body. *Put her down*, his cousin had said.

With bones as brittle as rotting wood, she looked as if she might turn to sawdust if he hugged her too hard. Her cheekbones and blue veins protruded through translucent skin. Gone was the luxuriant red hair she had always neatly arranged in a bun. Now, her nearly bald scalp showed through thin, gray hair. Still, her hazel eyes shone with kindness. Underneath the sheet, she wore only the pink flannel nightgown he had given her for her last birthday. Even in this state, she forced a smile, the crevices around her eyes as deep as tunnels.

His grandmother's face came in and out of focus, and a flood of emotions tore through him—disbelief, despair, guilt. He shut his eyes, praying it was all a bad dream. But when he opened them, he heard, "Dear God," as if a voice had come from outside himself.

Hank's mother had died of cancer when he'd been just five, and his dad had moved Grandma Kitty in to live with them. For him, she was more a mother than a grandmother. She had sugar cookies waiting for him when he returned from school, and she'd attended all his high school football games, sitting in the bleachers with a homemade afghan thrown over her legs. Hank had learned his love of animals from her as much as from his father. She had never turned away a stray and had volunteered her time at the local animal shelter where she'd taken Hank on weekends as a boy. "They give you unconditional love and exist on a higher spiritual plane," she'd said. Even as a child, Hank had understood what she meant. Now, as if sensing her love for animals, Ling Ling jumped inside the crate, purring and butting her head against Granny's cheek.

Could he have prevented this if he'd worked less and had spent more time with her?

He steadied himself against the crate and stroked her wiry hair. "Granny, who sent you here?" She'd gone to live with his Aunt Betty last year after she'd fallen and broken her hip. He could imagine Aunt Betty sending her away for extermination. She didn't even have time for her own children.

Granny gazed into his eyes and tried to speak. Just like the rabbit before her, she trembled from the cold as Hank tucked a soft blanket around her.

"I'm here to help you," he said, desperate to assuage his guilt and to make things right. He leaned down and kissed her cheek. But who was he kidding? He glanced up at the camera in the ceiling, ever watching. She knew what he did at the warehouse. He could see it in her eyes.

In all his years here, this was the first time he'd ever come face-to-face with a relative. He'd once put down a neighbor who'd been eaten up with cancer and then a teenager who'd lived on his street after the boy had been mangled beyond repair in a car crash. But this?

He closed his eyes and prayed for strength. So this was all

his granny's life was worth after she'd given so much of herself?

To hell with it, he thought. For a split second, he thought he'd rescue her. But then what? If he tried to save her, the authorities would catch up to them before he'd even make it home. He'd be taken away, jailed, and some stranger would unmercifully exterminate her.

She grasped his hand in her tiny, bony appendage and somehow conveyed her acceptance. It's all right, she seemed to be saying as she held his gaze. He steeled himself. The past ten years had prepared him for this moment. Even if no one believed it but himself, he served a valuable function. Treating every creature at the center with love and respect was his calling, his passion. Without a doubt, he provided the last glimmer of kindness any of them would ever know.

He leaned down closer, still looking directly into Granny's eyes. His voice cracked. "You're the best grandmother a boy could ever have had. I'm here to help you move into the light. I have to believe it will be peaceful and beautiful. Your suffering will end, and Grandpa will be waiting for you. Is there anything you want to say?"

Her lips barely moved, but her eyes conveyed the same love they always had.

Hank had the sensation of leaving his body as he quietly inserted the catheter into her arm. "Our Father who art in Heaven," he recited, and without guilt, he lifted the death serum and inserted it into her vein.

* * *

Discussion Questions

1. What, if any, scarcity scenario would justify this kind of treatment for loved pets and the elderly? How bad would things have to get (*if ever*) for this to be okay?

2. What aspects of the euthanizing process are most offensive to you; being shipped in boxes, being barred from seeing loved ones in their final moments, being left in the cold, being left alone, being euthanized at all, or something else?

3. The story seems to imply the world situation deteriorated very rapidly, making the care of pets and elderly family members prohibitively expensive. Given the new global reality, what, if any, regulations would you put in place for having children or buying new pets in the future? Do people have an inalienable right to own a pet, have a child, and choose when they die?

4. The narrator justifies his role in this process by saying he, unlike others, treats those he is about to euthanize with dignity. Is this a better option than nonparticipation in an unjust system? Does the narrator believe the system is unjust or simply tragic?

5. What would you do if you were the narrator in this story?

Cicada

Ishan Dylan

* * *

Dr. Kamilah Zhang failed to turn up for her eight o'clock physics lecture on a cold Tuesday morning, leaving her students to grumble about *unprofessional conduct*. One student, a philosophy major, even went so far as to suggest — *unethical*.

By nine o'clock, nobody on the planet was still talking about professionalism.

* * *

In the video, Dr. Zhang sat next to a bookshelf. Behind her was a sixteenth-century poster of the solar system. She wore a lab coat over a dark blouse and a strand of pearls.

"It's done."

She pushed ahead without pausing for the words to land, seemingly unaware of their momentousness. "I don't just mean proof that it's possible. The technology for interstellar travel is complete. It's ours. Today."

* * *

But we couldn't make that the headline, of course. Dr. Zhang hadn't published her calculations. We couldn't risk our credibility. Then again—as multiple coworkers vented to me—Dr. Zhang *was* a credible source. It was frustrating. We were about to get beaten to history by the grocery store tabloid aisle.

After an hour of pitches and one shattered coffee mug, the managing editor settled on my draft: *Prototype for Interstellar Travel Complete, Says Renowned Physicist.*

It was honest. Not too flashy. Journalists aren't supposed to make promises we can't support. Our responsibility is to the truth, not dreams. The public deserves the truth.

* * *

Kids deserve to dream.

"When we go to space, where do you want to visit first?" Jade tugged the sheets to her chin.

I pretended to think. "Let's go to Titan. Surface oceans and fourteen percent gravity. The perfect vacation spot."

That earned me the eye roll I was expecting. "You can't surf on Titan, Dad. They're hydrocarbon lakes, not oceans. It's not dense enough. You'd just sink."

"Oh. Silly me." Outer space was one topic I did not have to feign any ignorance on. "What about you?"

"I can't tell you," her face was deadly serious, "because I'm going to an undiscovered planet. I think I'll name it *Shiva.*"

"Wow. You've got this all figured out, haven't you?"

"Maybe not the name. But all the other planets are named after Roman gods, and that's not very fair."

"How about *Ma'at,*" I offered, "the goddess of truth and justice."

Jade looked at me pityingly, like I was the child who

needed explaining to. "But I already *have* a backup name," she insisted, "Planet Bobby."

Bobby was her pet hamster's name.

I chuckled and kissed her forehead. "I'm sure you can discover two planets, sunshine."

* * *

"She's got nothing!" my boss roared, "Nada! Zilch!"

"We didn't *say* she had anything," I massaged my temples, "just that she *claimed* to have something. I'll report the leak, okay...?"

I stared at the blank document for long enough that my coffee got cold. Finally, I managed to type a headline. *NASA Leak Proves Interstellar Travel Claims Fraudulent.* I stared at the words until they were just black shapes on a screen. Then I made a correction. *NASA Leak Suggests...*

Next, there was the question of why she did it. Everyone at work had their own theory. It fell to me to copyedit them into something usable. I came across more than one contemporary paraphrase of "female hysteria."

* * *

With Jade at school, the house was empty. I used to walk the dog when I needed to get outside. But Scout was dead. I wandered down the sidewalk without an excuse. That year, it was easy to pick out the newly gentrified streets. I only had to look for which trees weren't crawling with cicadas, trees that hadn't been here seventeen years ago.

I watched the tiny marvels squirm from the mulch. *Beautiful things from the earth as well.* The nymphs emerge with vigor. Only a month to breed, only a month, breed breed breed, they thought. *They don't need to know about the stars.*

April 13th. It would go down in history as the day when... well, *April 13th* happened. No explanation needed. *July 4th. September 11th. April 13th.*

"It's a fake. It's a hack, or a... photo-chop or something."

"Photoshop."

"Whatever. It's a hoax. Do *not* report on this."

I looked back at my monitor, at the same compressed JPEG that was probably loaded on every screen in the world. Rolling red hills. A landscape that, by appearances, could have been from Earth, but of course, that would be impossible. Visible plainly in the Martian soil, footprints spelled a phrase now overwhelming the servers of Google Translate: *Quod erat demonstrandum.* Translation: *believe me now?*

* * *

The FBI found her on a ranch in Wyoming. No spaceship, no magic gateway. Just her, a woman in a lab coat. A podcaster started a theory that Dr. Zhang somehow used the Mars rover itself to write the message—*She's some kind of genius, isn't she? Like, a hacker genius?* The accusation trended for several hours until the internet collectively realized that rovers don't have feet.

It was a striking front-page photo. A pile of shredded paper and scorched motherboards. During interrogation, reportedly, Dr. Zhang smugly informed the investigators that there was still one type of memory drive their technology could not search.

But not even the constraints of reality can stop a Congressional subpoena. Congress opened an investigation into Dr. Zhang's "destruction of government property" under Title 18, US Code § 1361, and article eight of the Outer Space Treaty.

That's what I had to write. The facts. If you really wanted to know what Kamilah Zhang was on trial for, you just had to check social media. Everyone was arguing the same question.

If she had the technology, why didn't she share it?

People fell into three camps. The first declared the April 13th phenomenon a hoax. The second, that Dr. Zhang was extorting the US Government. The third camp declared everything else, ranging from something about alien body snatchers to the sinister machinations of a particular ex-secretary of state.

There was really no point in theorizing. You could just wait for the Congressional Record to release their transcripts.

* * *

The Senate Subcommittee on Commerce, Justice, Science, and Related Agencies was ready to convene the moment Kamilah Zhang touched down in Washington. Congress even came out of recess for the occasion. Senator Huxley presided.

When it came time for her to speak, Kamilah Zhang leaned almost imperceptibly closer to the microphone. "The data from my laboratory are considered records. I made the decision not to refer them to the Aeronautics and Space Administration."

"So you willfully disregarded your duty," Senator Huxley continued, "your... *sacred* duty, which you swore to uphold—"

"That's where we disagree," Dr. Zhang interrupted. "Oppenheimer fulfilled his duty on paper, but what about his duty to the world? Of course," she said, beginning to lean away from the microphone, "of course, he owed his superiors answers. But he could have drawn out the search. Keep them looking into heavy water, for example... buy time for a peaceful end."

A remarkably optimistic view. But that wasn't what Senator Huxley took issue with.

"Destroying government records is treason."

"Please. Some decorum," Senator Hart spoke up. Blue pantsuit. Third in line for the Democratic nomination. "Look, Dr. Zhang. I understand. Here you are," she emphasized with a squint, "with the power to change history."

"I don't want to be Oppenheimer—"

"—and responsibility can be awfully stressful—"

"—I want to be Frederick Banting."

A pause of confusion turned into real silence as Dr. Zhang drew herself up. "Banting. The man who sold the patent of insulin for one dollar, who ensured that his research would save lives rather than generate profit."

"Then follow his example," Senator Hart insisted, "share your research."

"Insulin today costs $360.25 per month," Dr. Zhang replied. "This economy didn't deserve Banting's trust. It will have to earn mine."

"Dr. Zhang," Senator Huxley interjected, "have you had any affiliation with the Communist Party of China?"

"Mister Senator, I think I've made very clear my position on any such profit-driven entities." Kamilah wouldn't let him goad her into producing any sound bites. "Look. I am willing to disclose some details from my research. They are necessary details to understand my decision."

The room quieted.

"The technology that I have developed can transport

matter anywhere in the universe. Senator Hart, imagine what could be done with that kind of capability..."

"We could have clean energy, better waste management—"

"I agree. We could have benefits for all mankind, which is to say—not profits. But is that what Amazon and Exxon-Mobil will think of, Senator? How will you respond when corporations start hosting off-world fulfillment centers far, far away from US jurisdiction?"

The Congressional Record doesn't include air quotes in its transcripts. You'll have to guess where she put them.

"The federal government exists to regulate private industry, Dr. Zhang," Senator Hart said. "It exists to address these very concerns."

"With all due respect, Senator. The purpose of a machine is what we use it for."

* * *

When the FBI took Dr. Zhang into custody, the editorial board called it an "unprecedented breach of judicial norms." They imprisoned her so that she couldn't give her discovery to any foreign governments. That's what we were saying.

I was assigned to write a piece reminding everyone to be very concerned about precedents. Even if you didn't agree with Dr. Zhang, her civil liberties were our own.

It needed to be said.

I would leave it for someone else to say. I decided to call out of work.

* * *

I was on another walk when I heard something hiss beneath me. A cicada helpless on the concrete, its broken legs waggling in the air.

Normally, I'd squash it. Call it a mercy killing. I stared down at the concrete.

We didn't have to be trapped here. There was someone who could help us. *Someone too busy arguing with millionaires on C-SPAN*, I fumed.

The newsroom and the editorial board hadn't been on speaking terms since the announcement. But it was the only thing I had the energy to write.

OPINION: Kamilah Zhang Thinks Her Politics Are the Center of the Universe. She's Wrong.

* * *

I was expecting my coworkers to be angry. It was only fair. Who knew how many hate messages had been lobbed at them because of what I wrote?

What I wasn't expecting was for my boss to walk in with a buddy-buddy smile plastered across his face. I furrowed my brow.

"*Great* timing. Really had your finger on the pulse for this one."

I didn't understand his sarcasm until he dropped an early draft of today's front page on my desk.

Dr. Kamilah Zhang Dead of Apparent Suicide in Federal Custody.

"Good luck out there, Krish. You'll need it."

* * *

Someone had to drive Jade to school. I tried to ignore the scathing looks. A few days ago, all these PTA parents in their smart watches and yoga pants had silently agreed with me. But that wouldn't show up if you googled their names. Not like my op-ed.

I had it out for her all along. That's what social media thought. Why else had I refused to report on Dr. Zhang between the first announcement and her death?

I started taking my walks late at night when the streets were empty. I slept while Jade was at school. I didn't have to worry about work since quitting, but I still couldn't escape the endless theorizing of my coworkers.

If they couldn't have the technology, nobody could. So they killed her.

No, they're dissecting her brain to figure it out. That's why we haven't seen the body.

I couldn't speculate. Only one question consumed my nightly walks.

Why did she tell us if she knew we couldn't meet her demands?

Guilt gnawed at me. A woman was dead, and I was mourning her research.

* * *

"What's that?" I pointed at the piece of poster board in Jade's hands as she climbed into the backseat of the minivan.

She turned it around. *Galileo* was written in bubble letters across the top.

"Nice! Are you gonna study space someday, like he did…?"

"Maybe," she replied glumly. "Ms. Kleinman said it was too late to change my presentation topic."

"Oh. Okay."

* * *

Once Jade was in bed, I flipped open my laptop.

It was just a school project. But it reminded me of something that I couldn't name. It was on the tip of my tongue.

My fingers hovered over the keyboard. I typed the only thing that ever crossed my mind when it was otherwise blank.

Kamilah Zhang.

42,800,000 results. My cursor hovered over the video thumbnail.

Click.

"It's done," her voice came through the speakers.

Click. Muted.

I didn't want to listen, to fool myself into thinking she was there and talking to me. That would mean I could apologize. I looked at the wall behind her. Something had been strange about the poster. Now I saw what. Earth was at the center, surrounded by concentric gold rings.

Galileo would go down in history for defending heliocentrism until he died, imprisoned for heresy. Religion versus science. The passion of Christ versus the passion for truth. Martyr versus martyr. I stared at the poster behind Dr. Zhang.

It was a message. A time capsule.

Everyone liked to imagine that they would side with Galileo. Especially journalists. After all, our first duty was to truth, even if we don't like where it leads. Or the enemies it leads us to.

* * *

Jade asked if she could stay up past her bedtime to join me on my nightly walk.

"Wait up!" she called out a few meters behind me. She was on her hands and knees, parsing through the wet grass.

"What are you doing?"

"Looking for bugs. New ones. There could be a brand-new kind of bug right here! I read that over eight hundred insect species are discovered every year."

I didn't even think about correcting her. Kids deserve to dream. I nodded along, half-listening.

"Bugs bugs bugs bugs bugs."

I stared at the tree trunks, covered with the translucent, amber carapaces where cicadas had crawled from their exoskeletons.

I stared at the empty husks and frowned. They leave behind their old bodies. They do not hold onto old weight to fly...

We never saw her body.

* * *

Discussion Questions

1. The narrator (*Krish*) says, "Everyone liked to imagine that they would side with Galileo." What does this mean? Why would people side against new science? Why might you side with, or against, Galileo (*or Dr. Zhang*)?

2. What do you think are the ramifications of Dr. Zhang's discovery, assuming it is true? Do you think it would be a net positive, or negative, for humanity?

3. Why do you think Dr. Zhang wanted to prove her discovery to the world only to deny providing it? If you were in her situation, what would you do? Do you think an inventor who withholds world-changing technology deserves civil liberties, or do the needs of the many outweigh one individual's liberties?

4. If you had a world-changing discovery that you wanted to guarantee would get out into the world in the most nonprofit-driven way, how would you do it? Under what, if any, circumstances should world-changing discovery be driven by profit motives?

5. What do you think happened to Dr. Zhang?

The Pool

Celia Lisset Alvarez

* * *

It had been about ten years since I'd driven down West Flagler. Even when Jack and I moved to Orlando, the apartment complexes on both sides of the street were already in disrepair. I still remember them when my parents and I moved here in 1974. They stretched from about 47th Avenue to 67th, all built more or less in the 1950s. Some were never works of art, but I always liked the circular one right on 47th or the one with the impressive two-story colonnade around 60-something. They were all usually one-bedroom apartments, no doubt built with the steno pool in mind. Speaking of pools, they all originally had one in the center court. By the late '70s, most of these had been filled in, paved over, turned into a grassy area, or—worst-case scenario—parking. There were rumors of a kid who'd been electrocuted during a thunderstorm. But the truth was less and more dramatic: with the wave of immigrants in the '60s, the buildings had become slums, and pools were expensive to keep up. And for what? The people who lived there had no time to sit in the sun.

Such a shame. There used to be a time when you could be poor and still entitled to a decent life. If I looked closely, I could still see the outlines of the pools. Cement borders around the ones that were a mess of yellow grass and weeds or cracks in the ones that had been paved over. Parked on. Forgotten.

I convinced Jack to buy me the one with the colonnade. At this point, we didn't need to profit from it. It could be my little project; I'd restore it to its original glory, pool and all, without raising the rents a cent. I didn't want anyone moving out or even moving in. I just wanted them, or maybe their kids, to have a place to take a swim or at least sit in the sun before or after going to work or school.

There was no such thing as a meeting. Some of the residents owned their apartments by this time, but I made it explicit in the letter I sent (in both English and Spanish) that the remodeling plans would not cost them anything. I did not expect the flood of requests I received: every apartment needed something, from new screens on the windows to new pipes, new appliances, more parking, an elevator that wouldn't trap someone at least once a month, bigger laundry and storage rooms. There were crumbling stairs and cracked tiles. Mold. Nobody mentioned a pool.

I made a list. I hired a contractor, a good one. We would start from the inside out: getting rid of mold (there was asbestos, too), leaks, termites. I put the residents up in hotels. Jack looked at the bills and raised his eyebrows, but that was all he did. It was the residents I had to fight—they did not want to get rid of their popcorn glitter ceilings or linoleum floors. Though they had wanted new appliances, they had not realized their new refrigerators would not be avocado green. They did not want their carpets pulled up. "You want to make all the apartments look the same," one of the older women, a widow who had lived there since the '70s, said. "I love my apartment just like it is." If not for the mold and termites, which put city codes on my side, I might not have been able to get anything done.

I discovered several first-floor dwellers had been feeding stray cats in the alleyway behind the building where the parking was. There were dozens of cats of all ages and breeds under cars, in the dumpster, skipping down the halls. I had them rounded up and fixed, vaccinated. Two more widows accosted me during one of my inspection visits, crying. "Animal!" They spat at me as if I had put them all down. There was a no-pets policy, but I have always loved and had pets, so I modified it. You could have up to two small pets per apartment, but you had to keep them inside. All you had to do was claim them from the shelter. Nobody did. I kept two of them for myself, a pair of calicos I named Hope and Faith.

I got rid of the rickety old elevator and installed two new ones on either side of the building. "I have to walk so much now to get to the elevator," one of the tenants who lived in the middle of the building complained. She was in her eighties and used a walker.

"But you live on the first floor," I said. "Why do you need to use the elevator?"

"My daughter lives on the second floor."

There was nothing I could do about that. But I added a new laundry room on the second floor and a second storage room on the first in vacant apartments. Although they cost a fortune, Jack was okay with the impact windows and doors because we got a big discount on the insurance.

Finally, we began on the pool.

"When is all this noise going to stop?" one of the men complained. "We have been living in terror for months."

The pool was originally quite large, oval, with a surrounding stone courtyard where there could be tables and loungers. It would have to be smaller this time, the contractor explained. We would never pass inspection unless we installed a safety railing around it.

"A safety railing?" I asked. I pictured what it would look like. Hideous. When I was a kid, my godparents lived in one of these buildings. We didn't have safety railings around pools. Your father would pick you up and throw you in the deep end. That's how you learned how to swim. Sure, some kids drowned when no one was watching. But usually, there was always someone watching. Now there was no getting around it. Parents couldn't be trusted. No railing, no pool. I caved. It was still pretty big.

The courtyard around it should not be stone, Mitch, the contractor, argued. "Too unstable," he said. "Too many elderly residents. It's a lawsuit waiting to happen."

"Okay," I said. I trusted Mitch and had become used to compromising at this point. "What do you suggest? Nothing too expensive." Jack's eyebrows were reaching his hairline by now, and that had receded significantly.

"Well," Mitch said, scratching his head. "I guess that puts tile out of the question. Concrete. We can dye it, stamp it, whatever you want. I got a guy." Luckily Mitch had lots of guys. Once, I had gone with him to Home Depot early on a Saturday. He held up three fingers out his window, and three guys leaped into the back of his pickup. They didn't even ask what kind of work they'd be doing or how much they'd get paid.

Soon, the pool was finished.

Jack had to travel to Washington right around that time, and I'd gone with him, so I'd missed the grand reveal. I wasn't able to make it down to Miami until the pool had been in use for a few weeks.

Driving up to the building, I looked expectantly out the window, craning my neck for the first glimpse of the pool. I had purposely gone around noon on a Saturday, thinking that would be the most likely day for the residents to be enjoying it. To my surprise, the pool was deserted. It had definitely been used, however. Towels flapped in the wind from the balconies on both sides. Leaves floated on the water. Empty soda cans, beer bottles, and fast-food packages littered the tables I had arranged around the pool, and one of the loungers was on its side.

I sent a letter. In English and Spanish.

In response to complaints about the cost of putting the towels in the dryers, I had the coin slots removed. But more complaints kept coming. Someone on the second floor had adopted two little yapping terriers that barked all day while she was at work. Dog shit had been found on the grass border around the pool courtyard. The men were smoking in the pool area, and the mothers were concerned about their children inhaling all that secondhand smoke. Signs had to be put up.

I got a call around midnight one Sunday. I was in Orlando. It was from Dolores, the lady in her eighties from the first-floor center apartment. Her living room window had a clear view of the pool.

"I can't sleep!" she screamed. "Those kids are still out

there. They're smoking pot! I can smell it from here, and it's making me sick!"

I called Ernesto, the super. "Okay," he said, "but this is not my job. You should call the police."

"I don't want to call the police," I said. "These are my tenants. Besides, Dolores says they're just kids."

"Just kids? Tenants, eh?" Ernesto said sarcastically. "Look, Ms. Carrie, one or two of these 'kids' might be your tenants, but what you got out there is a gang."

"What?"

"You heard me. Tattoos. Piercings. Loud music. Drugs. I wouldn't be surprised if they were armed."

"Jesus," I said. "Just please try asking them to leave nicely. If they don't comply, you can call the police."

Ernesto called the police. Turns out none of them were my tenants. They had just snuck in. Some of them were minors. The police suggested we put a locked gate around the property. Jack's eyebrows retreated into his hair.

But that was not the worst of it.

Before Ernesto went to confront the thugs (that was Jack's word), if he ever did (I suspect he called the police from the safety of his apartment), Dolores took it upon herself to get rid of the pests on her own. She put on her housecoat and ambled to the pool area, pushing her walker in her slippers.

She slid on a puddle and fell on the concrete.

I first heard of it around 1:00 a.m. from her daughter, Patricia, who called me from the hospital. My first thought was a broken hip, instant death, but it was a broken shoulder. "I hope you're happy," Patricia said. "Eighty-two and had never broken a bone in her life." She held the phone so I could hear Dolores screaming. It was loud.

Of course, there was a lawsuit. Luckily, we were able to settle out of court, but Jack had had it. "What exactly are you getting out of this, Carrie?" he finally said. Dolores had to go to a rehab facility. I was crying. "It seems like nothing but aggravation."

I hired an assistant for Ernesto. He came in every day at sunset to clean up around the pool and lock the gate. Nothing else happened for about another three months, other than the usual complaints about there not being enough parking. To make room for the pool again, I had been forced to restrict the parking to one spot per apartment and only two visitor spots. In the interim, Dolores had returned. "My grandchildren have no place to park, so they don't come to visit me anymore."

Also, Ernesto noticed that tenants from the nearby apartment buildings were using our laundry rooms. I reinstalled the coin slots. The towels returned to the balconies.

It was around 8:00 p.m. in mid-July when I got the call from Lalo, the kid I'd hired to keep the pool area safe. I was spending the summer in Miami with family, so when he said, "I think you need to come over," I did.

There was a burlap bag at the bottom of the pool.

"What is it?" I asked Lalo.

He was a skinny kid, very brown, always in board shorts, no shoes. He gave me a look. I noticed his hair was wet. "I didn't know if I should bring it up or what," he said.

"Please," I asked.

He dove into the pool without hesitation. Whatever was in the bag was heavy; he struggled to bring it up. When he got to the edge of the pool, he swung the bag onto the concrete. It landed with a dull thud. Then he scrambled out and knelt in front of it. It was tied with a white rope. "You sure you want to see this?" he asked.

"You called me over, didn't you?" I was getting a little exasperated. I could feel my heart pumping in my chest. I couldn't guess what was in the bag, but it couldn't be anything good.

Lalo nodded, untied the rope, and held the bag open for me to look. I bent over and gasped. It was the two yapping terriers and a bunch of rocks. Not rocks. Concrete. Pieces of the concrete that had once filled the pool, which the contractors had failed to completely haul away and had been littering the parking lot for months.

"Take them away," I said.

"What do you want—"

"Just take them away—I don't care—figure it out."

* * *

I suppose it was Lalo or Ernesto who found the dogs' owner and delivered the news. There was an animal cruelty report filed, but, of course, no one was ever charged.

I remember when we moved out of our first apartment in this country. It was right after the front lawn got paved. We moved to a duplex just a few blocks away. It was still just a 1/1. We were still renting. At the time, I couldn't understand the decision.

"Just sell it," I told Jack, who was more than happy to do so. I didn't return to Miami for a long time until my godmother died, the one who had lived in the apartment building with the pool when I was little. She, too, had eventually moved to a duplex and then bought a house in Westchester. After my godfather died, she moved into a condo complex—with a pool. By that time, she was too old to use it. It was hard for her to walk, and it was always so hot.

* * *

Discussion Questions

1. Was Carrie (*the property owner*) wrong to want to fix up the complex and make it nicer? Should she have simply left the complex in its dilapidated state and focused on making money from it? Should she have evicted everyone, renovated the empty complex, and gotten all new tenants?

2. When the units were being remodeled, the tenants complained the new refrigerator wasn't 1970s avocado green and that the shag carpet was replaced with new flooring concepts. Why weren't the residents more grateful for the housing upgrades?

3. How do you know when complaints from your tenants are worth listening to and when they should be ignored? Which tenant complaints in the story were legitimate, and which should have been ignored?

4. At what point, if any, in the complex renovation process should Carrie have met with the tenants to hear their thoughts and feedback? Why didn't she?

5. Inertia and resistance to change—even seemingly positive change—dominate tenant's attitude. What lessons, if any, from Carrie's renovations could be applied to city, state, and national governments trying to make positive policy changes?

Drag Brunch

Mark Bessen

* * *

On Friday, Kyle arrived in the crowded foyer of Swift's Attic in downtown Austin, itching for a bitch sesh. His friend, Jay, an unreasonably beefy muscle bottom he'd met on Grindr, waved him over to their table, where Kyle harrumphed into his seat. After the dumpster fire of a week he'd just had, he needed to extinguish the flames with some well liquor and good shit-talk.

"Can you believe this?" Kyle said, passing his phone to Jay over charred edamame and ice-ball cocktails. He'd just been uninvited from his soon-to-be-former best friend Hannah's bachelorette weekend via a text.

"It's just such a stupid excuse." Kyle popped a pale green bean out of its furry shell, busying his hands while his phone was otherwise occupied. "Saying she wanted a 'girls' trip.' So basic. Like, fifties housewife gender binary where's-my-dowry basic."

"Don't you hate weddings anyways?" Jay asked.

"That's not the point. *Tara* was invited, and Hannah doesn't even *like* Tara. And having her Maid of Honor tell me? She didn't even have the balls to tell me herself."

"Hannah has always been... The bottle blonde seeped in a little too deep."

"Sure, she like, drives a Mustang, but we've been friends for forever."

And they had. Even now, both thirty and on track to start their Real Lives—Hannah in some suburban enclave, Kyle in his apartment on Austin's east side—Kyle really thought they were closer than this.

"You're dealing with a lot right now," Jay said. "I'm just not sure this is worth your energy."

Kyle knew Jay was right. It *was* just a stupid bachelorette weekend. There was so much more important fucked-uppery in the world. Parents at the school where he taught tenth-grade English had petitioned to ban forty-eight books, citing concerns of "indecency, profanity, and egregious lewdness"—meaning, for the most part, they involved queer people; he'd just gotten back from sponsoring a student protest of a track meet because another district had banned a trans girl from racing, even though she wasn't very *good*; Texan politicians were on the news making vacuous arguments about grooming and protecting kids from drag queens instead of gun violence or climate change. The phrase "deviant lifestyle" had even reemerged in conservative politics like a bloodthirsty anachronism.

But it was all so abstract. What was he supposed to do, scream into the void about ideology? This bachelorette bullshit gave him something concrete to focus on. Rather than perseverate over the sweeping injustices beleaguering the Texas

Homosexual, Kyle could fix his ire on his morally bankrupt bridezilla ex-best friend.

"And Kyle, she treats you like her woke accessory. You thought you were her bff, but to her, you were always the gbf."

Straight girls sucked.

The bachelorette party would be leaving Austin for Miami soon. After Jay got up to go to the bathroom, Kyle started scrolling mindlessly through Insta until he saw a post from Tara that looked like something Pinterest had vomited up.

Hannah's Bachelorette Extravaganza!
May 3-5 • Miami Beach

Friday
7pm: Check in at Airbnb in SoBe, beys! Let the White Claws and tequila shots floweth!
9pm: Dinner rez at Nobu—she's serving fish ;)

Saturday
12pm: Brunch at Bacon Bitch—don't forget your sunglasses, bitch!
2pm: Beach day! Meet near the rainbow flag just south of 11th
7pm: Dinner at Santorini. Dress classy, ladies!
10pm: Gay clerbing! Start at Twist and see where we end up

Sunday
1pm: Drag brunch at the Palace!
4pm: Fly back to Austin :(

"Is this a fucking joke?" Kyle asked, his stomach clenching around soybeans and bourbon as Jay sat back down. Kyle showed him the post.

"Jesus," Jay said, shaking his head. "It's like they think they're going to the zoo."

* * *

The seven bachelorettes lounged around Gate 24 at Austin-Bergstrom International Airport, their bottom halves a mix of form-fitting Lululemons and retro Juicy sweatpants, matching pink T-shirts on top. Daniela's was printed with "Maid of Honor," the rest of the bridesmaids—Katie K., Tara, Caity C., Rebecca, and Sophie—labeled accordingly, and HRH Hannah's shirt said "Bride," set apart by gold glitter. They were wearing the T-shirts ironically, though, Daniela thought, no one else knew that.

Daniela, for her part, had enough self-awareness to be mortified by the gaucheness of the gaggle. She hated this kind of Live Laugh Love affair and suspected that even Hannah was a little embarrassed. Daniela had been surprised when Hannah asked her to be the Maid of Honor, assuming the role would go to Hannah's sister or her gay bff Kyle, and worried she'd been chosen less out of intimacy than logistical prowess since she worked as an event organizer.

Daniela recrossed her legs in the leather-on-metal airport chair and checked a few last-minute work emails, then set her Slack to "Out of Office." Good timing: her edible was just kicking in. They were all a little tipsy from the shots they had before they left for the airport. Daniela had stopped at one, but Sophie, the woo-girl of the bunch, had also covertly filled a flask with shots from the airport bar and was swigging from it now.

On her phone, Daniela looked over the itinerary that Tara had just posted to Instagram. Tara had volunteered to make the itineraries, and Daniela had been thrilled to offload a task, but she did wish she'd done a bit more quality control. All the drag references and gay slang felt like salt in the wound for Kyle, who she'd had to uninvite from the trip. She liked Kyle—he was real, even if he was sometimes insufferable. And Hannah's "girls' trip" excuse was flimsy at best. But what was she going to do? It was Hannah's gig. Hannah's mom was springing for the whole thing, so at least Kyle wasn't being put out. Daniela would honor her maidship, even if she begrudged it.

"Girl, let me see that rock!" said Rebecca, one of the bridesmaids who Daniela still struggled to distinguish. Rebecca grabbed Hannah's hand and let out a mock gasp. Then, she asked, "Where's Kyle?"

Fuck.

"Is he meeting us in Miami Beach?"

Daniela had forgotten to text the updated guest list to the out-of-towners on the trip.

Daniela looked at Hannah, who sat back in feigned calm and said, "I just thought he'd throw off the vibe, you know?"

Tara chimed in. "I've heard this drag brunch is epic."

Daniela was surprised by Tara's savvy redirection and worried she'd judged her too harshly. Her eye rolls would have been better directed at Sophie, who added, "I hear Ross Matthews goes there all the time."

"And Lisa Vanderpump." This was Caity C., who had auditioned for *The Bachelor* three times. "I wonder if any of the queens from *Drag Race* will be there."

"Have you seen the new season?" Rebecca asked. "The

queens are icon*ique*."

"It's so cool there's a straight queen!" Katie K. said. "I'm so glad the show is becoming more inclusive. He's so talented."

Daniela dug through her backpack for an Ambien, hoping to get some rest before they arrived in Miami—and to be unconscious to the flight attendant's raised eyebrow about their matching garb.

"Ugh, I'm so excited for our girls' weekend," Sophie said, apropos of nothing. "I'm *so* done with guys."

* * *

Hannah opened the door to the five-bedroom SoBe condo her mom had rented for them and let out a sigh of relief. She needed this: a good-vibes-only trip, time to relax and escape the wedding stress. This trip would be her safe space, free of judgment.

The girls looked around the gorgeous beachy rental—soft blues and whites, a matching set of glass coffee and kitchen tables, a stack of towels at the end of every bed—then paused when she saw the palm-tree-shaped floor lamps that Kyle had called "tacky bungalow realness but not a dealbreaker" when he'd helped her find places to stay.

She needed to get Kyle out of her head, or he'd ruin this weekend trip, his presence insinuating itself into every conversation like a phantom limb. Yeah, she should have told Kyle more than a week ahead, that was bad, but she just didn't have the energy for that kind of convo. And she knew it had been a dick move to make Daniela do the uninviting, but if Hannah had told him herself, he'd have asked for an explanation.

Some part of Hannah was a little sad that Kyle wasn't on

the trip—he provided endless, easy entertainment—but she was also a lot relieved. Kyle was a loose cannon (as he'd proven at that dinner with Trent), his words cannonballs aimed at creating as much wreckage as possible. She understood where he was coming from, and for the most part, she agreed with him, but she wasn't going to throw a wrench into her family dynamics. Hannah cared about social issues as much as anyone, but she wouldn't be a bitch about it.

"You okay?" Tara asked Hannah, extending a plastic shot glass toward her. Tara had already changed for dinner, which reminded Hannah she needed to get ready. "Seems like you're in your head."

"I'm fine," Hannah said. Tara was annoyingly perceptive but not terribly tactful.

"Are you worrying about Kyle?"

"Wedding stuff."

Not entirely untrue. Hannah had always intended for Kyle to be in the wedding, despite the ups and downs their friendship had weathered over the last decade. When she presented the list of bridesmaids to her wedding planner, a long-time friend of her mother's, Kyle had been on it as a brides*man*.

"Your mother was hoping for something more traditional," the wedding planner had replied, returning the amended list. "It would throw off the whole aesthetic— weddings are all about the pictures."

The bridal party would feature an ombré of matching dresses in descending hues of purple, from eggplant to pastel. Where would a tux fit in?

Hannah called her mother immediately.

"I'm not paying to have your grandparents scandalized," her mother said. "I don't think that's too much to ask."

Classic, Hannah thought, using money to enact her will—just like she had done to get her to go to SMU. Hannah had wanted to go to UT, but her parents didn't want their annual alumni donations to go to waste, so a Mustang she became.

"Remember, this wedding isn't just about you," her mother said.

Hannah started to protest, began formulating in her mind a speech about gender normativity and backward ideas. But she paused because, on some level, she shared her mother's ideal of the picture-perfect wedding. And also because Kyle had been a real headache lately.

What was she going to do, she thought now, as she applied her wingtip eyeliner, turn down the hundred grand her parents were paying for the wedding? She'd be better off having them pay, then donate twenty grand to the ACLU, or, like, Human Rights Campaign, if Kyle wanted to talk about "social impact." She just never found the right time to *tell him* he was out of the wedding party.

Hannah shut her worrying away with a snap of her makeup mirror.

"Okay, ladies," she said, waving her mom's platinum credit card. "Let's get some sushi."

* * *

Kyle slept on it, hoping he'd wake up purged of his resentments, but instead, they seemed to have multiplied in his subconscious, and he was fuming. He texted Hannah to see if they could talk, but no answer. He refilled his coffee mug from his French press, coffee grounds floating like bits of bark on the surface. He gave it until eleven before he called for the first time—noon for her, a reasonable hour. The phone rang six times and then went to voicemail. He texted again. Called again. By the third call, it went straight to voicemail. He wanted to give Hannah the benefit of the doubt—well, he wanted to murder her, but he also wanted to give her the benefit of the doubt—but he had to talk this out. They'd been best friends for *years*. Surely that warranted a conversation.

He went to Black Swan Yoga to try to sweat out a decision about how to handle it. As he flowed through sun salutations, he ruminated on his friendship with Hannah. She'd been the first to make him feel included at their shitty conservative high school. The first person he'd come out to. But had she just been looking for her Kurt from *Glee*? Was he really just the gbf, like Jay said, easy to cast aside when he became inconvenient?

They'd been fine until she started dating... *him*. Fucking Trent. That douchebro. He was a lawyer for the oil company Hannah's dad had worked for. Kyle had gone to dinner with them a couple months prior, bribing Jay into coming along. The four started off their dinner at Launderette with chitchat about the wedding and bachelorette party, which Hannah was late in planning. Kyle had suggested Miami Beach as a fun destination, easy to book last minute. At that point, Kyle had still been in the wedding party, but he still found the wedding small talk intolerable—and decided to address Trent instead.

"So," Kyle had asked, "how do you justify working for an oil company that is actively driving climate collapse? Is it really as simple as wealth accrual?"

"Whoa there," Trent said, holding up his hands. "Coming in hot."

Jay tipped back his cocktail.

"Kyle," Hannah warned.

"What?" Kyle said. "You said he was in the Federalist Society in law school. I figured he'd be up for a little debate."

"Hey, I'm socially liberal. I support gay rights. At least I'm not a Republican," Trent said.

"Oh come on, you're a lawyer. Don't pretend to be so obtuse as to think that fiscal conservatism is compatible with being 'socially liberal.' And you're a Libertarian, which is arguably worse."

"How is that worse?" Hannah asked.

"Because he thinks it's better," Kyle said.

He backed off after that Libertarian jab, for Jay's sake (well, and after a kick in the shin). Had that one dinner been what led her to uninvite him? He'd thought his friendship with Hannah was still on solid enough ground to weather political differences. At the time, he'd even thought, *Well, at least Trent's pleasant enough*—polite to waiters, perfectly fine at basic conversation. But with the benefit of hindsight, wasn't it actually *worse* that Trent was a nice guy? Somehow more nefarious that he smiled and laughed but spent his days making the world a worse place to live in? Even if he supported "gay rights," Trent had dropped the phrase "no homo" more than once, and that was with Kyle there. What did he say when there were no queer people there? And Hannah?—she just let it all happen.

Maybe Kyle had just been her gay pet. The fruit for the fruit fly. The hag's fag.

As he walked from yoga to the vegan kolache place, Kyle tried calling Hannah again. He considered calling Daniela but didn't want to use her as a messenger like Hannah had, that coward. So he called Jay, who was on his way to a shift at the airport, where he'd fly back and forth from Dallas until he worked his way up to a more optimal route.

"It's basically a millennial hate crime to cold call, you know," Jay said.

Kyle ranted about Hannah for a good ten minutes uninterrupted. He seethed about the encroachment of gay bars by entitled straight women. He couldn't even go to a drag show without fighting through a bachelorette party. Was no space sacred anymore? The same bridal parties that used gays as entertainment looked away—or worse, looked and said nothing—as queer folks systematically had their rights stripped away. Was the irony of celebrating *marriage* at a gay bar, when Obergefell was being debated in the news, lost on them? What a symbolically insipid institution marriage was. For fuck's sake, even watching *RuPaul* had gone from queer escapist fantasy to revenge porn now that it had been infiltrated by breeders. The latest season had a straight dude contestant—what?—just so the show could promote itself as having the first drag queen who couldn't say "faggot" without committing a hate crime?

Jay finally cut him off. "You know I, too, am a *homosexual*, right?" He pronounced it *home-uh-sec-shoe-uhl*. "Girl, either do something about it or get over it. Hang on, I'm going through security."

Kyle wasn't sure what there was *to* do, but he knew he wasn't good at just getting over things. Didn't he have a duty to stand up for himself? For the queer community?

Finally, Jay was back. "I don't know how to help you, girl." A pause, then, hesitantly, "But if you want, you know I can get you a flight out there."

* * *

On Sunday, the seven gals rented Citi bikes and rode along the strand past batido carts and thong bikinis until they arrived at Palace for drag brunch. As soon as they stepped inside, like gay magic, the whole party shifted dialect.

"Yasss queen! This is going to be uh-*mah*-zing!"

"Get it gurliez!"

"Werk bitch, those sunglasses are stunting."

Daniela heard it happen and started studying the program on the table as a reprieve from eye contact.

PALACE
Today's Queens!

Jenny Greg
When this fitness queen isn't using her -2% body fat to bench press bridesmaids, she's personal training at Gold's Gym (or in the steam room).

IG/Venmo: @JennyGregLifts

Daniela looked up when she heard the girls debriefing about the night before. They'd gone to Twist, the gay dance club they'd found on a blog about the best bachelorette party activities in Miami Beach, but things hadn't gone quite to plan. Neither of the Katies had gotten in because they were both wearing sandals (too many broken glass incidents, they were told), and Sophie was turned away because she started drunkenly screaming at the bouncer about the absurdity of such a rule in a beach town. The remaining girls were met with abundant side-eye once inside, and another bachelorette party at the club sucked all the energy out of the room as it colonized the dance floor. Still, that hadn't stopped Hannah's crew from wooo-ing until their feet blistered.

"The guys there weren't exactly friendly," Rebecca said, possibly trying to make the rejects feel better, but more likely having failed to read the room at Twist, Daniela thought.

"I mean, we need a safe space, too," Hannah added. "I guess that's the trade-off for not being hit on."

Daniela looked back down at the program.

Estefania Luz

She's back with a BBL and tits to match! Let's hope she doesn't sweat them pasties off! Or does. ;)

IG/Venmo: @Estefaniaaa

A waiter walked up to their table with a tray of mimosas, wearing the Palace uniform: tan booty shorts and muscle-tight T-shirts emblazoned with the restaurant's motto: *Every queen needs a Palace*. Almost all the waiters were Latino, and Daniela imagined them wondering what she was doing walking around with this flock of blondes.

"Oh my god, he's so cute," Katie K. said less-than-discreetly as the waiter walked away.

"What a waste!" Sophie whisper-yelled, already two shots deep and now searching for meaning in the bottom of her glass.

"Right? All the good ones are either gay or married."

"Or gay married!" Caity C. chimed in.

Sarah Tonin

As long as her Zoloft is slapping, Sarah's slapping back with original bops like Crying in a Wig *and* The Sunken Place (Between My Tits), *now available on iTunes.*

IG/Venmo: @SadSarahTonin

Three other bachelorette parties were seated throughout Palace, and Daniela was sure the brides were sizing each other up. One of the other brides had a picture of her husband-to-be taped to a popsicle stick. Was that a thing? Daniela looked over at Hannah, but she couldn't get a read on her expression behind her oversized Ray Bans.

Sophie waved the waiter back over and asked him how he kept his "badonkadonk" so tight. "A lot of squats and a lot of good sex," he said, humoring her by twerking in her direction before asking if she wanted a refill.

"Okay, read me, henty!" Sophie replied, holding out her glass.

Daniela cringed and dropped her eyes back to the program.

Tiara Monet
She's the dancing queen of Miami Beach, and she's ready to make your head spin.

IG/Venmo: @TiaraMonetMIA

Tonya Hardon
Watch out, or she'll break your shins and then fuck your boyfriend.

IG/Venmo: @ITonyaHardon

The girls ordered their breakfasts—a choice between

psychotically pink guava pancakes, chicken chilaquiles, or eggs benedict—all served with bottomless mimosas. No one ordered the pancakes—too many carbs—but Hannah added on a bottle of Veuve.

"Ugh, I just feel so at home here!" said Rebecca. "I'm basically a gay man trapped in a woman's body."

"Clearly begging to be let out," Hannah said, presumably aiming for snarky but landing on snide.

"A real gay Rachel Dolezal," Daniela added so that Hannah's comment wouldn't just float there, cruel and lifeless.

And your host, the legendary

Tiffani Phenomenon
She's been hosting drag shows since Stonewall, but she's still 39—hope you know your drag her-story!
IG/Venmo: @TiffaniThePhenom

Their food arrived concerningly quickly. The waiters continued to shuttle around pitchers of mimosas that they could almost balance on their perky derrieres. Daniela wasn't sure why she turned in the other direction, but she did, and she was the first to see him. *Fuck.* She didn't have time to intercept as Kyle walked into Palace and slid into his seat at the only table set for one.

* * *

Hannah did a double-take, hoping it was any other twink in a too-tight Target tee and six-inch inseam shorts, but it was Kyle, and he was walking up to her. As soon as she heard his piercing voice, the bubble of her blissed-out vacay weekend popped.

"Hi, Hannah," he said. "Can we talk?"

"What are you doing here," she said. What was this fake casual act he was pulling? He'd just flown out here and led with, "Can we talk?"

"You weren't answering my calls." Kyle wasn't gesticulating like usual, and his voice sounded off, freaky.

"Please leave." It took everything in her to keep her tone quiet. Icy.

"I'm going to watch the show."

"Come on, please? You flew all this way just to make me feel bad?"

"Why did you uninvite me, Hannah? Why'd you kick me out of the party?"

"You know, it's like, certifiable to fly all this way. It's fully unhinged. *Psycho*." She could probably call the police and have him arrested for stalking.

"Come on, Hannah. Be real for once."

"Why do you care so much?" Hannah asked. "It's a bachelorette party. You hate weddings."

"Because we were best friends for years. Because I cared about you. I *loved* you!"

As Hannah heard Kyle deploy the past tense, she realized she'd been using it for years.

"Kyle, come on, I'm not going to do this here. Now."

"Fine. Save it for that homophobic neofascist melted Ken doll that Daddy picked out for you."

He knew how to jab right where it hurt. Two years ago, her father told her he had colon cancer, and six months after that, he was dead. But not before telling her, "Trent is a good man," and to Trent, "Take care of my Hannah." Shortly after, they'd gotten engaged.

"Jesus, Kyle, is this how far you've slid? You're such a social justice warrior now you can't even tolerate the idea of people you disagree with?"

"He voted for Trump!"

"That doesn't by default make him a neofascist. You can't hold every individual accountable for, like, big systemic failures." She huffed. "I'm not having this conversation," Hannah said.

"Classic. Whatever. I guess it makes sense that you'd want one last hoorah before you settle into suburbia with that where-were-you-on-January-sixth, nazi-paraphernalia-collecting oaf. And the drag brunch? The gay clubbing? All of it's just entertainment for you, huh? What, did your dad know RuPaul through fracking or something?"

"Don't fucking talk about my dad."

Her friendship with Kyle had been on life support for years. It made them both look too closely at themselves through each other's eyes—her, a fair-weather liberal, an apologist for conservatives; him, a moralistic bullshitter too convinced of his own oppression to give people a chance. Now, they brought out the worst in each other, which was its own strange and powerful intimacy. Like seeing someone without any skin, their network of nerves exposed, radiating pain at the slightest breeze.

Hannah took a breath. "Kyle, we haven't been 'best friends' in a decade. We were in *high school*. You're too fucking much now. You've *always* been too fucking much. You drag everything down around you. You have to *stop* with this holier-than-thou bullshit!"

Just then, the hot, muggy air thickened with the clapping of wooden hand-held fans, the waiters creating a mechanical chorus that silenced the restaurant. The silhouette of a three-foot beehive wig appeared in the dressing room door, and Palace erupted into applause.

* * *

The table of bachelorettes shifted uncomfortably to make room for Kyle, who was forced into a seat among the party to avoid disturbing the show. The energy between him and Hannah was enough to break Florida off the continent and send it drifting, dick-shaped, into the sea. He felt himself clutch the stem of his mimosa flute like a dagger. He wanted so badly to hurl the sticky elixir in Hannah's face, to watch the orange juice drip out of her overly bleached hair, hair the color of complicity and gentrification and gay best friends, to right the scales of justice by a couple ounces at least. Instead, displaying heroic restraint, he tipped his glass back into his mouth and gestured for a refill. Then another.

Kyle's stomach churned as Tiffani Phenomenon floated down the aisle to the front of the room like a seven-foot-tall linebacker walking en pointe, a huge sequin purple train trailing behind her.

"Oh my god, is that Bob the Drag Queen?" asked Caity C.

Rebecca delicately corrected her, saying they just had similar makeup, but Kyle knew the only thing Tiffani had in common with Bob was her skin tone.

Kyle drank some more, then focused his attention back on Tiffani as she announced the performers. A queen in knee-high bright-pink stripper heel boots held together by matching duct tape climbed up a structural support pillar and death-dropped eight feet to the ground. Even through his velvet rage, Kyle gay-gasped. The next danced an athletic salsa, culminating in so many in-place cartwheels Kyle felt like he was staring into a windmill. Estefania Lux racked up tips by dancing with the bride at another table, twerking her BBL'ed ass on the bride, then twerking away when the bride grabbed what she presumably thought was a breastplate but was actually Estefania's tit, as revealed by a burlesque number ending in nothing but tasseled pasties. To get through all of it, through the *yas queens* and *werk hentys* and *oh no she betta don'ts* from the crowd, Kyle searched for the bottom of his bottomless mimosas.

After half an hour of dancing numbers and lip syncs, Tiffani was back in the center of the room, announcing an intermission to refill drinks and take out more cash for tips. Now was his chance. Kyle stood up, walked over to Tiffani, and slid the bedazzled mic from her acrylic claws.

"I've got something to say," he said.

"This isn't an open mic, honey," Tiffani chided to hesitant chuckles from the audience. "Come on down from there." But Kyle was already climbing onto the table he'd abandoned, ready to deliver his polemic from this makeshift pulpit.

"I've got something to say," he said again, gathering his thoughts in a final swig of mimosa, his vision blurred and his moral certainty coming into focus.

"Let me tell you something about appropriation," he began. The audience groaned, but he went on. By the time Kyle would board his plane in a few hours, aching and ashamed, it would all blur together. But he remembered talking about the bachelorette party drag show industrial complex. The antiquated, patriarchal financial institution of marriage. The banned books, the bathroom bills, the slow trans runner who wasn't even allowed to lose. "And this fucking minstrel show?" he added—this he would regret later, reflecting on how Tiffani had put her hands on her padded hips in the Tik Tok video— "All these talented queer people performing their art for a bunch of drunk bridesmaids, and you're handing out *ones*?"

Then, as the waiters and queens mulled around below him, some snapping along and others with arms crossed, he turned to Hannah. The purportedly well-intentioned suburban white girl, the most insidious of them all, just out there collecting her tokens. But just as Kyle was about to reach his apotheosis, to bridge the gap between personal and political, to connect this drag brunch to the broader systemic flaws it represented, his foot slipped off the edge of the table.

As he tumbled to the floor, Kyle's eyes met Hannah's, and he saw that she was a stranger to him now, maybe always had been. She just stood, frozen, watching the show. Tiffani lunged forward and broke Kyle's fall, his head landing on her glittered arms and his gaze on the ceiling, which was painted with a re-creation of the Sistine Chapel. But here, Adam had been rendered as a muscular jock, blessedly better endowed, his outstretched finger reaching toward a long purple nail that, when Kyle traced it back to its source, revealed that God herself was a drag queen.

* * *

Discussion Questions

1. Hannah's mother refused to give her $100,000 for the wedding and bachelorette party if Kyle was a bridesman. What should Hannah have done in response to this threat? Is Hannah allowed to be self-focused on her wedding day?

2. Can morals be implemented sporadically, or must they always be followed? Could Hannah have excluded Kyle from the wedding but donated $20,000 from the wedding coffers to the Human Rights Campaign and have that be considered a moral compromise?

3. Given the story's facts, how would you describe Hannah's support of LGBTQ equality?

4. What should Kyle have done in response to being excluded from the bachelorette party? Does he have a duty to stand up for himself and the queer community by flying to Miami to confront Hannah with her hypocrisy? Is that why he is doing it?

5. Are drag shows, minstrel shows? If the majority of the people in a drag show are straight, does that then make it a minstrel show?

The Walnut Tree

Michael Shainsky

* * *

When they told him at work that he'd be accompanying a group of American tourists, Nikolay wasn't particularly excited. This coming Saturday happened to be his only chance to take his car in for servicing. Sergey, his mechanic, had Sundays off, and it was high time somebody changed the oil.

Maybe I'll manage to find time during the week, Nikolay figured, *get off work early and change it. Come to think of it, how can one ever find the time for work, day-to-day routine, and on top of it all, self-improvement? And time isn't the only thing in short supply—what about money for Mark's private school? And diamond earrings for the wife on our fifteenth anniversary? And I need it all right now, not sometime in the future when the time or money happens to turn up. Damned if I know. One thing is clear—you've got to balance it all, stay on top of things all the time. Or life will kick you downhill all the way.*

Nikolay was a manager at Vostok tour operator. He was his own boss, true, but recently there had been a lot of work.

Tourists came in droves, wanting to visit the famous cities of Uzbekistan: Samarkand, Bukhara, Khiva. And, of course, Tashkent—the capital, where Nikolay's company was located. Nikolay's primary responsibility was to coordinate logistics: pickups and drop-offs at the airports, booking hotels, buses, attractions, and restaurants, coordinating local guides and tour directors, and designing tour itineraries. Sometimes he had to accompany tour groups himself, especially when they needed someone who spoke English.

Saturday would be just that kind of day. At twenty to nine in the morning, he drove up to the Hilton Tashkent City hotel, parked his car, and walked around the building to the spot where tour buses collected and dropped off their cargos of tourists.

The bus his company had chartered for the trip was already parked there. Kudrat, the bus driver, saw Nikolay, got out of the bus, and shook hands with him. They had worked together a few times before and were on good terms. Kudrat was a good guy and a pro. He was the head of a large, traditional Uzbek family, and tips—especially in US dollars—were a serious boon to the family's financial well-being.

It looked like the whole group was there, and Nikolay began distributing name tags. Yes, everything checked out; no one was missing. Nikolay always appreciated the American habit of punctuality.

Today's destination was the famous mountain beauty spot Lake Urunghach. This was the penultimate day of the group's two-week visit to Uzbekistan. The plan for the next day was a farewell excursion around Tashkent, and on Monday, they would fly back home. Before such a long, taxing flight, it would be a good idea to have some R&R outdoors. The tour director assigned to that group, who had been with them for the whole itinerary, had called in sick, so Nikolay was asked to take them to the lake. There, he would organize a barbecue for them and then take them back into town in the evening. That would give the tourists a whole day off, with no obligatory sightseeing.

Or very little.

Their first stop was Tepar, a village in the mountains, about an hour and a half outside the city.

The bus stopped at the end of a gravel road on an empty, unpaved patch of ground. The twenty-first century seemed to have bypassed Tepar altogether. There were no traffic signs or lights on its narrow, winding streets. Not that there was much need for them—most of the traffic consisted of dogs, sheep, and goats, which would have been oblivious to them anyway. A lone rooster ran out onto the road, chased by a boy, who deftly grabbed it by the tail then took it away—probably home—leaving just a few feathers to drift to the ground.

The houses here were made of adobe bricks. Quite unprepossessing on the outside and fairly basic inside, these houses provided shelter for the village's three hundred or so inhabitants. Tepar was famous for its delicious mountain honey and incomparable apples, but lately, the livelihood of the villagers had come to depend more and more on tourism. With the rise of the Internet, people had started coming here in droves to see the main attraction of the area—a giant walnut tree.

Today was no different. About forty people got off Nikolay's bus and immediately went to browse in the quaint gift shops that had popped up, one after another, in response to the growing demand.

The hottest items were painted models of the walnut tree, fashioned to scale from clay, along with numerous likenesses of the famous tree on posters and in paintings by local artists. *As always,* thought Nikolay, *demand for the arts stimulated artistry. Be it in Florence during the Renaissance, in classical Vienna, or here in Tepar.*

The studio of a glassblower was also popular among tourists. Here, eighty-eight-year-old Saeed-aka, a master artisan, crafted glass vases, carafes, and pots with the image of the tree branded on them. Awestruck, the visitors took photos and videos of the birth of these fragile pieces of art. The most prized and sought-after item of all, however, was a foot-tall glass sculpture of the walnut tree. It was like crystal, sparkling and glittering in the light—like divine beauty itself—arresting the gaze and, it seemed, able to touch one's very soul. Thanks to the pictures featured in travel magazines and on websites, Saeed-aka could barely keep up with the orders, selling some to visitors and shipping others to different corners of the world.

Among the simple adobe houses stood a visitor's center. Inside, was a framed, blown-up copy of a page from *The Guinness Book of World Records* depicting the tree with the inscription: "The largest walnut tree in the world. Location: The Village of Tepar, Uzbekistan." In the middle of the building's only room was a guestbook on a stand with a few pens lying next to it. In the guestbook, visitors had written their names, the countries they came from, and occasional comments. A hand-written note on the opened page read: "We visited Saeed's glassblowing shop, and it blew us away! He also sings while weaving his magic. Uzbeks are talented and noble folk. This blessed land seems to give birth to generous and happy people, some of the best fruit on the planet, and great singing voices with rich overtones—a befitting reflection of their rich soul."

An hour or so later, Nikolay gathered the group by the visitor's center and announced: "And now we're going to meet the actual star of the show. Follow me, and I'll show you the famous walnut tree itself." He took the tourists down the narrow and winding central street. The weather was stunningly beautiful. Unpleasantly hot days were rare at the beginning of summer in Uzbekistan, and in the village of Tepar, some six thousand feet above sea level, it was blissfully mild.

Walking in single file, keeping to the side of the cobblestone road, the tourists snapped pictures of domestic animals, which stubbornly refused to yield to the occasional car or bicycle. Toward the end of the main drag, a short unpaved driveway peeled off to ascend a moderately steep hill. As the visitors made it to the top, a small adobe house came into view. In front of it stood an enormous walnut tree in all its splendor. It was so big that it dwarfed the house. The canopy of the tree overhung the rather large yard and a barn a hundred feet away. Like the tentacles of a giant octopus, some of its branches even reached over to the neighboring houses across the street.

In the shade of the tree, an old man was sitting on an *ayvan*, a large, low wooden platform. The platform was covered with a thin, colorful cushion, and in the middle of it stood a low wooden table. Children ran around, laughing and cheering. Occasionally, a grownup would intervene, telling them to quiet down. The noise would subside for a while but soon resume at an even higher volume. One after another, neighbors, relatives, and kids went up to the old man to wish him a good day.

Laughter hung in the air, and the joy was genuine and infectious.

The group approached the old man, and Nikolay introduced him. "Ladies and gentlemen, please meet the owner of this fabled house, Mr. Azamat-aka Muradov, who turned one hundred and two in March." The assembled group applauded. Nikolay then exchanged a few words with the old man and allowed the tourists twenty minutes for pictures. The beautiful mountain lake was just a half-hour's drive away.

As soon as they had left behind the last house on the main street, a mountain pass rose up in front of them. The bus began to climb it at a rapid clip, but suddenly, Kudrat glanced at the dashboard. A red blinking light had come on.

"Something's wrong?" asked Nikolay.

"The engine is overheating," Kudrat said, his voice betraying a certain tenseness. He drove a bit further, then pulled over and shut off the engine. "I'm going to take a look." He took a pair of gloves from the glove compartment, opened the door, and got out.

Nikolay grabbed the microphone to inform the passengers that they had encountered a technical issue. He and the driver would take a look at it, and hopefully, they would be on their way shortly.

He followed Kudrat off the bus. The driver was standing at the back of the vehicle by the engine compartment. He had opened the hatch and was shining a flashlight inside. He examined some hoses and joints, touched the couplings here and there, making sure there were no leaks, then returned to the cab to start the engine. The temperature gauge began to crawl up. Leaving the engine running, Kudrat got out and quickly walked back around the bus. He peered at the running engine.

Suddenly, he pointed at the radiator and said to Nikolay, "Look, the fan isn't running!" He then ran to the cab and shut off the engine.

The tourists had already left the bus, which was too hot to stay inside without the AC, and were milling around. Kudrat called his company and conferred with someone on the other end for a long time.

Meanwhile, Nikolay announced that the bus company was going to send a mechanic soon and asked everybody not to venture out onto the road. People began strolling up and down the side of the street, chatting.

An hour passed. The midday sun had grown fairly hot, and the tourists, one after another, made runs inside the bus to grab the bottles of water stored in a cooler on the rear seats.

An older man came up to Nikolay, asking him where he could find a restroom. Normally, Nikolay's tour company used buses with an onboard toilet, but this bus didn't have one since it wasn't a long trip. *For Pete's sake,* he thought to himself, *if this guy were Russian, he'd just go behind the bushes and be done with it!*

They walked down the side of the road in the direction of the village they had just left. After about ten minutes, they came across a gate in an adobe wall surrounding a house. As he knocked on the gate, Nikolay noticed that the man was hopping from foot to foot. "Just a few more moments," he told the man and knocked harder. An old woman opened the gate. She immediately guessed what the trouble was and motioned to them to come inside.

"Come on in, come on in," she said.

"It's just him." Nikolay nodded at the other fellow.

"That's all right," said the woman. "You come on in, too."

Nikolay declined, not wanting to bother their hosts. He explained that their bus had broken down—just up the hill a ways—and they were waiting for the mechanic to arrive. He glanced in the direction of the bus, and suddenly his jaw dropped—the entire group was marching downhill toward him.

The group was already approaching. Nikolay had begun to collect himself, having come to terms with the unavoidable, when he received a second shock, far more jarring than the first: an enormous tractor wheel was rolling downhill, headed straight for the group. Nikolay began to shout and wave, warning the people to get out of the way and move to the side of the road. Only one man, walking quickly ahead of the rest, failed to heed Nikolay's warnings. Just as he reached Nikolay, even before he could ask where the bathroom was, the huge wheel sped past like a juggernaut, nearly grazing his back. The old woman, now in a state of shock herself, pointed inside the house with a trembling hand, and the man made a dash for it.

"Was *that* part of your bus?" she asked Nikolay.

The rest of the group stopped by the gate. Sensing that the danger had passed (but glancing at the mountain pass every now and then—what if there was another wheel on the way?), Nikolay addressed the group.

"You know, the only facilities here are inside this home. Let's not inconvenience the hosts with so many people. How about we wait for those two gentlemen to come out and then go back to the Walnut Tree House? They know us already, and there are public toilets right in the backyard."

When the two men returned, Nikolay thanked the old woman profusely and led the group down the street, occasionally glancing behind him in case there were any other surprises coming their way. A few moments later, he noticed that Kudrat was hurrying to catch up with them. "They say they can't get in touch with the mechanic," he said, panting. "It's Saturday; he probably turned off his phone. Said they'd send another bus. They'll call back when they find one. None of ours are available. They're trying other companies."

At the Walnut Tree House, Azamat-aka was sitting cross-legged on the *ayvan* and speaking animatedly to a group of young children that had gathered around him. They sat on the platform with him like little ducklings, all wearing neat uniforms, and listened intently, their mouths agape. Now and then, the old man sipped tea from a shallow bowl that he regularly refilled from a small teapot. "And so we picked the walnuts and sent them to the frontline," Azamat-aka continued. "And on every bag, we wrote: 'For Victory!'"

Lowering his voice, Nikolay told the group, "These are kids from the local elementary school. Their teacher brought them over to learn the story of the walnut tree from Azamat-aka."

A few older kids raced around in the yard, playing and enjoying themselves. When Azamat-aka had finished his story, the younger kids jumped down from the *ayvan* and joined the older kids running around in the yard. From time to time, grownups came through the gate to take some of the children away or just to greet the old man. *Must be neighbors*, thought Nikolay.

The old man was very wrinkled and thin but full of vim and vigor. Like a magnet, he attracted more and more visitors. A teenager came up to the old man and greeted him respectfully, followed by an adult, who approached the old man and hugged and kissed him. It was clear that these encounters were heartfelt, and all parties were happy to exchange a few words.

A little while later, Nikolay asked for the group's attention. He announced that the driver had just spoken to the bus company and they were looking for a replacement bus. "I'm sure you're hungry," he added. "Let me see how I can organize lunch for you." He walked off and talked to the hostess for a few minutes. Then they both approached the old man to confer with him. Nikolay returned to the group. "Here's the plan. There's some barbecue meat on the bus, some greens for a salad, and beverages. The hosts have been kind enough to offer us the use of their barbecue grill. We will be able to have lunch right in the shade of this magnificent walnut tree. How do you like that idea?"

The tourists applauded.

"Excellent. And so that we don't have to carry the coolers ourselves, our generous hosts have also offered to let us use their donkey cart. Anyone volunteer to be the donkey?" People laughed, and some hands went up. "Just kidding." Nikolay motioned toward the corner of the house, where a cart harnessed to an irresistibly cute donkey was standing. "Please meet Dennis the Donkey." Everyone clapped in excitement and began taking pictures of the animal. Dennis, apparently unused to such a ruckus, started braying and backing away, nearly smashing the cart into a clay oven. A teenage boy, probably a relative of the hosts, dashed over to the skittish animal and tugged on the reins until Dennis calmed and stood still. Nikolay hopped into the cart, and they started off, Kudrat walking alongside.

About half an hour later, the three of them returned to the Walnut Tree House and were greeted with another round of applause. Dennis pulled the cart, now loaded down with the big cooler and crates of beverages. Nikolay and Kudrat walked beside it, carrying another large cooler by the handles. They unloaded everything next to the barbecue grill and, with the help of Azamat-aka's great-grandson, lit up the coals. Soon the wonderful aroma of shish kebab began to spread around the yard.

It wasn't long before Nikolay summoned the tourists to help themselves to the meat. They came up one by one, forming a small line. Having worked with groups of American tourists, Nikolay had always admired how organized and well-behaved they were.

Everyone took a skewer with meat and a piece of flatbread and served themselves salad on a disposable plate. Then they each took a beer or some soda and began eating with gusto, sitting on the grass beneath the tree, clearly enjoying themselves. Evidently, everyone was happy with the simple but delicious menu.

As evening approached and it grew darker, the smoke from the grill grew whiter. Almost imperceptibly, a velvety summer evening seemed to steal in beside them underneath the enormous walnut tree. Cool, crystal-clear air wafted down from the mountains around the village and filled the lungs.

The hosts turned on a few lights. Now there were fewer kids playing in the yard, but adults kept coming in and out.

Nikolay conferred with Kudrat now and then, but the news from the bus company was far from encouraging. They couldn't find a replacement bus, and they said that if one didn't become available soon, they would send a dozen cabs instead.

The tourists didn't seem to mind the change of plans. Their collective mood improved steadily as the number of empty beer cans grew. Nikolay took a few skewers of meat to the old man and invited his family to join the feast.

Everybody seemed to be in high spirits. Soon, a large wineskin appeared on a table near the barbecue grill. The old man had asked his great-grandson to bring it out. The tourists started helping themselves to the wine. Full and happy, some even tipsy, they began to approach the old man one by one. With Nikolay's help, they asked him about his life and about the tree.

By now, it was completely dark. Only a few bulbs cast their light on isolated patches of the yard. The illuminated branches of the tree appeared mysterious, almost mythical. The giant canopy seemed to stretch into the sky and merge with it, touching the stars.

When the party was in full swing, the lights suddenly went out. There was confusion, then silence. Nikolay went to find out what the problem was and when they expected the power to return. Nobody could say. Thirty minutes passed, then an hour. There was still no electricity. Then a neighbor came over and said that the problem was with the power generator and that the power wouldn't be restored until morning.

Tepar had its own hydroelectric station, occupying a small wooden booth on a riverbank. The container was painted toxic green and housed a generator the size of a microwave oven, which was driven by the water from the river, diverted via a pipe that poured it over the blades.

A few boys were sent to the local grocery store with

Dennis, the cart again harnessed to him, to pick up some empty boxes and crates lying around outside. They returned no more than a quarter of an hour later. The donkey and cart were so loaded up that the poor animal was barely visible. In the magic of the summer night, amplified even more by the smoke swirling around the barbecue, one could easily have imagined that the boxes and crates were moving on their own. The only giveaway was Dennis's long ears.

In pitch darkness, occasionally cut by the flashlights of cellphones, the boys placed a few boxes and crates next to the barbecue grill and lit them. The fire slowly began to catch, growing and growing in size and intensity.

Then a group of musicians arrived. They were young people, members of a local folk ensemble. They played an assortment of national instruments, including two huge *karnays*—ten-foot-long brass horns, whose bellowing could wake the dead. All of them wore modern clothes, mostly jeans and T-shirts. Settling not far from the fire, the musicians began playing and singing popular Uzbek folk songs, primarily dance tunes. Nikolay learned later that they had been sent by the bus company.

The *karnays* pointed into the sky and roared so that the glass in the windows trembled. The tourists had never before seen or heard anything like this. Quite inebriated by now, they began dancing, trying to copy the moves of the intricate national dance through which their hosts were weaving. Their attempts looked fairly comical, yet natural enough. The fire flared higher and higher, and gradually the area around it became as bright as day.

At one moment during a break between songs, one of the

tourists came up to Nikolay and asked him to translate. He wanted to talk to the old man. The tourist, who looked to be about forty, had blond hair and was tall, well-built and in excellent shape. They found the old man sitting cross-legged on the *ayvan*, just as he had been before. And just as before, he poured tea from a small china pot and sipped it. But this time, the tea shone a deep red in the blaze of the fire.

"Wine? You want?" the old man asked when he saw Nikolay and the tourist.

The tourist was dumbfounded. "You speak English?"

"Nah," the old man continued in Russian and nodded to Nikolay, prompting him to interpret for him. "Just know a word or two. The most important ones." He winked at them and poured some wine into two very small, shallow bowls. "Please, have a seat. What brings you here?"

"Good evening," said the tourist. "I'm Steve. I hope you don't mind my asking, sir, but how do you manage to look so youthful and to be so full of life and joy at such a venerable age?"

"It's very simple. It's all because of the tree," the old man said, pointing at the enormous canopy above the house.

"The tree?"

"Yes, yes, the tree."

"You mean I need to plant a tree in order to be happy? I already have several in my yard."

"And they don't help?"

"No, sir. Even a big house with a pool, several luxury cars, and vacations six times a year don't help." Steve sipped some wine from the tiny bowl. "I feel pretty miserable when I'm not at work. And even work is more like a distraction from the misery. It's not something I truly love."

The wine had started to go to his head, and although he knew he had gotten a bit carried away, he somehow trusted the old man. He sensed that Azamat-aka had a large and open heart and that he was not afraid for it to be disturbed. And unlike people with small hearts—barely big enough for themselves— he was not going to brush Steve off or make an excuse and leave. So, Steve continued his improvised confession, getting more and more fired up.

"Where I come from, people don't talk to each other much... except through a lawyer. I am only forty-two, and I already feel like an old man. Totally overfed, over-entertained, and lacking a purpose in life. And lonely. Living my life for nothing, feeling neither joy nor heartache. Now, tell me, how is it that you don't seem to have any of the things that I have—you barely have anything at all—and yet you are happy and surrounded by so many people?"

After this outpouring, both men were quiet for a while. Then Azamat-aka began to speak.

"Once upon a time, when I was a little boy helping my father tend this very yard, I planted a walnut seed in this soil. Right in this soil." The old man pointed down, then folded his palms in front of his face as a sign of gratitude to God. "I watered it, and after some time, it sprouted. My joy was boundless. It grew as I grew. It grew so big that it provided plenty of shade on hot summer days, and the villagers would come to gather underneath it. Then the war broke out. Even though there was no fighting here, we all felt the pain of it. Many of our children went to war and never came back. We gathered under the tree and prayed. Food grew scarce, and people came to eat the walnuts. They would take some home, grind them into flour, mix the flour with water from the river, and bake flatbread. That's how the whole village survived the war. My children, their children, and now the grandchildren and great-grandchildren all grew up under this tree. They all came to understand that the tree was very special, strong and beautiful, growing bigger and bigger, and that its strength helped many people. The villagers found shelter under it after an earthquake that nearly destroyed the whole village. They were afraid to go back to what remained of their homes in case there were more quakes, and they slept under the tree for the whole summer that year. It became the heart of the village. After the fear had settled, people still gathered here to talk and share their news, to drink homemade wine. Children from the entire neighborhood came to play and study under this tree. Then, long after they grew up, they still returned from cities and towns around the world to say hello and to treat themselves to walnuts and drink wine with me."

The old man poured more wine into the bowls.

"You have it all figured out, don't you?" said Steve, scratching his head, surprised and bewildered. "You are quite an accomplished man. You seem to have no loose ends in your life. Or are there? Is there anything else you would like to accomplish?"

"Yes, there is. I want to learn English."

"English? Here in this village?"

"Yes, in this village. Every day, we have more tourists, and no one around here speaks English. They're opening a hotel soon. We already have two restaurants. An art gallery. Donkey rides. We need an English teacher."

Just as Steve, with the edge of his imagination, pictured

himself in this role, a resonant female voice rang out:

"I'll be happy to teach English." A girl, laughing, approached the old man and kissed him on the cheek. "And you'll be sitting next to the fifth-graders in my class." The girl looked no older than thirty, perhaps thirty-two at most. She had a pretty, round face and long black hair. Her white sundress, cinched at the waist with a thin black leather belt, outlined her absolutely amazing figure. She exchanged a few words with the old man in Uzbek, and then, noticing Steve's spellbound gaze resting on her, she spoke to him. In perfect English. "Good evening. How are you?" Steve was awestruck. He couldn't take his eyes off her—which was obvious to everyone, including the girl. There was an awkward pause.

"You... speak English?" Steve said, trying to regain his composure.

"On occasion," the girl replied, laughing. "I'm doing a master's degree in Cambridge. I'm home for a visit on the summer break."

Steve was so stunned that he nearly put his foot in it by saying, "May I stay with you for your summer break, too?" He pulled himself together, however, and said, "A master's degree, huh? Wow."

"Yes, I just have one semester left," the girl said. She looked at Steve with curiosity. "I'm flying back the day after tomorrow. Well, I have to go now. Nice meeting you!"

"Nice meeting you too! Hope to see you again someday," Steve said, mesmerized, watching the girl as she left.

"My great-granddaughter," the old man said proudly. "Our Sevara's a smart girl. Beautiful, too."

At that moment, a loud scream and what seemed like the

sound of dishes breaking could be heard coming from the house.

"What was that?" Steve said, startled.

"Oh, don't pay any attention to it. That's just my older brother causing trouble. He always does that when he has a bit too much wine," said the old man.

Oh, thought Steve, *so that's it! That's the secret formula for a long and happy life. Authentic human interaction mixed with pristine air, water, and a little bit of wine. Not too much, though...* He grinned. Then, as though in a trance, he left to find a quiet spot, took out his phone, and dialed a number.

"Jack? Hi. Listen, I'm not coming back. Sell the law firm, or run it yourself."

The musicians struck up another tune. There was still no sign of the bus, but the tourists didn't seem to care. They had forgotten all about the broken bus and the lake and were having the time of their lives. Billows of aromatic smoke once again filled the yard, and a light breeze carried the enticing scent into the neighborhood. The hosts were cooking pilaf on a wood stove. With lamb! Ah! And mutton drippings! Mmm! Another wineskin appeared next to the large cauldron.

Steve had just poured himself some more wine and taken a few sips when he felt his cell phone vibrate. The music was so loud that it overpowered the ringing. The phone buzzed in his pocket, in sync with the stirring tune. He answered the phone with his standard "Steven Hotchkins speaking," but he couldn't hear the other party. He asked the caller to hold and quickly walked toward the gate. When he was outside the yard on the street, he was finally able to make out the voice of his partner on the other end of the line. "Steve," he said, "it's obviously up to you, it's your life, but we may have a multimillion-dollar case coming our way."

"Is that so?" said Steve. "What kind of case?"

"A lady stopped by the office yesterday. It seems her husband came home and discovered that her favorite lap dog had bitten their old gardener on the hand. The gardener tried to shake it off and accidentally tore the little bow on its head. The wife demanded that the husband fire the gardener, pronto, screaming that she'd spent half the afternoon tying that bow so nicely, to which the husband replied that her dog was just as much of a bitch as she was. She got mad—at the insult to the dog!—and filed for divorce. Wants to take *everything* from her very rich husband. And you know who else stands to get a good portion of that *everything*."

"Oh? You mean you didn't give her a bottle of wine, then tell her to go home and drink it with her husband and forget about the whole thing?" Steve said, chuckling.

"Yeah, well, quit fooling around. We're talking serious cash here. Come back." His partner hung up.

At any other time, Steve would have found this story amusing. But not now. He stood alone on the narrow winding street, inhaling the heady smells of the summer evening. Sounds of revelry were still coming from the Walnut Tree House, but the rest of the village was dark and quiet. Steve stood there, lost in thought. His whole life passed before his eyes. Was it too late to try living it another way? What if the best part was still ahead of him?

A bus trundled up to the house, slowly and silently, and stopped by the driveway. The driver jumped down and walked up the hill toward the Walnut Tree House. Steve snapped out of his reverie, looked at the bus, then at the figure of the driver getting smaller and smaller as he neared the house, and thought, *I guess it just wasn't meant to be.* Then he, too, walked back up the driveway.

As he approached, the music grew louder; he could hear people calling out. When he entered the yard, he froze in disbelief. The flames from the bonfire seemed to reach up to the sky. To the accompaniment of the music, people from his tour group were jumping through the fire in what resembled a frenzied, ritualistic dance. One of them held a tambourine in his hands. He took a running start and jumped through the conflagration, all the while shaking the tambourine and howling something in an unknown tongue. Another tourist turned out to be a fire-breather. He broke off a board from a burning crate with a single blow of his palm, grabbed hold of it, and stuck it, still aflame, in his mouth. Light shone through his eyes, smoke came out of his ears, and the hair on his head stood on end. A woman of about fifty in tight leggings—probably a former circus acrobat or maybe a gymnast—also took a running start and jumped over the fire, cartwheeling through the air. She was holding a plate of pilaf in her hands and didn't spill a single morsel of rice. Dennis, the donkey, was bobbing his head and braying in sync with the music, pausing only to drink from a pan. Azamat-aka's five-year-old great-grandson regularly refilled the pan with beer from a can.

Steve stood by the gate next to the bus driver who had just arrived. Steve cast his gaze on him and, in the flickering of the bonfire, saw his eyes had grown so wide that he looked more like a horse than a human being.

It took Nikolay a great deal of effort and persuasion to put a stop to this bacchanalia and begin to herd everyone onto the bus. Some had to be carried by their arms and legs, others had to be dragged, while others managed to walk on their own two feet, albeit unsteadily.

The following Monday, Nikolay and Kudrat took the group to the Tashkent International Airport. The tourists were ecstatic with their impressions of Uzbekistan in general, and especially with their aborted trip to the lake. Both the driver and the guide received generous tips. They thanked the tourists from the bottom of their hearts and wished them a safe flight.

Only when he got into a cab at the airport to go home could Nikolay take a deep breath. Finally, he could relax. All the stress, which was almost a given on these trips, was behind him. Yet again, he had left a tiny bit of his soul with strangers and had made them happier. But was *he* happy?

From the cab, Nikolay called Sergey, the mechanic, to find out whether it would be possible for him to change the oil in his car today. Listening to the phone ring, he thought, *It's unlikely. The guy is always working, day and night.* A woman, probably his wife, picked up the phone. She was sobbing, and her speech was barely intelligible, but she managed to convey the news that Sergey had passed away the night before after suffering a heart attack.

Nikolay let out a sob of grief.

"What's the matter?" said the cab driver.

"Someone I know died. Unexpectedly."

They drove in silence for a while. Then the driver said, "Could happen to any of us."

"Yes," said Nikolay. "At any moment, everything could come to an end." And, lowering his voice as though talking to himself, he added, "So, be kind to others, don't expect anything in return, and live life to its fullest."

Steve was on his way to check in for his flight. He thought about Sevara, the old man, the windfall legal case, and his loneliness. The check-in line was short, and he had plenty of time to spare. After he had checked his luggage, keeping only his small backpack with him, he slowly wended his way through the airport, following the "To All Gates" signs. He felt listless and lacking in purpose.

Suddenly, in one of the hallways, he saw ahead of him a tall, slender woman with long black hair in a white sundress. *Could it be her?* he wondered, and his heart began to race. Pushing people out of his way, apologizing left and right, he hurried toward the receding figure. She melted into the crowd a few times, only to reemerge again. He would recognize her anywhere: that white sundress, that waistline, and that long black hair! Speeding up, Steve bumped into an old man in a traditional Uzbek robe pushing a cart full of melons. The melons spilled out, rolling all over the floor. The old man yelled something at him, and though Steve did not understand a word, he guessed these were mainly four-letter. While he was apologizing and helping chase down the melons, *she* disappeared. Steve ran down the hallway, not knowing which direction to choose. Eventually, he realized all his efforts were in vain. He took off his backpack, threw it on the floor, and sat down on it in despair, lost and dejected. People walked around him, keeping their distance.

He was brought back to reality by a young woman tripping over him and nearly falling, who voiced her annoyance in a language much like that of the old man with the melons.

Steve realized he had been sitting in the doorway to a ladies' room. He got up and walked away, absentmindedly looking around, searching for signs to the boarding gates. Suddenly, right in front of him, out of nowhere, Sevara appeared.

"Oh, it's you! Are you leaving, too?" she said, surprised.

"Hi," said Steve, astonished, looking her straight in the eye. And after a short pause, he added, "Yes, I'm leaving too."

She returned his stare with her large, pitch-black eyes. Her gaze was so intense that he felt his head start to spin.

"Isn't it incredible! Just two days ago, you said we'd see each other again someday, and here we are," Sevara exclaimed. "When's your flight?"

"Not for a while yet."

"Mine's been delayed." She looked at him as though studying him.

"Want to grab something to eat?" Steve said.

"What a lovely idea. It's lunchtime."

They found a small restaurant and sat down. There were very few customers. The waiter promptly brought green tea, hot, fragrant flatbread, and fresh herbs. Steve and Sevara settled into a conversation. At first, there was some awkwardness, as though each party understood that this brief encounter at the airport would be the last. But gradually, as they learned more and more about each other, the conversation livened up.

They sat and ate, lost in conversation—two travelers at a crossroads, reveling in the joy of discovery.

They barely noticed the passage of time. Eventually, their conversation took a more practical turn.

"What are your plans after you graduate?" Steve asked.

"I'll return to the village and teach English in the local

school."

"Oh, come on! With a Cambridge degree?"

"I know it sounds strange. They offered me a teaching job at Cambridge, and even closer to home, at Tashkent University. The salary is decent. They say I could be on my way to professorship. But... it's just not for me. I want to be useful to the people in my village."

"Interesting," Steve said. "When you decide on a job, you choose people over pay. We mostly choose money."

"You too?"

"Yes, me too. At least, I used to..."

"And now?"

"Not anymore. Money, success—it's a lost cause. When you finally get to the end of the race, you find there's no happiness there."

"Where is it, then?"

At that moment their conversation was interrupted by a loud flight announcement. When it quieted down, Sevara asked, "When did you say your flight was?"

"It's already gone," said Steve, totally calm. "And yours?"

"Mine too."

Both remained silent. She looked intently into his blue eyes and he into her black.

* * *

Discussion Questions

1. What do you think happens next in the story? What is Steve's future? Sevara's?
2. Why do you think the tourists had more fun at the Walnut Tree than they likely would have had at the lake? Why do you think tourists are more likely to sign up for a lake trip than a meal and drinks under a walnut tree?
3. Why do people often prioritize possessions over connections and experiences if we know connections and experiences bring us happiness?
4. Do you think Nikolay had a good time as well, overseeing the tourists and the bus repairs? What was different about Nikolay's and the tourist's experiences?
5. Do you think there are people in the village that are as unhappy as Steve, or is unhappiness a big city problem? What actions are required to try living another way?

The Pill

Thea Swanson

* * *

Marlee stopped taking the pill when she was fifty-two. She had been bleeding each month—albeit hardly and close to tar—so she figured she was fertile, sort of, that something would attach itself to her uterine lining even if not completely thriving. She thought herself to be a woman who could have babies easily and forever if she didn't take measures. She had had two, and each one had been planned insofar as the condom was removed that month for that purpose, and one spermatozoon had made contact both times on the first try, digging their pushy little heads into her waiting eggs so that the following month, the test read positive. At her recent mandatory checkup with her new primary doctor, Marlee went over the facts of her body quickly to get the meeting over with, and when mentioning the pill and then receiving the pause, Marlee said, "I'm still bleeding," and was told, "That's because you're taking the pill," and Marlee said, "Oh."

Marlee was not stupid. She had earned a master's degree

in business administration and had applied decades of fundraising expertise in development offices in Seattle. Moreover, she acquired great wisdom, leading and sometimes winning household wars for close to thirty years. The correct day to stop the pill was not on her mind. When Marlee was thirty-eight, she learned she was anemic from bleeding too much, and the pill lightened the flow. Who knew the reason she had pressed her cheek to the kitchen counter was not from cooking yet another meal but from oxygen deficiency? The pill allowed her to do many, many tasks.

Her new doctor typed Marlee's spoken data in her digital record.

"I'll stop then," Marlee said.

"Your hormone replacement therapy could be pills—the most common, but there are patches and creams too." The doctor peered at the screen. "You don't have high blood pressure or any—"

"Can't I just stop taking the pill?"

The doctor regrouped. "You could, but you may find the sudden change difficult. You might find the hot flashes and night sweats unbearable."

"I've been having night sweats for years."

"Then you're probably already perimenopausal. You could try it and see how it goes." The doctor tapped the keyboard. "If you suffer too much, we can look at your HRT options." The doctor stopped typing and looked straight at Marlee, causing her to straighten her sitting posture. "After one full year without a period, you will not need protection from pregnancy. Use something else in the meantime."

Marlee finished her pill pack, and all blood ceased. Emotionally, she was exactly the same. It was clear she had already gone through menopause. A few years back, she'd wake at two a.m., sweat pooling around her torso, and she didn't think of menopause. As far as she knew, the cessation of menstruation was the turning point. She had never talked about these things with her mother or any woman, had not looked them up. If her OB/GYN, whom she avoided regularly, ever mentioned menopause, she couldn't remember.

Marlee's sex drive also ceased the day she stopped the pill. During the previous decade, her libido had been a thing she'd conjure when necessary or if nudged by the touch of her husband. Occasionally, she'd view an image that would titillate, causing warmth to rush to the vulva, and if completely alone, which was close to never, she'd close the bedroom door and indulge in two minutes of lushness, then grab her jeans she had stepped out of and go on with her day. Sex, to her, had been, for quite some time, an interruption of things that mattered. There were things she wanted to do in any given twenty-four-hour period, and boosting her husband's self-confidence, which is what sex had become for the past ten years, was not on her list, though it always seemed to make its way there. Yes, her life had been one of tending to others. Five seconds of orgasm—and the two hours of building up his ego beforehand with coffee or beer and attentive listening—robbed her of a beautiful morning run or three absorbing chapters before sleep.

Without the pill, her conjuring resulted in nothing. No matter the fantasy or body part, she could not be moved, save for a distant, focused, brief rise and fall. And if it was just her body that was of concern, she would have celebrated with a bath, a candle, and Pinot Gris—a bath that was not to prepare oneself for the pleasure of another but simply because it felt good to Marlee. A bath from beginning to end with only Marlee in mind. No shaving and staying in the water till sleep. But there was this other body that used hers for its purposes. Love and affection, sure, but coming at her were also body parts, and she was feeling like an apparatus now more than ever. Hostility brewed within her, surfacing in private moments on her lips and brow. How many years must a woman be a tool for all to use? And when the day would come that she wasn't of use, she was sure to shuffle in her pastel pants through the halls of a nursing home, tossed away.

With menopause came a knowing. Commercials advertising male supplements she now viewed with pinpointed judgment that she sounded through the living room with a clear and heretofore untried resonance—"DO THE MATH. YOU'RE FIFTY. LET IT GO."—resonance fueled by two irritants: one, this call for increased stamina should interrupt Rachel Maddow's researched unraveling of the Trumpian horror of the day; and two, the woman in the commercial who would supposedly "like it too" was in her twenties while the man speaking into a mic to reporters (of this newsworthy event???) was in his forties. "SHE DOESN'T CARE ABOUT YOUR FUCKING PENIS. SHE THINKS YOU ARE AN OLD MAN." Marlee felt the rapscallion blood of satisfaction flow through her body after saying these words aloud as her husband sat on the other end of the couch, scrolling and saying nothing.

Yes, it was as if a great veil had been lifted to reveal the behind-the-scenes mechanism running this great show of the world or as if she had crept into the underbelly of it all to see the ragged slaves pushing the enormous cogs around and around, and she shook to the core when she realized she had been one of these cog-pushers all these years.

Lying in bed after sex one evening, Marlee asked (by all appearances out of curiosity and not for her survey of one), "Why do older men take Viagra?"

"Self-confidence. If I can get it up, I feel like a million smackers."

"It's okay if you can't get it up. It's a natural thing to stop getting it up."

"That seems so sad."

"That's where hugging comes in. Sex doesn't have to last forever."

"Yes, it does. Forever!" Her husband shot his fist in the air. Sex was an accomplishment. To achieve the accomplishment, he needed the mechanism: Marlee.

She turned over, grabbed her robe, and hauled herself to the bathroom to let semen drip out of her body for the millionth time and to pee to avoid a UTI while he grabbed his phone to scroll.

* * *

The general understanding in Marlee's society (USA, 2022) was that committed partners were to be sexually available for one another. That relationships required mutual sexual satisfaction. That Partner A touches or pulls or licks Partner B's part to make them feel something pleasant, even if Partner A feels as sexually dead as defrosted chicken while engaging in the act (but Partner A cannot express this fact to Partner B because it would destroy him. Instead, Partner A has to continue to do things and be things for Partner B. Partner A is feeling a swirling tempest form as month after year passes while she must continue to build up her fucking husba—Partner B.)

It's not that Marlee hadn't been aware of inequality and sexism and the patriarchy; she had experienced all of this from girlhood to this day. It was just that her new clarity uncovered the *degree* to which the world was saturated.

Getting ready for work, Marlee added color to her lips, and for the first time ever, her lips looked less than full, looked a bit thin. She lightened them with pink gloss and hated the anxiety she felt at the knowledge that her lips were closing in on themselves—a natural thing, but this natural thing meant dying, and to the office, it meant not as pretty. She hated that people looked at one another and labeled: pretty, ugly, young, old. Ultimately, she wished her lips fuller not because she wanted a man's approval but because she wanted her job and was afraid someone would take that away if every aspect of her physical being wasn't just so. But, as she dusted brown eyeshadow on her white roots, she thought the truth: If she lived alone with the bears in a cabin and had no monetary concerns, her lips would simply need to be moist so they wouldn't crack, and a smudge of coconut oil would do. And her hair, she'd never color because it was a royal pain in the ass. Though she'd probably still draw on her lost eyebrows until she was a bona fide old woman (shuffling, bent).

But she had a job. A damn good job with lots of money, relatively speaking, compared to years ago, and no credit card debt and a decent 401(k). The house was almost paid off. If needed, she could live by herself in her own apartment and be completely fine. Comfortable. If she wanted, she could move across the water, solo. She finally understood the archetypal woman with cat—both self-sufficient, each doing their own thing, neither asking the other for much. Here is kibble. Here is ear. A good book. A sweater. Bliss. No one needed to be jerked off to confirm they were still a man.

She capped her moisturizing lipstick and headed out the door. She'd park at the park-n-ride and catch a short bus to the ferry to Seattle.

Though the Bainbridge Ferry trip was always a tranquil journey, Marlee's new hormonal equilibrium created such peace within her during this day's trip that she had the idea, while lifting her gaze from her laptop to the placid Puget Sound, that she had reached the perfect human state. No pubescent flourishing, no adolescent appetite, no maternal worry, and no elderly frailty—which she imagined to be a trapping, holding a lifetime of wisdom inside a diminishing shell. Here, now, in her seat on the ferry, Marlee could think and do for herself without a single human or hormone pulling at her mind or body or heart.

The ferry docked, and the passengers headed off, Marlee leading the pedestrians. She had been standing at the door along with other fast walkers as the boat approached the pier. Some were runners, wearing gear, and some had buses to catch, like Marlee, but Marlee's preparedness was more than just her desire to be punctual; it was also due to the intoxication she always felt when hurtling through the city streets—especially now, having worked remotely for two years during the pandemic. Two months ago, she had picked up where she had left off, speeding like she used to, climbing Seattle blocks to her next ten-minute bus ride. Others would take the bus at the stop closer to the ferry, but she chose the walk, which she considered an essential part of her day, rain or shine, to keep fit and to be whipped to attention by the haphazard breezes from Elliott Bay, an umbrella always at the ready in her backpack.

Her route had changed since before the pandemic, both the streets she took and the streets themselves. Tall boards either hid or replaced tourist shops down Alaskan Way, creating a barrier between pedestrians and construction behind the boards on the water's edge. The change had started before the lockdown, when the Alaskan Way Viaduct, deemed unsafe, had been demolished. But in the sickly lull of this new world disease, while people and businesses died and waited and hoped, a tattered presence clung to these Seattle streets. An ominous and invisible presence, Marlee also felt. Maybe large rats crawled up through manholes at night. Maybe ribby dogs slunk low to the pavement. In the early morning daylight, a chalky feel lingered in the air, perhaps dust still holding on from the old viaduct, perhaps dirt wafting from the dragging of the many steps of the many homeless people who on some streets outnumbered the working ones because the working ones were working at home. Marlee thought as she avoided Marion Street because of a large tent-home of a street person and seeing many such people meandering and scratching all around, that most likely, there were not more homeless people as some were saying; we just saw more of them since the working bodies didn't block our view.

Marlee stayed on Alaskan Way then walked up Madison, always jaunty at 8:00 a.m., now more than ever with her newly acquired equilibrium, and when she made it to First Avenue, she paused at the light, which she always tried to beat but never could. Across the street, in front of the Henry M. Jackson Federal

Building, stood numerous people, mostly women, holding signs, and she knew at that moment this was the day: the Supreme Court leak had flooded her land. A few people in a room had decided, after discussions, that yes, the government could decide what to do with Marlee's body. As a matter of fact, fifty little governments could decide what to do with Marlee's body, depending on where she paid her mortgage.

The light at the street changed, but she remained. A woman with white hair and sloping shoulders held a sign at her belly. A man with no hair and floppy jowls held his hand-painted sign above his head. This crowd would grow.

The light changed again, and Marlee continued her walk up to Third Avenue much slower than before. She was one of the lucky ones: to live in a progressive state and to be too old to conceive.

Lucky or not, she still felt the weight of it all, knew the ramifications for the entire nation. She knew, too, that she would not be truly at peace until her own body was completely hers. *Sorry, hon. Don't take it personally, but I just don't want to have sex anymore.* Can you imagine? She thought the question in a mental conversation with herself. She shook her head as she trudged uphill, knowing that by simply uttering those words, a wedge would be drilled into her marriage. She had to choose to either be true to her body or to keep her husband content.

A construction truck rolled up the street. Fifty-two, and leers still landed on her body through vehicle windows, appraising what they felt was theirs to rate. How much inspection had she endured in her lifetime?

How many men's bodies had come her way? The ones she had invited and then regretted the arrival? The ones that persisted until she gave in? The necks that had hovered rhythmically over her face while she cried? The ones she was too young and drunk and lonely to walk away from? The diseases she should have? And the little pink daily pills she had thankfully popped from Planned Parenthood when she was eighteen, not because she was guided by a mentor or mother or nonexistent social media but quite by chance because a fellow student at school mentioned she was going. She had said it matter-of-factly with no shame or secrecy, and Marlee took on her aspect at that moment, wore it the day she entered the building. It had been a new thing to try on: *I would like to go on the pill.* And the response was easy and without judgment, just medical questions, income questions, an easy sliding scale, an exam, professionalism, information. The pill had protected her from her own unmoored, naïve, and lonely adolescence. Marlee didn't think much of herself all those years ago. The satisfaction and affection of the male of the month, her benchmark. It was the eighties. No one told young, skinny Marlee otherwise. No one told Marlee it was okay if a man didn't like her. Everyone told her men had to like her, and if they didn't, then she was worth little.

If fifty-two-year-old Marlee and eighteen-year-old Marlee should meet at an intersection like the one she was approaching, at Third and Madison, younger Marlee would smile, then look down, and she'd make room for older Marlee to walk. Older Marlee would smile in return and see the deference and feel tenderness for this young person, and she would break a little with worry that this girl-woman would be walked over, mostly by men, and ignored by women who would not know what to do with her because she was a little too pretty to have around and a little too nice and a little too lost. *Hey,* older Marlee hoped she would say, *You don't have to put up with that. Do you have some time? How much time do you have?* Older Marlee hoped she would stop everything she was about to do in her day and say, *Do you have all the time in the world for the most important information?*

Marlee crossed the street and walked to the end of the block, to Third and Seneca. She waved her ORCA card over the reader, and it accepted her fare with a beep. She was expected at a two-hour breakfast meeting with the board members. She readjusted her mask as the 70 bus made its way up the street. It squealed in front, and the doors opened. She saw her reflection in the glass, a working woman wearing a light-blue mask under tired eyes, a woman who had little say in the scheme of things, yet her life had meant something to at least a handful of humans, and lately, more than ever, it meant something to her.

Let's go, Marlee. She turned around and walked the way she had come. *There is so much you need to know before you make all those bad decisions. Let me give you some guidance, a plan book you may or may not follow completely, but at least it will give you possibilities.*

Marlee made it to First Avenue and joined the crowd. She had no sign. She had such thoughts, though. Finally, the time had come. Women did not need men. A woman's livelihood was more important than a man's kindness or smiles, which were fleeting. Her dependence would be her downfall. She needed to make her own money, and doing so would give her power over herself. This was the key, she was sure.

And as she read the sign "Our Bodies, Our Lives," she thought of the many times she wanted to leave her marriage.

How she wasn't happy but had settled because she had these babies who became kids who loved their dad, and they loved her, too. She didn't want to hurt them—their sweet brows and their tenderness—and she knew if she were to leave, then her children would never be the same, and she just couldn't do that. So she stayed, committed to making sure they had a good life. She's been at this for twenty-five years, and she then realized, quite suddenly and with horror, that having a baby was potentially, quite possibly, probably, and yes, most definitely, a long, long road to complete dependence. And she cleared her throat and opened her mouth.

* * *

Discussion Questions

1. Do you think a married spouse has an obligation to have sex even when they aren't in the mood? What if they are never in the mood?

2. What do you think is the cause of Marlee's lack of interest in having sex with her husband? Is there something she can change about her life to regain her sex drive?

3. Barring a medical condition, if a person doesn't ever want to have sex with their partner, does that mean their relationship is failing, or can couples have a fulfilling, sexless relationship?

4. Do women who make more money, have more self-confidence, and seek less approval from men naturally want less, more, or the same amount of sex?

5. Marlee says children are a road to dependence. What does this mean, and do you agree?

Author Information

The Worst Thing You Can Do is Nothing & Visions Of Midwives

C.S. Griffel holds an MFA in creative writing and an MA in Rhetoric. She currently teaches creative writing and composition at the University of Mary Hardin-Baylor. Her fiction and nonfiction has appeared in *The Talon Review* and *Great! Storybook*. She is currently interested in writing neo-gothic and speculative fiction.

The Chair of Opportunity

Cory Swanson lives with his wife, two daughters, and the ghost of an old, blind dog named Kirby in Northern Colorado. He teaches music by day and writes by early morning, playing guitar in the evening. At night, he doesn't fight crime. Rather, he sleeps like most people. Facebook *@speculativemeculative;* Instagram *@coryswansonauthor;* X (Twitter) *@author_cory*

M.I.N.D. Your Marriage

Kim Z. Dale (she/her) is an information security specialist and writer. Her essays and short stories have been published in multiple anthologies, including ones from Belt Publishing, Death Knell Press, and Kendall Hunt. Her one-act and full-length plays have been performed most frequently in her current and previous hometowns of Chicago and Pittsburgh. X (Twitter) *@observacious; kimzdale.com*

Understanding Ice Cream

Earl Smith is a political and social theorist who lives in Southwest Washington. He received a PhD in Political and Social Theory from Strathclyde University in Glasgow, Scotland, an MMS from the Sloan School at MIT, and a BA from the University of Texas. An itinerant, he has lived all over the world, played the great game (intelligence) internationally, founded six companies and two non-profits and lived in Manhattan for almost two decades. *www.Dr-Smith.info; www.SmithTales.com*

Glad All Over

Lee Dawkins is a lawyer and writer, with a degree in politics. He was born in London and now lives in the South West of England with his wife, daughter and a crazy Labradoodle. Lee writes across a range of genres, including literary, speculative and philosophical fiction. He is the proud owner of George Orwell's stapler.

Thorn

Erik Fatemi lives in Arlington, Virginia. A former newspaper editor and columnist, he now lobbies the federal government on behalf of nonprofit health groups. His fiction has also been published in *JMWW*, *Identity Theory*, and *WWPH Writes*. X (Twitter) *@ErikFatemi*

What We Talk About When We Talk About Reincarnation

Edward Daschle (he/him/his) is a student of fiction in the University of Maryland's creative writing MFA program. He grew up in the Pacific Northwest, land of serial killers and Sasquatch, deadly mountains and overcast skies. His fiction also appears in *Grim & Gilded*, *Stoneboat Literary Journal*, *Defunct*, and *OFIC Magazine*.

The Draft

Jan McCleery spent her career as a software engineer start-up founder, and applies her independent woman experiences in a man's world to her writing and thought processes. Jan became a California Delta activist and formed a non-profit to fight the "water wars." Jan has also published nine books, including her recent spy novel series. *www.FromTheDuckPond.com*

Final Determination

Lea Pounds holds an MFA from the University of Nebraska. She likes writing and reading stories that lead people to see things in a different light. She has been published in *Sandhills* and *The Novice Writer*. Lea lives in Omaha, Nebraska. When she's not writing, she's in the garden or watching true crime stories. *www.leapounds.com*

More

Julia Edinger (she/her) is a queer writer from Northwest Ohio currently living in Southern California. She works in journalism. She has had writing published by *The Mill*, *Bridge*, *Pamplemousse*, *Variety Pack*, *Paragraph Planet*, and more. When not writing for work or pleasure, she is exploring the mountains with her partner and her pit bull, King. X (Twitter) *@julia_edinger*

Hard Metal

Porter McKoy (she/her) received her Ph.D. in philosophy from The New School. She lives and writes in NYC about the dirty glamour of desperate times. X (Twitter) *@PorterMcKoy*; Instagram *@porter_mckoy*; *www.portermckoy.com*

The Things We Give

Allison Padron is an M.A. in Writing student at Rowan University. She lives in New Jersey with her husband and her three cats, Basil, Sushi, and Tofu. In her free time, she enjoys reading, knitting, and visiting national parks. *X* (Twitter) *@apadronwriting; www.allisonpadron.com*

Three Blocks

Kathryn LeMon earned her BA in creative writing from Kenyon College and is presently an MFA candidate at the Ohio State University where she serves as the Production and Online Editor for *The Journal*. She is the winner of *Flash Frog's* 2023 Blue Frog award in flash fiction. Her work has appeared or is forthcoming in *Flash Frog*, *Gigantic Sequins*, and elsewhere.

Euthanasia

Kelly Piner, Ph.D., is a Clinical Psychologist who in her free time, tends to feral cats and searches for Bigfoot in nearby forests. Her writing is inspired by Rod Serling's *Twilight Zone*. Ms. Piner's short stories have appeared in *Litro Magazine*, *Scarlet Leaf Review*, *The Last Girl's Club/Wicked News*, *Rebellion Lit Review*, *The Chamber Magazine*, *Drunken Pen Writing*, *Storgy Magazine*, *The Literary Hatchet*, Weirdbook, *Written Tales* and others. Her stories have also appeared in multiple anthologies.

Cicada

Ishan Dylan is a conservation biologist and fiction writer from the Chesapeake area. His work is forthcoming in *Exposition Review's* 'Lines' issue. (X) Twitter *@IshanDylan; ishandylan.com*

The Pool

Celia Lisset Alvarez is a writer and educator from Miami, Florida. She holds an MFA in creative writing from the University of Miami and has four collections of poetry: *Shapeshifting*, *The Stones*, *Multiverses*, and *Bodies & Words*. Her most recent publication is the anthology SMEOP 2: HOT and has forthcoming work in *Talon Review*. She was the editor of the *Prospectus: A Literary Offering*. *www.celialissetalvarez.com*

Drag Brunch

Mark Bessen (he/him) is a queer writer based in Austin, Texas, originally from Southern California. He holds a BA in English from Stanford, and his fiction and essays have been featured in *Epiphany*, *The Offing*, *Taco Bell Quarterly*, *New South*, *Tahoma Literary Review*, and elsewhere. (X) Twitter *@MarkBessen*

The Walnut Tree

Michael "Mikhail" Shainsky is a Russian born American author living in Los Angeles, librettist and composer. He is also a world traveler and cycling enthusiast—when he finds the time between being a dedicated parent, entrepreneur and Executive Director of the Dr. Joseph Shainsky Foundation, a nonprofit providing free sightseeing tours to US veterans. (X) Twitter *@MikhailShainsky*; Facebook *@michael.shainsky*

The Pill

Thea Swanson is a feminist atheist who holds an MFA in Writing from Pacific University in Oregon. Founding Editor of *Club Plum Literary Journal*, her dystopian flash-fiction collection, *Mars*, was published by Ravenna Press in 2017. Pushcart prize nominee and is published in places such as *Chicago Review of Books*, *World Literature Today*, *Mid-American Review* and elsewhere. X (Twitter) *@thea_swanson*; Instagram *@swanson.thea*; *www.theaswanson.com*.

Additional Information

Reviews

If you enjoyed reading these stories, please consider an online review. It's only a few seconds, but it is very important! Good reviews mean higher rankings. Higher rankings mean more sales and a greater ability to release amazing new stories.

Monthly Magazine

https://www.afterdinnerconversation.com

Purchase our growing collection of print anthologies, "Best of," and themed print book collections. Available from our website, online bookstores, and by order from your local bookstore.

Podcast Discussions/Audiobooks

https://www.afterdinnerconversation.com/podcastlinks

Listen to our podcast discussions and audiobooks on Apple, Spotify, or wherever podcasts are played. Or, if you prefer, watch the podcasts on our YouTube channel or download the .mp3 file directly from our website.

Patreon

https://www.patreon.com/afterdinnerconversation

Get early access to short stories and ad-free podcasts. New supporters also get a free digital copy of the anthology *After Dinner Conversation–Season One*. Support us on Patreon!

Book Clubs/Classrooms

https://www.afterdinnerconversation.com/book-club-downloads

After Dinner Conversation supports book clubs! Receive free short stories for your book club to read and discuss!

Social

Connect with us on Facebook, YouTube, Instagram, TikTok, Substack, and X (Twitter).

Special Thanks

It is with a profound sense of nostalgia and accomplishment that I address you in the wake of our latest "Best of" edition, a mere year after the previous one. In the ever-evolving landscape of literary expression, the past twelve months have felt like a lifetime, marked by the transformative emergence of Chat-GPT and the inevitable influx of AI-generated spam submissions.

Yet, I am delighted to report that discerning these synthetic interlopers remains a task of relative ease. The more significant transformation, however, lies in our own evolution, a maturation akin to the ripening of fine wine or the blossoming of a seasoned artist's oeuvre.

In this period of growth, we have had the privilege of enlisting the talents of a professional graphic designer, the incomparable Shawn Winchester, whose contributions grace our monthly covers with a touch of sophistication befitting our publication. Our volunteer staff, now seasoned with years of dedication, bears witness to the enduring commitment of individuals who have woven themselves into the very fabric of our magazine.

Allow me to express my deepest gratitude to R.K.H. Ndong, our Story Editor, and the dedicated team of Associate Acquisitions Editors – Tina Forsee, Pyrros Rubanis, Y. Len, Noelle Canty, K. Roberts, and Deborah Serra. Their collective efforts, alongside the dedication of our volunteer readers and the unwavering support of our Patreon community, have elevated our literary endeavor to new heights.

Looking ahead, 2024 holds the promise of nine carefully

curated "themed" books, each a collection of ten previously published short stories unified by a common thread. The meticulous work of Kate Bocassi in polishing these compilations is a testament to our commitment to providing quality content for classrooms and bookshelves alike.

On the digital front, our Substack has flourished, rapidly gaining ground, while our monthly magazine has earned the distinguished ranking of #7 out of 3000+ literary magazines on ChillSubs. Regrettably, our podcasts are presently on hiatus, awaiting the opportune moment for their revival.

In a significant stride, we have transitioned to a nonprofit model, marked by our inaugural end-of-year fundraising drive. This milestone has empowered us to increase our compensation for writers, fostering an environment where creativity is valued and sustained.

Reflecting on the past five years, I hesitate to liken our publication to a mere tween; rather, it stands as a Junior or Senior in High School, navigating the complexities of its identity with a newfound sense of clarity. While uncertainties persist, we have mastered the art of opening our lockers and savoring lunch off campus with time to spare.

On a personal note, I extend heartfelt thanks to my wife for her enduring patience and provision of health insurance, to my sister for her flexible job schedule, and to everyone who has showered us with their patience and love.

Here's to the journey ahead, marked by literary brilliance, artistic expression, and the collective spirit that propels us ever forward.

(Yes, I wrote the section above, then had Chat-GPT rewrite it "in the style of a literary magazine." Like I said, it's still super easy to

spot AI writing... Just look for someone writing like an over vocabularied pretentious d-bag.)

Thank you!

Editor-in-Chief

www.ingramcontent.com/pod-product-compliance
Lightning Source LLC
Chambersburg PA
CBHW052030240626
47153CB00006B/2029